CW01642095

PERFECT PLANS

J.T. TIERNEY

CURTISS STREET
PRESS

For Sue, James, and Tom

~ with love

Chapter One

The Human Variable

Sofie Chen sensed someone's life was about to change. She just wasn't sure whose—his or hers. But watching the tall, twenty-something stranger in Margo's office meticulously align his chair to some invisible grid, Sofie felt it—a barely perceptible shift in energy, a subtle reordering of molecules, the tiniest redirection of fate.

"This is Ryan Porter," Margo said, gesturing toward the man, who rose with careful precision. "Ryan, meet Sofie Chen, one of our senior coordinators."

On paper, Ryan Porter's job application was baffling: two applied mathematics degrees from Caltech and what seemed to be a broad base of knowledge—but no hospitality background, no event-planning experience, nothing remotely conventional.

"It's good to meet you," he said, maintaining what seemed like a deliberate distance between them and extending his hand at precisely forty-five degrees. His handshake felt exact, a careful midpoint between greeting and grip.

"Likewise," Sofie replied, noting his gray eyes evaluating her—not in the usual way men did, with that quick territorial scan, but as if she were a particularly appealing data set.

"Did you know the tint of your blazer was Pantone's Color of the Year in 2023? Viva Magenta, RGB 18—"

"Ryan," Margo cut in gently. "You were about to tell me more about your earlier background, before your university years. You were raised in ... Alaska?"

A flicker of pride—or perhaps nostalgia—crossed his face. "Yes. My parents run the University of Alaska's Nordvik Research Station. They study marine mammal migration patterns and pack-ice dynamics." After a thoughtful pause, he added, "I assisted with data collection and analysis."

"Fascinating," Sofie said, genuinely intrigued. "And now you want to coordinate conventions? That's quite a pivot. Have you ever worked in event planning?"

Ryan's fingers twitched slightly. "No. But I've conducted observational studies of group behavior, spatial negotiation, and crowd dynamics. Conventions seem like a highly concentrated version of those phenomena—with high stakes and complex variables."

"Don't forget the lanyards and coffee breaks," Sofie said, amused with herself.

She glanced again at the intricate convention schedules Ryan had submitted with his application—color-coded matrices, precise metrics, meticulously mapped crowd flows. Overkill, perhaps, but after managing countless events nearly derailed by human unpredictability, Sofie valued exactitude. This guy would bring that. In spades.

She thought about the parade of job candidates she'd helped interview over the years: the overeager kids fresh from event-planning programs, their voices full of nervous energy; the transfers from hotel services and other hospitality sectors; the corporate refugees looking for a more "creative" career; the party planners who thought organizing a sweet sixteen qualified them to manage a convention of two thousand forensic accountants.

She'd never interviewed anyone like Ryan Porter. He was entirely unique.

"What drew you to apply for this particular position?" she asked.

"It aligns with my interests and skill sets," he replied simply. Then, more quietly, he added, "Also, a therapist suggested I could benefit from a job involving more frequent human interaction."

Sofie couldn't help the smile that broke across her face. There was something so refreshingly raw, honest, and transparent about his response. She felt it again—that crystalline something in the air. A presence, representing change. What she saw across the table wasn't just a brilliant oddball. It was almost a reverse image of herself.

She'd spent years honing an impression of flawless professional control—clipboard in hand, blazer crisply pressed, never missing a cue. But it was always a performance. Always. And it struck her then, as she watched Ryan Porter carefully align his pen and tablet with the edge of the desk, that he wasn't performing at all. He was just being. In the precise, straightforward way he knew how. There was no polished script, no desperate attempt to fit himself into what he thought they wanted, no claimed passion about organizing conventions. Just the clear-eyed truth, and a flicker of vulnerability that made her like him instantly.

She also detected in him a need similar to her own—a need to be perfect. She understood the kind of pressure and stress that entailed. The constant recalibration of self in an effort to avoid failure, the fear that one misstep might unravel everything. And she knew all too well how exhausting that was—and how it often went unnoticed by others, unless they harbored that same need themselves.

Margo raised an eyebrow, silently asking Sofie's opinion. Sofie nodded toward the hallway.

"Would you excuse us for a moment?" Margo asked Ryan.

In the hall, Sofie lowered her voice. "Margo, what's the story here? Is he ...?" She made a vague waggling gesture.

"Neurodivergent? On the spectrum? Possibly," Margo said. "I don't know. I didn't ask. Maybe. Or it could be his isolated upbringing. Maybe a bit of both. Who knows? Does it matter?"

Sofie started pacing. "It might," she said. "A big part of our job is managing emotions. Reading people. He has a mental file of the codes for Pantone colors. I just ..." She hesitated, searching for the right words. "I don't want us to set him up to fail. That would be cruel, Margo."

"Yes, but I don't believe he'd fail." Margo smiled warmly. "When was the last time you saw someone approach our job in a completely new way? We've got plenty of people who can handle the emotional side. Ryan could give us a structured way of managing chaos." She studied Sofie closely. "Besides, he's exactly what you think we need around here."

Sofie felt suddenly exposed, surprised Margo had sensed her private frustration with their chaotic methods. "How would you know that I—"

Margo smiled. "Oh, please. I've often seen you working here late in the evening—at a whiteboard, painstakingly categorizing, mapping, strategizing. I know what that's about. And I agree with you that we need better systems." She patted Sofie's arm.

Through the glass wall, they saw Ryan waiting, spine perfectly straight, fingertips tapping a precise, metronome-like rhythm on his tablet as he examined the room's angles—as if calculating how many tenths of a degree off true right the corners might be.

"Margo, forgive me, but I can't stop thinking about this guy in relation to some of our emotional, unpredictable clients. Yesterday, the Quilting Society president nearly declared war on the Scrapbooking Guild. She brandished pinking shears because she thought the other group had better lighting. How could this poor guy possibly deal with that?"

Sofie had meant it as a rhetorical question, but Margo calmly replied, "Let's ask him. See what he says."

Back inside, Margo stepped behind her desk. "Ryan, Sofie faced a dispute yesterday at a quilting convention—a conflict between two crafting groups fighting over shared space. How might you handle something like that?"

Ryan's face lit up. "Oh, interesting! I've actually developed a framework for resolving resource-allocation disputes," he said, "based on arctic fox den-sharing behaviors." His hands moved rapidly, sketching imaginary territory maps in the air. "If you think of each group as a fox skulk seeking optimal territory and adjust for resource-scarcity variables ..."

Sofie watched him, seeing the gears turn. He wasn't just analytical; he instinctively sought solutions, mentally sorting variables and considering ones others might've overlooked.

She felt an unexpected protectiveness toward this precise, earnest man from Alaska. She sensed the potential their combined strengths offered—her intuitive approach and his systematic analysis, her improvisational ease matched by his careful precision.

Her entire career had been built on making other people look good, anticipating needs, smoothing edges. Always the stage manager, never the star. Always holding chaos at bay with nothing but a clipboard and an unwavering smile, maintaining a flawless performance to mask her internal doubts.

What would it be like to work with someone who didn't perform at all? Who simply let himself be, without artifice or pretense?

Margo turned to Sofie, silently asking again. Yes or no?

Sofie took a deep breath, feeling the weight of the decision. She nodded. Thumbs up.

Margo smiled and turned back to Ryan. "I'd like to offer you the position. You can start on Monday. Your first assignments will be helping coordinate an accountants' conference, then the American Meteorological Society convention next month."

Something flickered in Ryan's eyes. "That's optimal," he said. "Weather systems parallel convention crowd-flow patterns mathematically. The models I've developed could significantly improve your spatial strategies at large events."

Sofie exchanged a quick, apprehensive glance with Margo. Hiring this guy would prove to be either a stroke of genius or a colossal mistake.

Margo shook his hand. "You'll be on Sofie's team. She'll also be your point person here at Prestige Events—she'll orient you to our systems, accounts, and clients. And generally get you settled."

Walking him to the elevator, Sofie asked, "Ready to dive in?"

Ryan tilted his head, as if processing the metaphor. "I'm an excellent diver," he said, earnest. "Though I generally prefer a more measured entry into new environments." The corners of his mouth twitched up, and Sofie saw it. A wry sense of humor, she thought. She liked him even more.

But as the elevator doors closed, she wondered just how measured Ryan Porter could remain when confronted by the unpredictable realities of convention planning.

Chapter Two

Optimal Conditions

Ryan inserted the digital thermometer into the water and watched the numbers climb. The optimal temperature for coffee wasn't negotiable—195 was weak, 205 was bitter. When you'd grown up in an Arctic research station where precision meant survival, you didn't cut corners. Even on the small things.

When the thermometer hit exactly 200.0, he began his pour-over ritual: 17.3 grams of coffee, evenly distributed, water poured in slow concentric spirals. The aroma was rich, reassuring. Rituals like this made sense. They grounded him.

His small Brooklyn apartment was equally calibrated. Every item had its place because chaos tightened his chest. Each succulent on the windowsill got rotated every third day, each mug arranged by thermal retention. Order felt safer than the alternative. So he worked hard to maintain it.

He took a sip of coffee. Sublime.

"Good morning, specimens," he said aloud to the succulents. They were thriving—hardy plants, built for survival. He felt a quiet kinship with them. "You're adapting nicely." He spoke kindly, believing the jury was still out on whether plants responded to human vocal tones and emotions. He believed in hedging bets.

Outside, the city surged with controlled chaos. Ryan walked briskly, maintaining his preferred thirty-one-foot buffer from other pedestrians. He'd optimized his route through systematic testing of 14 path variations. He knew the average walking speeds, street by street. He knew the statistical likelihood of being slowed down near major retail locations, construction areas, and school zones. The bagel shop on the corner was to be avoided at all costs.

On the subway, he automatically added data to previously noticed patterns of phone-checking and eye-contact avoidance. He catalogued a new observation: women looked behind themselves 67 percent more frequently than men. He doubted anyone else tracked these things, but for him, reading environmental patterns had been a survival instinct since childhood.

He'd long accepted the speculation about his being "on the spectrum"—was it biology or just growing up isolated among scientists? Even Caltech's psychologist couldn't say. Whether nature or nurture, this was how his brain worked. Demonstrably efficient, which should be all that mattered.

At age ten, after getting strange reactions from people outside the research station, he'd asked his mother about it.

"Ryan," she'd said gently, "you process things the way we study ice cores—you see every layer. That's a gift. But most people don't see the world that way. They skate on the surface. If you want to connect, you might have to loosen up around them. Be less precise about things."

He'd tried. In college, he'd reached the point that his roommate joked about his "almost passable normal-person conversation skills." Still, deep down, he preferred precision.

He arrived for his second day of work at Prestige Events fourteen minutes before his scheduled start. Exactly optimal, in his view. The lobby's lighting registered slightly too cool on his internal Kelvin scale, but he ignored it. New priority: professional integration.

The elevator doors opened. Ryan stepped out, tablet in hand, notepad tucked beneath one arm, spine straight. He adjusted his collar.

Sofie looked up from her desk.

"Good morning," she said.

"Good morning," he replied. "I adjusted for the humidity today—shoes with better traction."

She blinked. "Cool."

He meant to say more, but a crooked picture frame caught his eye. He resisted the urge to fix it.

By the time the morning staff meeting began, Ryan was seated at the end of the table, quietly assessing the spatial arrangement of chairs, the placement of the coffee urn relative to the electrical outlet, and the uneven distribution of sugar packets next to the cream.

Someone mentioned gluten-free caterers. Another person griped about a bridezilla. Ryan logged the tension variables, the speaker overlap rate, and the average eye-contact interval.

He'd never worked in an office before—just labs, research stations, controlled environments. But this was a data-rich ecosystem, and Ryan Porter was ready to prove his systematic approach could revolutionize event planning.

What the data couldn't predict was everything else.

Chapter Three

Stacked Events, Fractured Realities

"A what?" Ryan blinked, his mental algorithms recalibrating.

"A field trip," Sofie said, standing beside his desk. She wore a mini-backpack and an expression his facial-analysis matrix categorized as Mischievous Anticipation.

"Time to meet the beast in the wild," Margo added, joining them and holding what Ryan counted as her fourth coffee of the morning. "We're taking you on-site."

Ryan's shoulders tensed. On-site. The prospect of entering the field—where human chaos reigned supreme—sent a prickle of anxiety across his skin. He understood the importance of throwing himself into uncomfortable situations. How else would he stress-test his models against reality? But why hadn't they put this on his schedule? Told him about it earlier? The abrupt disruption echoed the dreaded fire drills at Caltech that obliterated his study plans.

In just three days at Prestige Events, Ryan had methodically mastered the office environment—95 percent proficiency with Outlook and a grasp of client-folder taxonomy within an acceptable 3 percent margin. Each properly handled document and memo had earned small nods of approval from Sofie and Margo. If they now felt it was time for him to go to an actual event, who was he to argue?

The walk to the Hamilton Regency was roughly ten blocks—unfamiliar urban territory full of honking traffic, the rhythmic click of heels on pavement, and the ambient hum of a thousand conversations bleeding together. What started as manageable anxiety grew more acute—not least because Sofie and Margo were serial violators of Ryan's internal rule about personal-space buffers. By the time they reached the hotel, his breathing had grown shallow, his mind racing through a branching decision tree of potential scenarios.

Cool air greeted them in the hotel lobby, and Ryan's senses immediately heightened. There was an ambient tension he recognized—like the time at Caltech when theoretical physicists were forced to share conference space with experimental physicists—each group barely concealing its disdain for the other's methodologies.

Now here it was again: a peculiar atmospheric disturbance that seemed to oscillate between mutual hostility and forced politeness. He spotted the source: two opposing registration tables occupying opposite sides of the vast atrium, approximately 27.5 meters apart.

On one side, the NASA Retirees Association Reunion, complete with space-shuttle models. Opposite, the Flat Earth Society's Annual Conference featuring a sphere labeled "THE BIG LIE."

Cognitive dissonance overwhelmed him. It was like trying to compute the square root of a negative number without acknowledging the existence of imaginary numbers. A cold sweat broke across his forehead.

Turning to Sofie, he said, "I thought your reference yesterday to unlikely, incompatible pairings was comedic hyperbole."

"You mean you thought I was kidding about this sort of thing?" she asked, raising an eyebrow.

"Yes! How could this happen?"

"Space is space," Sofie said with a shrug.

"The Flat Earthers booked the Roosevelt Wing first. NASA came in late and insisted on the East Wing. With the atrium open ... *voilà*. You get cross-pollination. Could've been the Ayn Rand Society next to the Democratic Socialists of America. That actually happened to me once."

Ryan's brow knitted. "Why would any rational management or planning system allow this?"

"Venues maximize revenue," Sofie explained. "If dates align and checks clear, they'll put weddings next to a dog show. It's about capitalism, not compatibility."

"Sometimes the clients are at fault," Margo added.

"Groups book late, insist on specific rooms, refuse to compromise. We try to avoid chaos, but we don't always have a say."

Ryan watched, concerned, as two men—one wearing an Apollo 15 flight jacket, the other a T-shirt reading "NASA Lies! Earth Is Flat"—brushed past each other with icy glares. His mind spun with potential confrontations.

"And you accept these conditions as standard operating procedure?" he asked, incredulous.

"Well, no," Margo said. "But we don't really have much choice. It's often unavoidable. And it can be a shit-show of epic proportions when the pairings create ideological friction."

The sudden profanity startled Ryan, reminding him of a physics professor who once threw chalk at a blackboard and shouted, "This is absolute fucking bullshit—and yet the math says it's true!" Ryan had admired the logic: when the universe itself made no sense, neither did polite language.

They rounded a column and spotted two Prestige staffers in sky-blue polos managing what could only be described as ideological tension.

"That's Jenny," Sofie said, nodding toward a petite woman intercepting a man about to hang a "Space Flight Is a Hoax" banner. "She's our confrontation whisperer."

Across the atrium, Todd—tall, calm, wearing a Bluetooth headset—redirected NASA retirees from a table of Flat Earth literature while texting hotel staff.

"Todd's more of a strategic deflector," Sofie said. "He'll

steer the retirees toward muffins while moving the Flat Earthers to a breakout room with 'better light.'"

Ryan watched, captivated. This was coordinated, adaptive response. Different from mathematical models—but still patterned. Messy, but deliberate.

A Flat Earther with a portable mic and speaker wandered too close to the NASA side.

"Watch this," Sofie whispered.

Jenny stepped in like a bat plucking a mosquito from the air. "Sir, your breakout session's starting down the hall. You'll want a good seat for the gyroscope demo."

The man hesitated, then veered away.

Ryan exhaled slowly. It was elegant social engineering. A living algorithm.

"That was very impressive. But I still can't help thinking this whole scenario represents massive system inefficiency."

"Better get used to it," Sofie said. "Hotels and convention centers are built to stack events—multiple ballrooms, movable walls, segmented catering teams. Like Tetris, but with lanyards and dietary restrictions. We try to match vibes, but honestly, the odds of a perfect fit are low. It's revenue-driven chaos." Her casual cynicism startled a rare laugh out of him. It reminded him of his quantum-physics professor's axiom: *The universe isn't broken; your expectations are.*

"But the chaos!" Ryan gestured toward a Flat Earther in pizza-box headgear arguing with a NASA rep.

"That's why *we* exist," Sofie said. "We're the buffer zone. We keep quilters away from sword enthusiasts. We stagger lunch so Romance Writers don't get trampled by the High School Football Awards."

Ryan pictured it. These were complex systems—less predictable than equations, but fascinating.

"Do our methodologies include distraction mechanisms?" he asked.

"Decoys? Absolutely," Sofie said. "Fake signage, potted plants, scent diffusers. Everything's fair game."

Ryan made a mental note to study olfactory influence on aggression.

"That's why we build flexible schedules," Margo added. "Stagger departure times. Hide certain groups like they're rival camps on *Survivor*."

The reality TV reference was lost on Ryan, but the underlying principle made sense: strategic separation of incompatible elements.

"Should I study conflict mediation?"

Sofie and Margo exchanged looks.

"Start with improv," Sofie said.

"Then maybe move on to hostage negotiation," Margo added.

Ryan blinked. Unclear if they were serious.

The three of them watched as Jenny and Todd gently separated two groups of opposing conventioneers marching toward each other like rival gangs in *West Side Story*.

"How do they stay so calm?" Ryan asked.

"You learn to roll with it," Sofie said. "Or you cry in a stairwell. Either one's fine, as long as you keep your radio on."

“And save any comfort drinking until the end of the workday,” Margo added.

Ryan nodded slowly, eyes scanning the swirling chaos. He saw something he hadn’t expected: amidst disorder lay fascinating complexity—disorderly, unpredictable, but undeniably compelling. Worth learning to work with.

Chapter Four

The Taxonomist

Sofie watched with fascination as Ryan meticulously arranged color-coded sticky notes across the conference room wall. The soft rustle of paper and the faint squeak of his marker filled the quiet space. She studied him as much as his organizational system—the tall, composed frame, the clean, practiced motions. He ran a hand through his cinnamon-brown hair without disturbing a single strand. His focus was magnetic: sharp gray eyes locked on each note's placement, brow knit in concentration.

He wasn't Hollywood handsome, but his facial symmetry was almost classical—high cheekbones, straight nose, and a sharp jawline that could've been carved by a sculptor with an architectural bent. His clothes, perfectly pressed and methodically coordinated, gave off the impression of someone who'd Googled "business casual" and followed the script to a T.

He reached up to adjust a sticky note that was, apparently, three degrees off true north. Each note represented a different session of the upcoming convention of the Northeast Public Accountants Association, positioned according to what Ryan called his "optimal spatio-temporal distribution matrix."

"See?" Ryan stepped back, gesturing at his creation with the reverence of a museum curator. "By applying the Fibonacci sequence to session scheduling, we create a natural flow that mimics efficient patterns found in nature—like the spiral formation of nautilus shells, or the arrangement of seeds in a sunflower head."

"Uh-huh." Sofie tilted her head, studying the pattern. She had to admit, there was something oddly beautiful about it. "And the colors?"

"Taxonomic classification," Ryan said, pointing to a cluster of notes. "I've coded Tax-law Updates in azure blue because studies show blue promotes trust and stability. Audit Procedures are in emerald green, associated with growth and precision. And the keynote speeches—"

"Are in 'caution yellow' because accountants find motivational speakers threatening?"

Ryan blinked. "No. Sunburst yellow, proven to enhance information retention—" He paused, looking at her more carefully. "That ... the 'caution yellow' comment ... was a joke."

"Gold star for recognition," Sofie said, smiling. After

three weeks of working with Ryan, she'd developed a fondness for his literal-minded sincerity. "But seriously, this is impressive—even if the accountants won't appreciate the Fibonacci sequencing behind their snack-break scheduling."

"Actually, I've modeled optimal caffeine-intake intervals based on circadian rhythms and—"

"Ryan," Sofie said gently, cutting him off before he could launch into full exposition. "Have you gotten a feel for the group dynamics? What about the social aspects?"

He brightened. "Yes! Margo's idea to send me to the Midwest Region's meeting last week was inspired. It allowed me to document accountants' behavioral patterns."

He pulled up a spreadsheet titled *Accounting Species: Taxonomic Classification and Behavioral Analysis.* "I've identified several distinct subspecies," he said. "The Tax Specialists tend to be territorial about premium seating near power outlets. The Forensic Accountants display pack behaviors, clustering in groups of three to five to discuss fraud detection methodologies. And the Audit Partners exhibit alpha dominance displays, primarily through subtle variations in suit quality and—"

Sofie held up a hand, trying not to laugh. "That's ... thorough. Thank you. How about we focus on Roberta Wilson? The conference chair?"

"Ah, yes. Subject Alpha-1." Ryan tapped his tablet. "Her emails demonstrate a 44.3 percent higher use of exclamation points relative to—"

"Probably because she's excited about the conference,"

Sofie interrupted. "And probably nervous. It's her first time as chair. She wants everything to go smoothly."

Ryan frowned. "My calculations indicate we've reached a 92 percent optimization rate for all scheduled activities. That's—"

"Irrelevant. Your estimates and numbers aren't going to calm her nerves," Sofie said. "Roberta needs to feel supported. That means connecting with her personally. Listening to her concerns."

"I see," Ryan said. "Should I prepare a statistical analysis of our support metrics?"

"No, but thank you," Sofie said, smiling. "Roberta's coming in at noon to review the setup. I usually take key organizers to that little French bistro around the corner. Breaking bread together, you know?" She smiled. "Tell you what—why don't you come along?"

Panic flickered across his face—the expression he made when confronted with rituals that defied quantification. Sofie knew what would come next: he would reach for data to calm himself. Sure enough, he opened a map on his tablet and said, "There are four French restaurants within a six-block radius of here. I could analyze their Yelp ratings, the price diff—"

"We'll take her to Chez Jeannier. They have great food and cozy booths where people feel comfortable talking."

"Is comfort quantifiable in this context?"

"Not everything is, Ryan." Sofie watched him carefully. She saw his uncertainty, the way he needed to get it right. "At lunch you can walk Roberta through your amazing schedule. And remember—she's not a subject. Not a specimen. Not a data point. She's a person who wants her event to go well."

Sofie gave his arm a quick pat, noting with satisfaction that he didn't flinch this time. Progress. "Now," she said, pointing at his laptop, "tell me more about your coffee-break optimization. But maybe with, like, half the decimal points?"

Ryan pulled up a different spreadsheet, and Sofie found herself drifting into memory. Watching him lay out his color-coded calendar and optimal panel placement reminded her of something long buried that still pulsed with unexpected pain.

She was ten, backstage at the Fairview Theater's summer production of *Guys and Dolls*. Her mother, Linda Chen, was running the show—stage manager extraordinaire, the unflappable queen of headsets and clipboard mastery. In the Chen family, theater wasn't just entertainment; it was a profession treated with near-religious reverence.

The backstage area had been a swirling chaos: mismatched costumes, late entrances, a props table that looked like a yard sale in a tornado, all underscored by the sharp smell of stage makeup and the musty scent of old velvet curtains. Actors panicked about quick changes, the lighting board operator nursed a hangover, and someone had spilled coffee on the sound cues.

Yet her mother had orchestrated it all—catching near-miss disasters, smoothing fragile egos. Young Sofie had watched in awe, adrenaline and admiration mingling in her chest.

"Theater is controlled chaos," her mother had said once. "Our job is to make disaster look like destiny."

But it wasn't always magic.

During the opening night of that same production, her mother had missed a single cue. Just one—Adelaide's entrance for "Take Back Your Mink." One missed signal, one unlit stage entrance, and the entire second act had teetered. The lead actress had improvised badly, throwing off the orchestra. A key scene fell apart. The audience had shifted uncomfortably in their seats, the spell broken.

The reviews the next day, though kind to the actors, had been brutal about the "technical mishaps." Her mother had read them silently at the breakfast table, her face a mask of composure that ten-year-old Sofie already recognized as a performance itself.

Later, at the post-opening reception, the theater board president had cornered her mother by the cheese plate.

"Linda," he'd said, voice pitched low but carrying in that way theater people's voices always did, "how does someone with your ... credentials ... let something like that happen?" He'd emphasized *credentials* like it was a slur. Like her mother's twenty years of stage management meant nothing in the face of one missed cue.

Sofie remembered her mother's face—the self-control, the slight tightening around the eyes, the way she'd straightened her spine an extra fraction of an inch. "It won't happen again," she'd replied calmly.

But later, in the car ride home, her mother had gripped the steering wheel so tightly her knuckles went white.

"You can be brilliant a thousand times, Sofie. They'll only remember the one time you failed."

That was the moment it clicked: you could execute flawlessly 99 percent of the time and still be defined by the 1 percent where you faltered. That was the moment Sofie learned that chaos, if not conquered, could turn on you like a wild animal. And that control—absolute, rigorous, preemptive—was the only shield against public humiliation.

The rest of the summer, her mother had arrived at the theater three hours early, checking and rechecking every cue, every prop, every costume quick-change. She'd developed plans for the backup plans. Color-coded redundancies. The show ran flawlessly. No one mentioned the opening night disaster again.

But Sofie never forgot the lesson: people only see the failures. The successes are expected; the mistakes are remembered.

By thirteen, Sofie was running backstage for the youth theater program. She mimicked her mother—early arrivals, constant checks, flawless composure. She did everything possible to anticipate and prevent disaster. By sixteen, she was stage managing full productions, earning a reputation for being "preternaturally composed"—a phrase she'd overheard adults use, not knowing composure was what she practiced like lines in a script.

Her father, who managed events for investment banks, had nodded approvingly at her developing skills. "Good," he'd said. "Real success comes from control."

The Chen family business was managing other people's moments. Making them perfect. Making the seams invisible.

Now, watching Ryan with his color-coded sticky notes and taxonomies, Sofie recognized her own drive reflected back at her—the need to anticipate, to classify, to control. But where she wrapped her precision in theatrical charm, he displayed his without pretense. There was something both unnerving and refreshing about his lack of performance.

"Sofie?" Ryan's voice pulled her from her reverie. "You appear to be mentally elsewhere."

She blinked, realizing she'd been staring at his elaborate display without really seeing it. "Sorry," she said, shaking off the memories. "Just ... thinking."

"About what?" he asked, with that direct curiosity that never seemed to recognize personal boundaries. In some ways, he approached others with the unvarnished directness of a five-year-old.

She considered deflecting, then offered a sliver of truth.

"I was thinking about why I appreciate your systems more than most people might." She gestured toward his sticky-note masterpiece. "My mother was a stage manager who ran shows like clockwork. I grew up backstage, watching her, learning about timing, precision, controlling chaos."

"That explains your efficiency metrics," Ryan said, nodding thoughtfully. "Though you integrate higher interpersonal flexibility."

Sofie smiled. "I think you just said I'm good with people. Thank you." Gesturing toward the latest spreadsheet he'd pulled up, she added, "And I must say, your schedule grid is a thing of beauty. Good thing, too—accountants aren't great at improvising."

He looked pleased. "I know. I've rated them low on my improvisation-tolerance index. Very low."

Sofie laughed and shook her head, but behind the humor, the image of her mother's tightly controlled expression at that reception wouldn't entirely fade. Somewhere deep inside Sofie, the old fear stirred—of missing the cue, being exposed, being the failure everyone remembers.

Maybe that's why Ryan made sense to her. They both lived to prevent disaster. The difference was, Ryan's systems were honest. Hers were wrapped in charm, wit, performance—the greatest of which was the illusion that she wasn't terrified of failing, of letting the curtain fall at the wrong time.

Chapter Five

Solutions Come Second

The hostess at Chez Jeannier led them to what Sofie had called a "cozy booth." Ryan assessed it at about 12 percent smaller than a standard restaurant booth. The tight fit made him hyper-aware of his proximity to Sofie, the scent of her perfume—citrus, underpinned by jasmine—more prominent than usual.

He reached instinctively for the laser measure in his pocket, then stopped, catching the look Sofie gave him. That slight lift of her eyebrows, the subtle seven-degree head tilt told him: *don't do it*. Reluctantly, he left it alone, even though part of him ached for the grounding comfort of numbers.

"This is just lovely!" Roberta Wilson said, her chipper tone falling right in line with his expectations. "I always walk past this place but never tried it!"

Ryan opened his mouth, ready to share the quick analysis he'd done on the restaurant's Yelp review trends over the past 26 months. But Sofie stepped in smoothly before he could start. She'd been doing that a lot lately. He understood she was trying to help—still, every time it happened, it left a small jolt of frustration behind, the same feeling he'd had back at Caltech when a professor dismissed one of his side projects as "off-topic" without seeing how it connected to the bigger picture.

"It's one of our favorite spots for meeting with organizers," Sofie said, flashing Roberta a warm, easy smile. "These private booths are perfect for going over details."

Ryan nodded, pleased to contribute something concrete. "The ambient noise level is 62 decibels," he said. "Ideal for conversation while still masking background sounds." A small ripple of pride went through him. He'd noticed that on his own, without prompting—the kind of environmental awareness his mother had always encouraged when he was young. *Patterns are everywhere, Ryan. You just have to look for them.*

Roberta blinked at him, her smile faltering for half a second in a way he couldn't quite decode or classify. Confusion? Amusement?

Sofie filled the gap with another easy comment. "Ryan's very detail-oriented," she said. "Which is exactly what you want when you're putting together an event this important."

A flicker of gratitude stirred in him. Sofie had a way of translating his facts and figures into something people actually wanted to hear. It reminded him of his father proudly showing off his childhood weather model to visitors, calling it "scientific promise" instead of what it probably looked like —obsession. Still, part of him wondered: what was wrong with talking about booth acoustics and privacy stats?

He made a mental note to figure it out later. Maybe it was what his mother had meant when she suggested he allow for more "conversational drift." For now, he focused on pulling up his condensed convention outline from memory.

He began, "I've optimized the schedule to ensure maximum efficiency—"

"Oh dear," Roberta said, frowning at the menu. "Everything looks wonderful, but I'm supposed to be cutting down on carbs!"

This wasn't on Ryan's list of anticipated lunchtime discussion topics. A small jolt of panic flashed through him. He quickly searched for relevant data, flipping through his mental files on nutrition studies he'd read last year when he'd gone down an internet rabbit hole into metabolic science.

He said, "Studies indicate that complex carbohydrates can actually improve cognitive function. You could factor that into your consideration, anticipating the coming differential in blood-sugar levels—"

"Ryan," Sofie said gently, cutting in before he could build momentum. Her voice was softer this time, less a brake and more a hand on his shoulder. "We're just ordering lunch. No need for all that." Then, kindly, she added, "But thank you."

"Oh." He was doing it again. Veering into the weeds. He still found it hard to know where the line was between being helpful and being ... too much. His college roommate had said Ryan was heavily into "info-dumping." He now felt that familiar sensation—the one you get when you miss a step on a staircase—that momentary lurch before regaining balance.

Ryan pivoted, trying to adjust. "The Salade Niçoise has the lowest carbohydrate content on the menu—about 12 grams, assuming a standard portion size."

"The Salade Niçoise sounds perfect!" Roberta said quickly, her smile a little tight around the edges. "And maybe we could go over the schedule while we wait for our food?"

Relief swept through him. Schedule optimization was safe territory. Numbers didn't get offended. Patterns didn't misunderstand you.

"I've developed a revolutionary approach to session scheduling based on the Fibonacci sequence—" he started, energized.

"What Ryan means," Sofie cut in again, still in that smooth, easy tone, "is that we've created a really intuitive flow for attendees moving between sessions."

Ryan bit back a correction. It wasn't intuitive at all—it was based on careful modeling of learning patterns and crowd dynamics. The need to clarify tugged at him. But Sofie's foot tapped his under the table. Another silent cue. *Don't.*

"The important thing," Sofie said, picking up the thread, "is that everyone will easily find their sessions and have time between them to recharge. It's all very thoughtful."

Roberta nodded, though her fingers tapped faster—130 beats per minute, by Ryan's estimate. Was it anxiety? Impatience? He thought about flagging it, but caught Sofie's eye again. *Let it go.*

He envied Sofie's ease with people. She moved through conversations the way he moved through equations—adjusting instinctively, sensing when to lean in or back off. What would it be like, he wondered, to move through the world that way? To understand people without spreadsheets and behavioral models, without having to run constant calculations?

The waiter arrived to take their orders, and Ryan was ready. He'd researched the menu in advance, weighing preparation times, spill probabilities, and nutritional balance. The memory of a disastrous French Onion soup incident during a lunch with his senior-thesis advisor still haunted him—stringy cheese on his chin, a stained shirt, a question he never got the chance to answer properly. The thought of it still made him wince.

"Sole Meunière, please," Ryan said. "Exactly eight ounces."

Sofie's smile tightened just a little, like she was trying not to react. Had he missed another unspoken rule? Was specifying portion size considered strange? Roberta gave him a look, too—one he couldn't quite code. Curiosity? Amusement? Mild concern? People's expressions were maddeningly fuzzy sometimes.

"About the keynote speaker," Roberta said once their orders were in. "I'm a little worried about Dr. Henderson. He's ... particular. He can be prickly about his requirements."

Ryan felt himself settle. A concrete problem. Good. He'd

spent two nights researching Charles Henderson's previous speaking engagements. He'd watched available video clips, read event planners' reviews and comments.

"I've compiled a comprehensive profile of his preferences and patterns," Ryan said, leaning in. "I've isolated five logistical variables affecting his satisfaction."

Roberta blinked. "Five?"

Ryan nodded. "His reported contentment is 72 percent higher when the podium is exactly 42 inches high and doesn't wobble by more than 1.5 millimeters on the diagonal. He prefers a Shure SM58 microphone—foam windscreen removed—with a backup lapel mic (on his left side, never right). He likes stage lighting kept at 2700 Kelvin; anything cooler and, quote, 'he looks embalmed.' He prefers the room temperature to be 70 degrees Fahrenheit—'72 is oppressive, 68 is punitive,' per his contract rider. And there is a clear trend toward better outcomes when his backstage green-room chair is armless, firm-cushioned, and not leather or imitation leather. 'No squeak factor,' his assistant once noted."

Roberta's expression had slid from curious to stunned.

Ryan continued, "I've already tested three chairs. One of them—"

"What Ryan's saying," Sofie jumped in, still smiling, "is that we're very attentive to speaker preferences. We'll make sure Dr. Henderson feels completely supported and satisfied."

Ryan blinked, thrown by the way Sofie was sanding down his detailed preparation into generalities. Not wrong, exactly—but not the full picture either. It left him feeling deflated, like he'd shown up with a precise blueprint and Sofie was turning it into a crayon sketch. He wanted to explain about the one chair that squeaked audibly at 39 seconds into a seated pivot, but Sofie gave him another one of her tiny micro-cues—a tilt of her head, a flick of her eyes —and he let it go. *People first. Data second.* That, he was beginning to understand, was Sofie's rule.

The conversation settled into a pattern: Roberta voiced concerns, Ryan offered solutions, Sofie translated. By the time their food arrived (his fish portion was closer to 9.5 ounces—annoyingly imprecise), the pattern had stabilized. But part of him still didn't understand why precise answers weren't more desirable.

"Well!" Roberta said, pushing her plate away at meal's end with a bright smile. "This has been so helpful! I feel much better about everything!"

(*Exclamation point count for the lunch: 27. His original model had predicted this.*)

"We're so glad," Sofie said. "And please don't hesitate to call if you have any questions. Right, Ryan?"

"Yes," he said. "I've established a dedicated email folder with automated response protocols for—"

"For staying in touch," Sofie finished. There was that foot tap again.

He smiled faintly. Once, during a Christmas visit home from college, Ryan had gone cross-country skiing with his father. He'd kept falling, unable to find the right rhythm—

until his father had suggested he stop thinking about the mechanics and just feel the flow of movement.

This conversation felt similar—like he was constantly off-balance, looking for a pattern that others navigated instinctively. But maybe, slowly, he was starting to get it.

After Roberta left, Sofie turned to him with a look he was beginning to recognize—the one that wasn't critical, just thoughtful, like she was trying to figure out the best way to steer him without bruising anything important.

"Ryan, you did great with the technical details," she said, her voice low and easy. "But remember what we talked about? About connecting with people? Sometimes people need to feel seen and heard before they want a solution. You need to remember that—and treat them like the star of their own story. Solutions come second."

Ryan hesitated. "I had answers for everything. The Fibonacci model alone—"

"Is brilliant," she said. "But timing matters. Empathy matters. Also ... maybe I stepped in too much. I'm used to stage managing. I should've let you perform. I'm sorry."

Ryan blinked. He'd never considered that Sofie might second-guess herself. That someone so fluent in human nuance, in the unwritten rules he struggled to grasp, could doubt herself, too. The realization shifted something inside him—something subtle but important, like when an equation you've been wrestling with finally balances.

Chapter Six

Stage Directions

Sofie's tiny Greenpoint apartment glowed in the soft light of string bulbs, its cozy clutter reflecting a life that had straddled the worlds of theater and event planning. Tonight, sprawled on her threadbare but beloved red-velvet couch—a thrift-store find she swore had once lived in a Broadway dressing room—Sofie was trying to explain the enigma of Ryan Porter to her best friend Val over Thai takeout and cheap wine.

"He calculated the optimal temperature for the accountants' coffee," she said, waving her chopsticks for emphasis. "Not just the brewing temperature—the serving temperature. He found a sweet spot where it's hot enough to keep them alert, cool enough to drink fast during breaks without throwing off the schedule."

Val, who'd known Sofie since their student days in the theater department at NYU, raised an eyebrow. "He sounds intense."

"Oh, he is. But also amazing." Sofie stood, needing to move as she thought about Ryan. It was a theater habit—blocking out her thoughts physically. Her snug apartment allowed for about six paces in any direction, but it was enough. "Last week, he defused a near-brawl between two groups at the Food & Beverage Expo—artisanal picklers vs. kombucha brewers. Some war about fermentation purity."

"What did Mr. Spreadsheet do?"

"He made a Venn diagram showing acceptable fermentation thresholds and posted it near the escalators like it was the Geneva Conventions. Then he made a flowchart for dispute resolution. First question was: Is your ferment fizzy or angry?"

"And that worked?" Val asked, clearly dubious.

"Well, nobody threw a jar," Sofie said, grabbing her wineglass. "That's a win in my world."

"Sofie ..." Val's voice had that careful tone she used when delivering tough notes after a show. "He sounds weird."

"I know, I know," Sofie said, deflecting Val's concern. "But good weird. He color-codes his spreadsheets, arranges his clothes by optimal workplace palette, compares convention groups to Arctic wildlife ... and somehow it's all just—"

"Adorable?"

"I didn't say that." She waved a hand dismissively. "I like him as a colleague. I admire his mind. The way he sees the world—like it's this vast equation waiting to be solved."

Val tilted her head. "Despite what you say, it sounds like you find all that pretty attractive."

"Val, you're not listening to me. I'm not into him like that. I just find him fascinating. He's like if a supercomputer and Mr. Darcy had a baby—raised by polar scientists. Brilliant and baffling—and, yeah, handsome. But different."

"Honey, let's remember: you have the worst taste in men."

"I do not—"

"Jason? The standup comedian who kept using you and your love life as a bit in his sets?"

"That was three years ago. And he wasn't using me as material. He was 'processing our relationship through art.'" Sofie used air quotes without irony.

Val smirked. "Okay. Whatever you say. ... How about Casey? The one who dumped you for the human Barbie?"

How could she forget? Casey had been her first serious boyfriend in college. He'd broken up with her after eighteen months for someone whose double-D cup size clarified what he meant by "wanting something different."

"Yeah. He always said I was 'too intense' about my work, too obsessed with making everything perfect." Sofie stopped pacing. "Funny thing is, at Prestige, that intensity actually helps. Even Ryan gets it—he said I 'employ theatrical techniques to optimize human emotional variables.'"

"How ... romantic." Val's tone was dry.

"No. Not romantic—accurate. He gets that my theater background shapes how I run events. It's not just about schedules and room layout. It's about emotional flow."

Val sighed, placing her empty carton on the coffee table. "Speaking of flowing emotions ..." Her eyes misted. "I got a rejection email from Manhattan Rep today. They passed on *Glass Menagerie*."

Sofie froze mid-sip. "No! That's impossible. Your direction was brilliant!"

Val shrugged, aiming for nonchalance but not quite hitting it. "Apparently they wanted something 'fresher' and 'more innovative.' Probably someone who thinks Williams needs EDM."

"Idiots. Remember that show last year that rejected you? Total karmic backlash. Their lead quit a week before opening."

Val smiled weakly. "Maybe the universe is saving me for something better."

"Like that experimental theater job you mentioned? With the warehouse space in Red Hook?"

"Yeah, about that ..." Val twisted a strand of hair around her finger, a nervous habit from their college days. "I'm no longer pursuing that. I'm ... actually thinking of moving to Chicago."

Sofie nearly choked on her wine. "Chicago! What's in—"

"Opportunity. A real assistant director position with Steppenwolf. Plus ..." Val's cheeks flushed slightly. "Remember Malcolm? The lighting designer from the Shakespeare in the Park program last summer? The one with the vintage motorcycle—"

"—and the impossibly perfect hair?" Sofie's eyes widened. "He's in Chicago?"

"Got hired as their tech director three months ago. We've been ... talking."

Sofie appraised her. "You've been sexting, haven't you?"

Val's cheeks flushed and she ducked her head, suddenly fascinated by her wine glass. "He wants me to visit."

"This is huge!" Sofie nearly toppled the coffee table in her excitement. "Why didn't you tell me sooner?"

Val looked up, vulnerability written across her face. "Because it's still new and scary and probably a terrible idea, given my track record with relationships and career moves."

Sofie winced. Val's last big move—chasing love and a job —had been to Seattle, where she'd spent eight miserable months watching her new boyfriend fall in love with someone else while working at a theater that specialized in "deconstructed classics"—which mostly meant actors in gray bodysuits pretending to be furniture.

"This isn't Seattle," Sofie said gently. "You wouldn't be dropping everything for someone you barely know. Besides, you've wanted to work with Steppenwolf forever."

"I know, but ..." Val hesitated. "But I'd be leaving you. Again."

The weight of their friendship hung between them. Since college, they'd been each other's constant in a sea of changing relationships, apartments, and career disappointments. Val's Seattle sojourn had left a hole in Sofie's life that had taken months to adjust to.

"You wouldn't be leaving me," Sofie said firmly. "You'd be moving toward something. There's a difference." She refilled their wine glasses. "Besides, at parties I'd get to dramatically declare 'my best friend's an assistant director at Steppenwolf.'"

Val laughed, the tension breaking. "What about you? Sticking with the lanyards and chaos? Or is there a Broadway plan I don't know about?"

Sofie looked around her cluttered apartment. Playbills from every show she'd ever seen shared shelf space with convention-planning manuals and her matchbook collection. Her walls were a collage of theater posters and whiteboards covered in event timelines.

"I don't think theater's calling me back." She paused, then chortled. "Remember that *Midsummer* we did in college? I made that elaborate cue matrix for tracking the fairy costume quick-changes?"

"God, that show was chaos," Val laughed. "The backstage soap opera? Three fairies and Puck all dating and breaking up mid-run?"

"Exactly. That's when I realized I was good at managing creative chaos. Mom always said theater people are just event planners with jazz hands."

Val grew serious. "Speaking of managing chaos ... I've been meaning to ask. Are you still getting those panic attacks before big events?"

Sofie's smile froze. "What? No. That was ... that was years ago."

"Bullshit. You can't fool me," Val said, appraising her friend. "You had that pyrotechnics convention last week. How bad was it?"

Sofie was quiet for a long moment, weighing the cost of

admission against the relief of confession. "Threw up twice in the venue bathroom," she finally said.

"Oh, for the love of—"

"Then reapplied my lipstick and went out to handle a dispute over the best ignition system."

"Jesus, Sofie. Does anyone at work know?"

"God, no. And they never will." Sofie's tone made it clear how utterly unthinkable that was. "It's just ... pre-show nerves. Lots of people get them."

"Not like yours." Val leaned back. "Ever since Chicago."

Sofie swallowed hard, the memory washing over her with unexpected force. Chicago. Her first solo event-coordination gig. The Small Business Leadership Summit—three hundred attendees, twenty-eight speakers, twelve breakout sessions. She'd spent weeks preparing, creating the most elaborate, minutely detailed timeline she could. Everything by the book, she'd kept telling herself, checking her watch obsessively. Every minute accounted for.

Then the panels ran long, schedules imploded, coffee arrived to empty rooms. The final blow came when she realized she'd placed the keynote speaker—the CEO everyone was there to see—in the wrong room. She'd sprinted through the convention center in her too-tight heels to find hundreds of attendees crammed into a space meant for fifty, while the main ballroom stood empty. Addressing the crowd as he stood on a chair to be seen, the CEO had caught her eye, raising a single brow that contained volumes of judgment. The shame had burned through her like acid.

"It was my fault," she said softly. "I should've done a better job."

"You mean you should've been perfect? Like your mom at her shows? Like your dad with his flawless galas?"

Sofie flinched. "That's not fair."

"No, what's not fair is watching you beat yourself up for being human." Val refilled Sofie's glass. "Remember what Angela told you afterward? 'Events aren't about schedules. They're about people. And people don't fit into spreadsheets.'"

Angela Perez—Sofie's boss in Chicago, who had somehow seen past the disaster to offer her a second chance. Who had taught her to recover when things went sideways, to improvise, to bend without breaking.

"Maybe that's why I'm drawn to Ryan," Sofie said slowly, the realization forming even as she spoke it. "Only professionally, obviously. His systems, his precision—they're like having a perfect script and a flawless stage manager all in one. Having him there offers the hope that maybe we can actually control the chaos, prevent disasters."

Val studied her. "Or maybe you're drawn to him—only professionally, of course ..." She playfully punched Sofie's shoulder. "... because with him, you don't have to pretend or perform. You just get to be competent. And human."

Sofie felt it—like getting hit with a prop that was supposed to be foam but wasn't. "Maybe," she said, then quickly pivoted. "Let's talk more about you and the technical director with the perfect hair."

Val allowed it, but her look said: *This scene isn't over.*

. . .

LATER, alone, Sofie stood at her window overlooking Manhattan Ave. The city glowed like a theater set.

She thought about her life here: the occasional bowling nights with friends from her theater days; the weekend brunches with fellow event planners, trading war stories about bridezillas and corporate team-building disasters; the endless parade of strange convention tribes that filled her days at Prestige Events.

And now Ryan Porter had walked into her careful story like an unscripted character—statistics and storm-gray eyes, decoding the truth behind her performance.

He wasn't her Romeo. But he was rewriting all her stage directions. And she kind of loved it.

Chapter Seven

Storm Front

"Oh God," Sofie whispered to Margo. "I bet he's doing the taxonomy thing again."

The Riverside Convention Center's Grand Ballroom had been transformed into meteorological ground zero, the air thick with the electronic hum of weather-monitoring equipment. Near the center of the room, surrounded by gleaming radar displays and digital weather stations, Ryan was deep in conversation with a group of meteorologists. He had his tablet out and was pointing at something, while a silver-haired man in a bow tie grew steadily redder in the face.

Sofie and Margo drew close enough to hear the escalating tension, but stayed far enough back so as not to intrude.

"I've classified the major predictive methodologies,"

Ryan was saying to Bow Tie, "and your approach appears to be an outlier. The statistical validity of using squirrel fur thickness as a primary indicator for long-range winter forecasts is approximately—"

"Squirrel fur thickness," Bow Tie spluttered, "has been used by the *Old Farmer's Almanac* for over two hundred years!"

"Which explains its 2.6 percent accuracy rate." Ryan tapped his tablet, the soft click barely audible over the rising murmur of disapproval. "About as useful as using the thickness of onion skins or corn husks as a predictor. So, would you prefer to be classified under 'Folk Methodologies' or 'Historical Weather Divination'?"

Margo winced. "Should we intervene?"

"Give him a minute," Sofie said, though her hand twitched toward her phone. "He might recover."

Ryan, unfortunately, continued. "I've created a comparative chart of various non-scientific prediction methods. Squirrel fur ranks slightly above reading coffee grounds, but well below migratory goose patterns—though, of course, none approach the accuracy of actual meteorological instrumentation ..."

"Listen, sonny boy, I've been forecasting weather longer than you've been alive!" Bow Tie was practically vibrating. "I suppose you think your fancy computers know better than generations of wisdom?"

"Yes," Ryan said simply. "By approximately ninety percent."

Sofie was already moving. "Dr. Whitaker! I'm so glad

you're here. We have a slight issue with the afternoon panel schedule ..." She deftly steered the furious forecaster away from Ryan.

She and Margo had thought the American Meteorological Society convention would be perfect for Ryan's first lead assignment. Weather patterns, data analysis, scientific methodology—it should have been a dream match. What they hadn't counted on was Ryan's eagerness to wade into the fierce tribal loyalties and bitter rivalries that divided the weather-prediction community.

Returning from her diplomatic mission, Sofie muttered, "Did you hear about the chaos in Room 204? Two groups got into a shouting match over competing El Niño models. Ryan tried to resolve it by suggesting they compare their mathematical proofs."

"Oh no."

"Oh yes. One side uses chaos theory, the other swears by something called 'pattern harmonics.' Ryan's exact words were: 'Your methodologies appear to be equally unsupported by empirical evidence.'"

Margo rubbed her temples. "If he can't handle meteorologists, how is he going to survive the World Clown Association next month? Or, God help us, BronyCon?"

"The Bronies might actually be easier," Sofie mused. "At least they're upfront about their peculiarities. The people here pretend to be rational scientists until you get them started on hurricane-naming conventions."

Across the room, Ryan was now animatedly talking with

a group of younger meteorologists. His tablet sat forgotten on a nearby table.

"That looks more promising," Margo said.

Sofie squinted. "Wait. Is he ... oh no. That's the radar-interpretation splinter group. They believe Doppler patterns contain hidden messages from aliens. Last year they tried to convince everyone that a supercell thunderstorm was actually an extraterrestrial communication cluster."

"And Ryan's talking to them because ...?"

"Probably analyzing their methodology. He loves documenting what he calls 'fascinating examples of human pattern-recognition errors.'"

Sure enough, Ryan's voice drifted across the room: "But the probability of radar artifacts forming naturally into recognizable linguistic structures is statistically insignificant. I've calculated the odds at approximately—"

"I should extract him," Sofie sighed. "I've gotten good at fabricating 'urgent situations' that require his 'immediate attention' elsewhere."

"Looks like someone else is going to extract him for us." Margo nodded toward a woman in a "CHEMTRAILS ARE REAL" T-shirt, approaching Ryan with the solemn intensity of a true believer.

To their surprise, Ryan smiled at the woman—an unguarded, genuine smile. "Oh! You're interested in atmospheric chemical dispersal patterns? I helped my parents track aerosol distribution in the Arctic. Would you like to see some mathematical models for particulate behavior in various atmospheric conditions?"

The woman blinked. "I ... what?"

"I have several fascinating datasets. Here." He pulled out his tablet.

To Sofie and Margo's astonishment, a small crowd of chemtrail theorists gathered around him, visibly enthralled as he launched into an impromptu lecture on atmospheric chemistry.

"Well," Margo said. "That's ... different."

"He's not arguing with them," Sofie realized. "He's not even telling them they're wrong. He's just showing them something more interesting than their theory."

They watched as Ryan pulled up a 3D model of Arctic wind patterns. The conspiracy theorists ooh'd appreciatively, nodding along as he explained cloud formation mechanics.

"Huh," Margo said. "Maybe we've been worrying about the wrong thing. We thought he'd struggle because he doesn't understand people's quirks ..."

"But maybe he's better with people when he stops trying to analyze them," Sofie finished, "and just lets himself be enthusiastically weird in their direction."

Ryan was now explaining wind shear using what looked like interpretive hand gestures. His audience leaned in, rapt.

"Still," Margo said, "the clown convention ..."

"Might actually work," Sofie said thoughtfully. "Clowns are basically performance artists with technical skills and complex taxonomies. If we get him talking about the physics of juggling or balloon-animal geometry ..."

"You just want to see him try to classify different types of clown noses."

"That too." Sofie grinned. "Besides, he's already making progress. This morning, he told me my organizational style was 'chaotic but effective.' And he meant it as a compliment."

"Speaking of chaos ..." Margo nodded toward the entrance, where several members of the *Old Farmer's Almanac* contingent were regrouping and casting suspicious glances toward Ryan.

"I'll handle the almanac crowd," Sofie sighed. "You might want to rescue Ryan before the chemtrail people start asking about his parents' Arctic research. One mention of government funding, and we lose all the progress he just made."

But a commotion from the technology pavilion pulled their attention. Dr. Fuqing Zhang, a young professor known for his experimental approach to weather modeling, was fine-tuning what looked like a miniature cloud chamber. A small crowd had gathered to watch as he made adjustments to the sleek silver device.

"Is that authorized?" Margo asked sharply.

Sofie checked her tablet. "It's listed as an 'atmospheric visualization system,' though I'm pretty sure the description didn't mention—"

A low hum filled the air, followed by a sudden chill that raised goosebumps on Sofie's arms. Above the device, moisture condensed into a swirling, growing cloud.

"Colleagues!" Dr. Zhang called out proudly. "Behold the future of weather simulation! The CloudMaster 3000 can recreate any atmospheric condition in miniature. Observe as I demonstrate a simple thunderstorm formation—"

Ryan, now nearby, froze mid-step. His eyes widened as the cloud—now the size of a minivan—began to rotate. A bolt of lightning arced from the cloud to a metal display stand with a loud crack. The acrid smell of scorched metal filled the room. Screams erupted. A wind system spun up fast, scattering papers like startled birds.

"Fascinating!" Dr. Zhang shouted, eyes gleaming. "Slightly more energetic than anticipated, but—"

"We need to shut it down!" Margo yelled.

"Oh my god," Sofie cried, turning to Ryan. "What do we do?"

Ryan's face had gone pale. A fine sheen of sweat glistened on his forehead. His hands trembled as he jabbed at his tablet.

"This ... this isn't in my risk matrix," he said. "I don't have a signal. And the Wi-Fi just dropped—I can't access the model."

He began breathing faster, shallow and uneven. His movements grew panicked.

"Ryan," Sofie said, grabbing his arm.

His shirt sleeve was damp. His muscles vibrated with tension. He didn't look at her. His eyes were locked on the useless tablet.

"Ryan." Her voice was firmer now. "You don't need the model. You grew up inside actual storms."

Finally, he looked at her. His eyes were wide, unmoored. "I don't know how to fix it without the numbers. They make sense when nothing else does."

"Forget the numbers." She squeezed his arm. "Trust yourself. Feel it."

The wind whipped louder. The chemtrail woman was screaming about government weather control. Thunder boomed above them.

Ryan inhaled sharply. Closed his eyes. For a moment, he stood perfectly still amid the swirling chaos. When he opened his eyes again, Sofie could see that something had shifted inside. There was clarity.

"It's the gradient," he said, voice suddenly calm. "The building's climate control is feeding it. We need to collapse the temperature differential." His gaze swept the room. Spotting the environmental control panel, he sprinted to it, then studied it like a code he was born to crack. "Sofie!" he shouted. "Get everyone away from the metal displays. Margo, open all exterior doors—we need to equalize the pressure!"

As Sofie herded panicked weather professionals toward the walls, she looked back at Ryan. He wasn't calculating anymore. He was *acting.* No tablet. No formulas. Just knowledge. Instinct. His fingers flew across the control panel, adjusting temperature and humidity in tight, deliberate bursts.

The storm system hesitated, the rotation slowing. The cloud mass began to shrink, condensing inward. With a last flash of harmless lightning, it collapsed in on itself, misting the crowd with a final damp burp that left the air smelling of rain and ionized particles.

Dr. Zhang stood in a puddle, blinking. "That wasn't supposed to happen ..."

Sofie jogged to Ryan's side. His hands were still trembling. Sofie felt the rapid rise and fall of his breathing when she placed a hand on his back. "You did it," she said gently.

He looked at her—really looked at her—and said, "That was terrifying." He exhaled. "Operating without a system is ..." His body shuddered.

Sofie smiled. "Welcome to how the rest of us live."

LATER THAT EVENING, the pavilion was nearly empty, filled only with the soft whir of vacuum cleaners and the distant echo of folding chairs being stacked. The air still held a faint trace of the earlier chaos—damp carpet and the lingering scent of ozone. Ryan stood alone near the control panel, staring at it. He didn't move when Sofie approached.

"Figured I'd find you here," Sofie said softly.

"I should've had a failsafe," he replied, eyes still on the panel. "I had no redundancy in my system. I failed to account for multiple critical variables. I should have anticipated—"

"You saved the room."

"I didn't shut it down correctly. I didn't follow procedure. I reacted." He turned toward her, eyes unguarded. "I guessed, Sofie."

She stepped closer, resting a hand on his arm. "Yeah. You were scared. But you acted. You solved the problem."

"I didn't like not knowing what to do," he said, barely audible.

Sofie felt the vulnerability in him like an exposed wire. Ryan, who built systems to keep uncertainty at bay, had been stripped to instinct—and had survived.

"There's a pub down the street," she said. "Let's go. No algorithms. No number-optimization. Just a drink. Or two. Or more."

He hesitated. She could see the calculations begin behind his eyes—alcohol content, blood sugar ratios, the likely impact of two drinks on logical reasoning.

Then he stopped. And nodded. "Okay," he said quietly. "Let's do it."

Chapter Eight

The Notebook

Ryan sat at his meticulously organized workstation, which stood in stark contrast to the cheerful chaos of the open-plan office around him. His desk was the only one at Prestige Events with a ruler permanently stationed at its edge—not for drawing straight lines, but for ensuring that his laptop, notepad, and framed photo of the research station maintained their precise 90-degree angles to the desk's perimeter. Three mugs, each labeled with their specific purpose (Morning Coffee, Afternoon Tea, Emergency Hydration), stood in ascending order of size. A small potted succulent—the only one that had survived the office's erratic temperature fluctuations—sat exactly five inches from the back right corner of his desk, its position marked by nearly invisible pencil dots on the wooden surface.

According to the email notification from Margo that went out at precisely 10:00 a.m., Prestige Events would be adding a new coordinator to the team. The message had included multiple exclamation points—a level of punctuation enthusiasm Margo usually reserved for genuine celebration. Sofie had replied with a string of emojis that Ryan had spent the past hour trying to decode. He found the dancing woman and facepalm combination especially confusing.

Margo's message made little sense to him. His own statistical analysis showed that their current staff-to-event ratio operated at optimal efficiency. Adding another variable to their carefully balanced system seemed unnecessary. Moreover, it had taken him fifty-four days to reach a comfortable equilibrium with Margo and Sofie and the others on staff. Starting that process over again with another person felt ... inefficient.

He reached for his Standard Office Interactions notebook—bound in blue leather, its pages divided into color-coded sections for each colleague. He had nearly filled the "Sofie Chen: Behavioral Observations" section, which was already three times longer than anyone else's. Perhaps he would need to start a new notebook entirely for this new, unknown hire who would soon disrupt their carefully calibrated ecosystem.

This personal interactions notebook was proving even more useful than he'd expected when he started it. He never imagined that it might supersede the utility of his taxonomy spreadsheet. But it had. The original taxonomy spreadsheet still existed—he'd spent too many hours categorizing behavioral subtypes to delete it now—but the sheer number of footnotes and exception cases had made it, in Sofie's words, "delightfully useless." She'd said this while peering over his shoulder last Tuesday, her fragrance momentarily overwhelming his olfactory senses. The way she said "delightfully" had made it sound different from when others dismissed his systems as useless. More like a private joke than a critique.

He was learning to recognize the difference. Just as he was learning other things about Sofie: the way she twirled her pen absently when thinking through a problem. How she hummed show tunes under her breath while reviewing contracts. The fact that her laugh had nine distinct variations. (He had cataloged them in a separate spreadsheet, though he wasn't entirely sure why he'd felt compelled to do so.)

These observations felt relevant to his work somehow, though he hadn't determined their practical application. Like how his productivity decreased by approximately 23 percent when Sofie wore her hair down. Or how his heart rate exhibited unusual patterns when she leaned over his desk to point something out on his monitor. He thought perhaps he should consult a medical professional about that last one.

Margo had said he was "growing into the role," which Sofie had explained meant he was learning to understand their clients as people rather than data points. He wasn't entirely sure that was accurate. He still saw them as data points. He just had a better appreciation for how wonderfully irregular data could be.

Sofie had already been instrumental in helping him navigate what she kept calling the "squishier" aspects of the job. When he'd struggled to understand why the World Clown Association had objected to his color-coded scheduling system (which, he maintained, was extremely efficient), she'd pulled him aside and explained that professional clowns spent their lives subverting exactly these kinds of rigid structures.

"They're not being difficult," she'd said. "They're being themselves. Sometimes the best organization is letting people feel comfortably disorganized."

He wasn't entirely sure he agreed, but he'd started adding flexibility metrics to his planning algorithms.

He turned to the green-coded section of his notebook, the one devoted to Jenny. Looking through it, he smiled, thinking about her genuine enthusiasm. He recalled the time the office-supply shipment had mistakenly included five hundred flamingo pens (non-retractable, ink quality: questionable). Jenny had adopted the pens with ironic enthusiasm. He'd caught her making a pair of them dance on the break room counter. "Look," she'd said. "They're doing the cha-cha." Ryan hadn't liked the little birds. He felt like they were mocking him with their tiny plastic eyes.

He'd cataloged how Jenny always referenced some part of her body when she adjusted the office thermostat ("My god, it's cold in here. I can't feel my knees"). He had come to like and even admire her vivacity—her bright energy. He could see that it wasn't a liability, but a kind of emotional superpower. Ebullient interest, it turned out, built stronger connections than polite detachment, even if the topic in question involved procuring freeze-dried duck treats or rhinestone-studded poop bags for the New York Pet Expo.

Her sunny disposition was relentless; she once described a plumbing failure mid-conference as "a learning moment—only with water features." Ryan still refused to follow her suggestion of starting each morning by "manifesting positive energy through interpretive dance." But thanks to her influence, he had, without thinking, once used the phrase "sparkle vibes only" in a Slack message. He immediately deleted it—but not before Jenny responded with a glitter GIF.

Flipping through the orange section devoted to Todd, Ryan was reminded of what in some ways was the most shocking thing his new colleagues had taught him—that sheer weirdness, strategically deployed, could be a strong asset to a team. Todd had a talent for defusing tense situations with off-topic asides—"This reminds me of that time I had to smuggle a live badger through airport security; don't ask." He had a way of leaving clients too confused to remain angry.

He narrated stressful moments like he was Sir David Attenborough ("And here we see the junior coordinator in his native habitat, surrounded by foam-core signage ...") and once calmed a panicking keynote speaker by offering a guided meditation in the voice of Werner Herzog. Against all odds, it worked. Todd was a marvel.

And sometimes, when the sheer strangeness of this job defied even his own systems, Ryan found it useful to review the field data—moments of spontaneous chaos that somehow worked. One of the most illuminating case studies of Jenny and Todd's shared absurdism came during what the team now referred to as *The Great Swag Purge.*

He and Sofie had come upon the scene on their way back to their desks from getting coffee in the break room. Jenny and Todd were standing in front of Storage Room B, the entrance of which was propped open with a traffic cone and cordoned off with neon tape like a crime scene. What lay beyond looked less like a storage closet and more like the ruins of a civilization that worshipped branded merchandise. Dust motes danced in the fluorescent light, illuminating layers of promotional sediment from conventions past. Years of leftover promo items had metastasized into a monument to misguided branding: towers of collapsible water bottles, crates of laser pointers that didn't point, pyramids of stress cubes in electric lime and 'corporate teal.' And tote bags. So many tote bags.

"What are you guys doing?" Sofie asked.

"Apparently we've reached *critical swag mass,*" Jenny said. "Margo wants us to clear this stuff out. Today."

Sofie hooked a tote bag on the toe of her shoe and dangled it like a biohazard. "Did these multiply in the dark?"

"They reproduce when neglected," Todd said. "Swag breeds." He ventured inside, Indiana Jones-style, and reemerged with a familiar item. “Remember this gem? *I Tote, Therefore I Am*? It killed with the Descartes Academic Society. Less so with academic humans.”

Jenny, who now had ventured inside herself, said, "I propose we sort things by—" She caused a small avalanche of rubber duckies when she tried to reach a bag of branded peanuts that bore an expiration date from the Obama era. "Sorry!" she yelled, as the duckies' cheerful yellow forms bounced around with tiny squeaks that sounded like deranged cheerleaders.

Ryan and Sofie had left them to the task, but returned later to see how the project was progressing.

Todd had the immediate area of the hallway segmented into two sections: *Functionally Useful* —piles of USB drives (mystery capacity), carabiners (non-climbing), and writing implements (mostly subpar); *A Carnival of Curiosities*—stress balls shaped like various professional symbols (gavels, stethoscopes, scales of justice), mugs with motivational Latin quotes, and an alarming number of branded lint rollers and golf balls.

When he noticed Ryan and Sofie looking at the assortment, Todd held up a calculator shaped like a tiny briefcase and frowned at its existential inefficiency.

Jenny, forced a little farther down the corridor, seemed to be spending most of her time trying on things and laughing. She sported a towering stack of hats that swayed with each head movement. "It looks like a novelty store threw up in here, don't you think?"

Sofie said, "Goodwill? Salvation Army?"

Todd held up something that looked like a business-card holder fused with a back scratcher. "You think even Goodwill wants this?"

Ryan leaned toward Sofie and whispered, “I'm starting to believe entropy isn't a threat here. It’s a strategy.”

Sofie grinned. “You’re catching on.”

Then, Jenny looked at a message on her phone and let out a guffaw. "The dental gods have saved us. Prestige has been hired to support the upcoming National Dental Hygienists’ Conference. They’re specifically requesting us to ‘enhance the swag experience.’”

The two of them exchanged a look—equal parts opportunity and mischief.

“We’re really gonna dump all this crap on dental hygienists?” Todd asked.

“They *love* little things,” Jenny said. “Branded chapsticks, compact mirrors, miniature floss samplers. They’ll think they’ve hit the jackpot.”

“But the branding won’t match,” Todd protested.

“Neither does this pineapple-shaped pencil sharpener from the *Equine Supply Chain Expo 2018,*” Jenny said, holding it up. “And yet it exists. ... Let's start re-sorting. Anything mint-scented, weirdly shaped, or ambiguously branded goes to them."

Ryan tilted his head slightly. “I'm not sure if we're facilitating a cleanup or enabling a deeply specific form of performance art.”

“Either way,” Sofie said, “it’s good for morale.”

“Look!” Todd cried, opening a box in the back corner. He

held up a stress ball shaped like a molar. Adopting the wide-eyed wonder of Owen Wilson, he said, "Whoa. Get a load of that! A stress ball *and* a molar. The universe totally delivers, man."

The whole episode had told Ryan more about his colleagues than several weeks of structured observation. There was no worksheet for what he'd witnessed—just instinct, irreverence, and a strange sort of synergy that couldn't be quantified. Jenny and Todd had taken a roomful of discarded junk and transformed it into a kind of communal folklore. There had been laughter, invention, shared absurdity. And Sofie, right there in the middle of it, encouraging the mischief while nudging it just enough to keep things on track.

It wasn't just functional. It was *alive.*

Now, with Margo's announcement hanging in the air, Ryan found himself calculating risks—not logistical ones, but social ones. Would a new hire understand the rhythms of this place? Would they appreciate that progress here sometimes took the shape of chaos before order? What if the new person didn't laugh at duck avalanches or see the creative potential in novelty lint rollers?

What if they didn't *get* Jenny? Or dismissed Todd's rambling detours as unprofessional? What if they interrupted Sofie mid-hum without realizing it meant she was problem-solving?

Would this new person treat Ryan like a curiosity instead of a colleague? Would they scoff at his notebooks, roll their eyes at his measured cadence, or—worse—try to "fix" him?

It wasn't that he feared change. Not exactly. It was that, for the first time in his professional life, Ryan Porter felt like part of something that worked. Imperfect, unpredictable, occasionally illogical—but still functional. Still whole.

And he wasn't sure how many more variables it could absorb before that balance was lost.

Chapter Nine

Off Script

After two straight days wrangling flammable egos at the American Gas Association's conference, Sofie needed to be where no one could lecture her about pipeline integrity or methane misclassification. This small Italian restaurant fit the bill—quiet at this hour, with warm garlic-scented air, flickering candlelight, and zero chance of encountering anyone from the Natural Gas Storage Subcommittee.

Ryan slid into the booth across from her, his movements as precise as ever, the fake-leather seat releasing a soft creak. He scanned the room—scattered late-night diners, a waiter polishing glasses with rhythmic focus—and gave a small, approving nod. "This was a good selection," he said.

Sofie smiled. "I do have excellent taste."

"Empirical data suggest you have an 83 percent success rate with restaurant choices."

She laughed. "Is that a real number, or are you just inventing statistics to charm me?"

He paused. "Does it matter, if the outcome is favorable?"

She rolled her eyes and grabbed her menu. "I needed this. I still can't believe the Renewable Methane breakout session almost combusted ... over cow-waste sourcing guidelines. It was like watching two rival directors fight over a Shakespeare interpretation."

Ryan sipped his water. "The likelihood of fireworks at that panel was high from the beginning. About 90 percent, I'd estimate."

She smiled. For weeks, she'd been working to figure out Ryan's analytical mind. Now, she was finally just ... enjoying the weirdness. "It's nice to talk," she said after a moment, surprising herself. "Without managing a crisis. Or needing to turn your statistics into something that won't terrify the general public."

"You're very easy to talk to," Ryan said. Simply. Like it was a data point he'd just verified.

Something warm unfurled in her chest. Her gaze drifted across the room, settling on a couple near the window. "Oh, look. Three o'clock," she whispered, "Must be a first date. He's trying way too hard. Look at how he keeps adjusting his shirt cuffs. And she's already checked her phone twice under the table. I give it twenty minutes before she gets a mysterious emergency text from her roommate."

Ryan glanced. "The statistical probability of a successful relationship with those variables—"

He was interrupted by the arrival of their waiter. Ryan ordered the arugula and fennel salad, followed by the branzino with lemon and capers. Sofie went for the caprese salad and the house-made pasta bolognese.

The server gestured toward the wine menu. "Might I suggest our excellent Chianti Classico? It pairs beautifully with our handcrafted pasta dishes and," he smiled at them like they were newlyweds, "life's more meaningful moments."

Sofie barely stifled a laugh. "You okay with splitting a bottle of wine?"

Ryan hesitated, then said, "That would be fine."

She smirked. "Look at you, being all flexible. Any preference? Red, white, something sparkling?"

He considered. "You ordered pasta bolognese, so a red would be the optimal pairing. Do you have a particular preference?"

"Montepulciano d'Abruzzo—earthy, smooth, perfect with pasta."

"Sounds like a reasonable selection," he said, dead serious.

As the waiter walked off, she leaned in. "That guy's definitely a struggling actor. He delivered that wine pitch like Hamlet's soliloquy. Only thing missing was the spotlight."

Ryan's mouth twitched again. "This is interesting. We take in the world differently, you and I. Where I noted the efficiency of the server's movement and order-taking, you saw an entire performance. Your world is full of characters and backstories—mine is full of data points and patterns."

His observation was so accurate—both about her and about himself—that it caught her off guard. And, if she was being honest, delighted her. "You're not wrong," she said. "When I look around me, I do see characters."

She nodded toward another table. "See that couple near the kitchen? Definitely food critics trying to be incognito. But they out themselves by taking tiny bites of everything and having intense whispered discussions."

"What about that family in the corner?"

"Three generations of Italian-American restaurateurs judging every dish against Nonna's recipes. Look how the grandmother keeps shaking her head at the marinara sauce."

"Is it impolite to say you're very weird?"

"Not as long as I can say the same about you." She set her chin in her hand. "Tell me—how did you become you? I've heard bits and pieces, but what was growing up in the Arctic really like?"

"Quiet," he said finally. "Very quiet. Not empty, just ... layered. The kind of silence where you can hear ice shift miles away. I used to watch the aurora for hours, trying to find patterns in the lights."

"Sounds magical."

"My mother called it my personal light show." His voice softened. "She encouraged my observations."

"And you weren't lonely?"

"I didn't realize I was supposed to be. Loneliness requires awareness of something missing. I didn't know I was missing anything. I didn't know any other way to be." He shifted in his seat, organizing his thoughts. "The station only had eight permanent researchers, including my parents. Everyone there approached the world through measurement and classification. When you're six years old, and the adults around you are measuring seal migration patterns to the half-meter or calculating atmospheric carbon levels to the third decimal place, you internalize the idea that precision is valuable. Normal, even."

"Yes, I see. So you learned to be exact," Sofie said.

Ryan nodded. "People sometimes assume that my parents must be cold and unfeeling. That's not true. But they're very focused on their work. They're passionate about knowledge, about understanding systems. They'd explain things to me endlessly—not to train me, but just because they wanted me to understand what they found so interesting."

"And you loved that."

He nodded. "I did." He smiled and took a sip of water, savoring some memory. "For my tenth birthday, they gave me my first spectral-analysis kit." A hint of warmth colored his voice. "Most kids get bikes or video games. I got tools for measuring and quantifying the world."

"No other kids around?" she asked gently.

"None. Just adults who thought in terms of variables and measurements, who rewarded questions with thoughtful explanations. When I made my first predictive model of snowfall patterns at age twelve, the entire research team reviewed it with the same seriousness they'd give a colleague's work."

"What about at school? Did you have friends there?"

"Home-schooled. I learned biology by tagging seals, physics by maintaining and monitoring weather instruments, math by analyzing ice core samples. My parents and their colleagues were my teachers. I had books. And access to the Internet and a vast digital library. But there were no other kids around. Just my curiosity and adults who treated questions like opportunities for deep explanation."

"Wow. So, no playground politics, no cliques, no social hierarchies. No passing notes to the pig-tailed girl sitting in front of you."

"Right. And you can see the result." His smile was self-aware, full of self-deprecation. "People sometimes ask if I'm 'on the spectrum.' But that implies a binary. It imagines a separate category rather than a range of human neurodiversity. By definition, everyone exists somewhere on the neurological spectrum. It's just a question of where."

That stopped her. She'd never thought about it like that.

"But I also think ... the way I am was learned. I was surrounded by systems thinkers, and I adopted that mental framework." His fingers traced an invisible pattern on the tablecloth. "By the time I entered more 'typical' social settings, my patterns were deeply ingrained, my methods already ... divergent. The way I processed information, the way I spoke, the way I approached problems—all of it marked me as different."

The waiter finally arrived with the wine, and the pair

quietly watched him uncork and pour, the soft pop of the cork followed by the gentle glug of wine filling their glasses. Sofie laughed aloud at one point when the waiter's series of flourishes seemed particularly absurd—the theatrical way he presented the cork for inspection, the elaborate swirl of the bottle. When he finished, Sofie plucked her glass from the table and raised it toward Ryan. "Cheers."

"And to you," he said.

She tilted her head. "And college? Was that a huge culture shock?"

"Yes." A deadpan response, though his eyes flickered with amusement. "I thought I was prepared. I'd studied human social dynamics. But I hadn't accounted for ... the gap between theory and practice."

She smiled. "Did you date? Hang out with girls?" She quickly recalibrated. "Or guys? ... Or were you too busy running advanced calculations on human behavior?"

"There was a girl in my advanced linear algebra class who asked me to coffee multiple times. I realized, too late, that she was thinking of them as dates." He paused. "By the time I figured it out, she'd moved on to someone more ... socially adept."

"Her loss."

Ryan's head tilted slightly, as if filing that response away for future analysis.

"At Caltech, there must've been others like you—students who saw the world through data."

"Some. But I was ... an outlier. More systematic and structured than most."

"Do you ever wonder who you'd be if you'd grown up somewhere else?"

Ryan looked at her directly now. "You mean with neighborhood kids and public schools and all those messy, unpredictable social situations children learn to navigate? Would I still sort my socks by weave density? Would I still create spreadsheets for optimal coffee-brewing temperatures?"

In that moment, Sofie saw a glimpse of something she suspected few people ever got to see—Ryan Porter, contemplating the complex variables that had shaped his identity. As if paying respect, the restaurant seemed to grow quieter around them, the soft murmur of other conversations mixing with the gentle clink of silverware and the distant sound of the espresso machine hissing behind the bar.

The conversational focus shifted to Sofie after that. He asked about her childhood, her theater experiences, her college years. And maybe it was the wine—smooth and earthy as it warmed her from the inside—or maybe being with Ryan somehow drew it out of her, but she told him stories she hadn't thought about in years. Playing every orphan in *Annie*. And the time she had to coordinate an entire show's scene changes when the stage manager got food poisoning. He asked questions. Real ones. And seemed genuinely interested by her answers.

When he asked her what she enjoys doing in her free time, she kept her answer casual. "Oh, I don't know ... bowling with friends. Or sometimes we go axe throwing. There's this bar in Williamsburg where you can do that."

"Axe throwing?" Ryan straightened with interest, like

she'd said the bar had a particle accelerator you could play with.

She smirked. "Oh, that gets your attention?"

He nodded. "It presents numerous variables worth analysis. Rotation rates, optimal force curves, kinetic modeling ..."

Sofie burst out laughing. "You know that most people just throw the axe and hope it sticks, right?"

"How inefficient." He frowned slightly. "A proper mathematical model could vastly improve accuracy."

She considered him. "Ryan Porter, want to come axe throwing with me sometime?"

He hesitated—calculating. Then nodded. "I'd like that."

She grinned. "Yeah?"

He nodded again. "I once created a thirty-page analysis of optimal spear-fishing techniques that my father never actually used. If I were to make an axe-throwing manual for us, I'd expect you to study it."

"Oh my God," she said, laughing. "You are a piece of work." She touched his hand, a quick brush of fingers.

But she felt it—the slight tremor in his hand, the surprising warmth of his skin, the way everything around them suddenly stilled. And for a second, she could have sworn he forgot to breathe.

Chapter Ten

The Mindfulness Mutiny

Like many office-wide calamities, this one began with an all-staff email from Margo.

> *Subject line: "Let's Breathe!"*
>
> Starting this morning, our unit is launching Mindfulness Monday—a brief, guided-breathing and reflection session from 9:00 to 9:20 AM every Monday in the conference room. Participation is mandatory for anyone who is in the office. Let's reset, recharge, and realign together. Bring your inner calm and leave your phones at your desk!

Ryan stared at his screen, calculating the loss of 30 minutes of peak cognitive function every Monday. "Oh, no," he muttered.

“Consider this a spiritual diagnostic,” Jenny said, spinning lazily in her chair. “Your soul needs a hard reboot.”

“I don’t have time to defrag my soul,” Ryan replied. “Also, how can mindfulness be mandatory? That’s logically inconsistent. Doesn’t enforced relaxation create a recursive stress paradox?”

“Maybe just give it a chance,” Sofie called as she passed with coffee. “What’s the worst that could happen?”

“Reduced productivity. Schedule disruption. The intrusion of unquantifiable ‘feelings’ into decision-making.”

“Sounds like utopia,” Todd said, joining them. “Except the feelings part.”

Ryan arrived early to the conference room, the space somehow still carrying the lingering aroma of Friday’s client lunch. He sat with his tablet on his lap, ready to log physiological metrics: heart rate, stress levels (subjective 1–10), ambient temperature, and productivity-loss indicators.

The others wandered in. At precisely 9:00, Margo entered wearing a “Peace, Love, & Planners” tee and sandals that slapped against the linoleum. She carried a small Bluetooth speaker blaring a loop called “Zen Cactus Wind”—an audio track that sounded, to Ryan, like a malfunctioning elevator.

“Welcome to our first Mindfulness Monday!” Margo beamed with the enthusiasm of someone who’d clearly watched several YouTube videos over the weekend to get some ideas. “Let’s begin by being still. Phones away, please. Eyes closed. Minds open.”

Ryan dutifully closed his eyes and immediately felt his

productivity anxiety spike. His stress level, which he'd rated a manageable 3 before entering the room, jumped to a 6.

"Let's do some deep breathing," Margo said, her voice taking on the unnaturally soothing tone of a meditation app. "Breathe in slowly through your nose," she instructed. "Feel the air filling your lungs. Release tension with each breath. Breathe in for four. Hold for four. Exhale for four."

Ryan tried to follow the instructions but believed the 4-4-4 pattern was suboptimal. His own research favored a 4-7-8 ratio for optimal parasympathetic nervous-system activation. Suggesting this aloud, however, seemed likely to trigger a social-anxiety cascade. He remained silent.

Seven minutes and thirty-three seconds in (he'd been counting), he cracked one eye open to check his watch. To his surprise, he discovered he wasn't the only one cheating. Jenny was stealth-typing on her phone, hidden under a spiral notebook. Todd was peeking at notifications on his Apple Watch—pretending to stretch, but periodically looking at the device, turned inside his wrist.

"Now let's practice mindful awareness of our surroundings," Margo continued, oblivious to the secret multitasking occurring around her. "Without opening your eyes, notice the sounds in the room."

Ryan heard the soft tapping of Jenny's fingers on her phone screen, the barely audible buzz of Todd's smartwatch notifications, and Sofie quietly humming—a tune he finally identified as the annoying hold music from their A/V vendor.

Meanwhile, his own stress level had climbed to a 7. The forced inactivity was making him acutely aware of all the tasks awaiting his attention. The Lincoln impersonators' convention needed final headcount confirmations. The romance writers' catering order required verification. The pet groomers' equipment list needed completion.

"Let's try a body scan meditation," Margo announced. "Starting with your toes, slowly bring awareness to each part of your body."

Jenny stage-whispered, "My body says it needs espresso, *stat.*"

Ryan tried to focus on his toes, but instead began calculating the long-term ergonomic effects of the conference room chairs on spinal curvature. His tension spiked to an 8 as he realized this meditation was preventing him from addressing actual workplace-wellness issues, like this objectively terrible seating.

At 9:17, Jenny's phone emitted a popcorn-like notification sound. Margo's eyes opened just long enough to shoot her a disappointed look.

At 9:20, a soft chime indicated the session's end, and Ryan immediately began documenting his findings. He logged his final stress measurement: 8.5 out of 10.

"Thank you for showing up for yourselves," Margo said brightly. "Now—how does everyone feel?"

"So relaxed," Jenny lied smoothly, discreetly sliding her phone into her pocket. "Very centered."

"Totally refreshed," Todd agreed, while his smartwatch buzzed with what was probably the fifteenth notification he'd received during their "mindful" session.

"Really peaceful," Sofie added, rolling her eyes for the benefit of the others.

"And you, Ryan?" Margo turned to him.

Ryan consulted his data, torn between honesty and social diplomacy. "The experience was ... quantifiably counterproductive," he said finally. "My stress levels increased significantly due to involuntary cessation of productivity."

Margo's smile faltered. "Maybe it just takes practice. Okay—everyone, go forth and mindfully conquer the week," Margo commanded.

Everyone fled the room like someone had yelled "Fire!" Back at their desks, the reactions came quickly.

"That was oppressive," Todd said. "Stillness is a form of violence."

Jenny leaned over Sofie's cubicle wall. "I reached a state of higher consciousness."

"You were texting," Ryan said.

"Of course," Jenny said. "How else could I stay spiritually in tune?"

By lunchtime, Ryan had emailed a 9-slide deck to Margo titled: *Mindfulness Monday: Quantitative Outcomes Report*. Slide 3 featured a bar graph labeled *Perceived Relaxation vs. Actual Productivity Loss*. Slide 6 included a pie chart titled *"Who Was Faking It?"* (Answer: 87 percent, plus one abstention).

Margo responded with a one-line reply: "No one is excused from next week." Thirty seconds later, another message arrived from her: "And whoever keeps setting the thermostat to 74—stop doing that. Immediately."

BY WEEK FOUR, the staff was in revolt. When Margo showed up at the conference room at 8:59, no one was there. A sign on the door read *CANCELLED.* She finally found them in the break room, where they'd started their own new Monday morning ritual—*Caffeinating and Complaining.* The rich aroma of fresh coffee and glazed donuts had replaced breathing exercises and any pretense of mindfulness. The space buzzed with animated conversation and the satisfied sounds of people mainlining sugar and fryer grease.

Ryan directed Margo's attention to the whiteboard, where a graph showed his accumulated data: *Time Lost vs. Serenity Gained: The Mindfulness Delta.*

Eyeing first the graph, then the donuts, Margo sighed. "Fine. Next week, we'll make it optional."

A cheer went up.

"It's too bad," Margo said. "Because it's good to be mentally present."

"I'm mentally present with this donut," Todd said, studying it like it held eternal truths. Then, in a Gollum voice, he added, "We are one with the donut, yesss, precioussss ..."

"I'd kill for a donut, but my fingers are frozen into claws," Jenny said, jabbing at the thermostat with hands balled like crab pincers.

Chapter Eleven

Four Score and Several Lincolns Ago

Ryan's internal urban-navigation system flared red: danger ahead. The sidewalk along Madison Avenue outside the Marriott Grand Central was clogged with what appeared to be a full-scale infestation of Abraham Lincolns. Black wool coats huddled in solemn formation, stovepipe hats swaying in the breeze. Ryan counted seven Lincolns, one of whom had opted for the pre-presidential beardless look—a choice that seemed to be causing considerable distress among the others. He caught the musty scent of vintage fabric and stage makeup drifting in the cool Manhattan air.

Sofie appeared at his elbow, somehow having bypassed his personal spatial perimeter undetected. "There you are," she said. "The Lincolns want their meeting room reconfigured. Something about wanting to recreate the Cooper Union speech setup? And they're refusing to discuss it with anyone who hasn't read the full text."

Ryan suppressed a smile. Finally, his encyclopedic knowledge of Lincoln's political oratory—studied during long Arctic winters—might prove professionally relevant. "I assume they'll want the original layout," he said, pulling out his tablet, already thinking where to find the relevant schematic. "The Cooper Union Hall had significantly different dimensions from those of our Maple Ballroom. I estimate we'll need to account for about a 25.4 percent variance in square footage."

Sofie gave him that look he'd once cataloged as Concerned Confusion but had since reclassified as Amused Tolerance. "Just ... try not to start another civil war over historical accuracy, okay?" she said, patting his shoulder. The gesture—unnecessary but consistent—occurred in more than half of their interactions.

"And Ryan? Remember what we talked about with the percentages?" She headed through the revolving door.

Right. She'd told him repeatedly that "normal people" didn't find statistical specificity soothing. He mentally rounded down and grimaced. He could hear his mother's voice in his head: *Ryan, in science we only round under protest.*

Inside the lobby, the Lincolns formed a perfect hexagon, blocking access to both the coffee cart and the elevators. The beardless one stood slightly apart, consulting a leather-bound volume that definitely hadn't been printed by 1860.

"Gentlemen," Ryan said, in a tone he deemed era-appropriate, "I understand we need to discuss the Cooper Union layout."

Six pairs of deep-set eyes turned to him. The seventh Lincoln was occupied at the coffee bar, loudly insisting to the barista that the presence of oat milk was an anachronism she should correct.

"Young man," the tallest Lincoln intoned, "are you familiar with the spatial requirements for proper oratorical projection in a pre-industrial speaking venue?"

"I am, in fact. The Cooper Union speech of 1860 was delivered in the Great Hall, with fifteen hundred attendees arranged in a semi-circular configuration to optimize acoustics within architectural limitations."

A ripple of approval moved through the hexagon. The beardless Lincoln took a step closer, tucking his book away.

"As you'll see," Ryan continued, "our Maple Ballroom presents certain spatial challenges that will require mathematical compensation to maintain historical authenticity while conforming to modern fire codes."

"Mathematical compensation?" The words came from behind him, accompanied by an alluring scent that his brain automatically categorized as Sofie-specific.

"Yes," he said, trying to focus on the Lincolns. "I've devised three different layouts that maintain the original proportions while optimizing sight lines and exit access."

Sofie stepped into view. "What Ryan means," she said, addressing the Lincolns, "is that he's found a way to make you all look presidentially perfect from every angle. Right, Ryan?"

The hexagon murmured appreciatively. Ryan opened his mouth to correct this oversimplification but felt Sofie's hand brush his arm—her standard signal for *quit while you're ahead.*

"Right," he said instead, though the imprecision pained him. "Shall we review the options in the ballroom?"

As the Lincolns filed toward the elevator, Sofie whispered, her tone patient, "Ryan, this isn't a geometry problem."

It was, actually. Everything was geometry if broken down properly. And if there was one thing he understood, it was spatial optimization.

Entering the elevator, Ryan took note of its weight capacity. During the 21-second ascent, he calculated the combined historical weight of seven Abraham Lincolns (at 180 pounds each, according to documented records), Sofie, and himself. He caught Sofie watching him with a twitch at the corner of her mouth. Her shoulder bumped his, a fleeting contact that carried the warmth of her body, making his carefully maintained spatial algorithms flicker and reset. It wasn't unpleasant—just distracting enough to scramble his concentration for a few seconds longer than he liked.

The elevator opened onto the third floor, unleashing its historical cargo into the hallway. Ryan had just begun shepherding the presidential procession toward the Maple Ballroom when a gasp erupted from the tallest Lincoln.

"Is that ... a Confederate?!"

Ryan followed his line of sight. At the far end of the hallway, a man in a gray uniform with gold braid was exiting the men's restroom, adjusting his elaborate hat. Ryan vaguely recognized him from an early logistics meeting—Kowalski, the guy obsessed with cannonball procurement standards.

"That's General Beauregard!" one of the bearded Lincolns bellowed, his voice ricocheting down the hallway. "Enemy of the Union!"

The man in gray looked up, startled. His eyes widened in alarm at the sight of seven Abraham Lincolns bearing down on him like stovepiped specters of vengeance.

"Actually," Ryan said quickly, stepping between the Union and Confederate lines, "that's Mr. Kowalski from the Civil War Re-enactors Society. They're meeting in the Oak Room to discuss battlefield authenticity standards. He's portraying General Pierre Gustave Toutant Beauregard, yes, but—"

Too late. The Lincolns were already marching toward Beauregard.

"Sir!" the tallest Lincoln called out, pointing a dramatically accusatory finger. "You stand on Union soil!"

Kowalski, to his credit, did not flinch. He swept his hat off with theatrical flair and executed a perfect Southern bow. "Indeed I do, Mistah President," he drawled, the accent thick as Mississippi mud. "Or should I say, Mistah Presidents? My, my, the Union must be truly desperate to require so many of you."

The Lincolns bristled. Ryan calculated the statistical probability of an actual physical altercation at 13 percent—and trending upward.

"Gentlemen!" Sofie said brightly, inserting herself into

the historical standoff. "What a fascinating coincidence! This is exactly how we planned to begin the 'Divided Nation' panel discussion."

Ryan blinked. There was no such panel scheduled. He made a mental note to retroactively insert it into the program.

"Yes," she continued smoothly, "an unscripted encounter between Lincoln and Beauregard—dramatizing the unresolved tensions of history. We'll follow this up with a debate."

The Lincolns' rigid postures softened slightly, their theatrical instincts clearly intrigued by this unexpected plot development.

"A debate?" Ryan asked.

"Yes," Sofie said, her voice picking up confidence as she improvised. "On whether historical reenactments should prioritize emotional authenticity or factual accuracy. Right, Ryan?"

He recovered quickly and nodded. It sounded like something they might actually schedule. "Correct. We've conceived it as a dialectical exploration of performative historicity versus documented precision."

Kowalski, clearly a seasoned improviser himself, picked up the thread. "Well now, I do declare! That sounds mighty interesting. Though I maintain, sirs, that the emotional truth of history cannot be captured through mere facts and figures."

The beardless Lincoln stepped forward. "And I maintain,

sir, that emotional truth without evidence is historical fantasy."

Just like that, the potential confrontation transformed into an impromptu philosophical face-off. Ryan watched in fascination as Sofie somehow herded all parties toward the Magnolia Room—conveniently empty—for what she was now calling an "unscheduled historical summit."

"That was impressive," Ryan told her once the Lincolns and the Confederate were safely engaged in debate, the tallest Lincoln already at the whiteboard drawing a Venn diagram of *Historical Accuracy vs. Emotional Impact.*

"Just basic crowd psychology," Sofie replied with a shrug. "People in costume are always looking for a stage. Give them one, and they forget about fighting."

"I'll add that to my conflict-resolution flowchart," Ryan said, making a note on his tablet.

But their Lincoln-related challenges were far from over.

Jenny sprinted up, clipboard in hand. "We have a problem with the luncheon setup!"

"Define 'problem,'" Ryan replied, already calculating probable variables: food shortage, equipment failure, staff conflict.

"The Lincolns requested a historically accurate mid-19th-century lunch banquet," Jenny explained, slightly breathless. "But they've just sent back the entire meal because, and I quote, 'Lincoln would never have eaten hothouse tomatoes in February.'"

Sofie pinched the bridge of her nose.

"Also," Jenny continued, "they're fighting about whether

Lincoln preferred apple or peach pie, and two of them nearly came to blows over whether the tableware was historically accurate. One is insisting we replace all the stainless-steel cutlery with period-appropriate bone-handled utensils."

"Where would we even—" Sofie began, then stopped when a commotion across the lobby caught her attention. Through the glass doors of the ballroom, she could see a new group arriving—five more Lincolns, costumed not in historical wool but in cinematic interpretations of Lincoln: Henry Fonda Lincoln. Daniel Day-Lewis Lincoln. Even Vampire Hunter Lincoln.

"The Lincoln Movie Portrayers Guild," she whispered. "We can't let them see each other. The Historical Authenticity Lincolns think the others are populist frauds. Last year in Boston, one of them challenged Daniel Day-Lewis Lincoln to a duel!"

The Movie Lincolns were approaching the ballroom. The Historical Lincolns were visible through the glass. Contact was at hand. Ryan's calculations gave them 17 seconds. That was either enough time to prevent disaster—or narrate the Gettysburg Address at auctioneer speed.

"Sofie," he said quietly, "presidential confrontation is imminent."

Sofie was already moving. She intercepted the Movie Lincolns with a brilliant smile, smoothly redirecting them toward the service corridor with promises of a "special red-carpet entrance befitting cinematic royalty." Ryan, meanwhile, hurried to the ballroom's control panel and dimmed the lights under the pretense of "testing the historical ambiance for the Cooper Union recreation." The Historical Lincolns were immediately distracted, debating whether gaslight would have cast more yellow tones.

Another disaster averted.

Later, leaning against the ballroom wall, Sofie gave Ryan a sidelong glance. "You know, after dealing with these Lincolns, I think I understand you better."

"How so?"

"They see everything through a hyper-specific lens. Every detail matters. Every variable. Every measurement. Sound familiar?"

"Are you suggesting I'm like a Lincoln impersonator?"

"Not in the beard department." Sofie laughed. "But there's a certain ... intensity of focus, a ... passionate precision. And honestly? It's kind of impressive."

Before Ryan could respond, Jenny's voice crackled over their headsets.

"Code Stovepipe, south corridor! I repeat, Code Stovepipe! The Movie Lincolns and the Historical Lincolns have made contact! Vampire Hunter Lincoln is challenging Gettysburg Address Lincoln to an oratory duel!"

Sofie met Ryan's eyes. "Time to defend the Union."

They ran.

Chapter Twelve

A Combustible New Element

"I'm sorry, who did you say we're interviewing?" Sofie's coffee cup froze halfway to her lips, the warm ceramic suddenly feeling heavy in her hands.

"Trevor Hoyt." Margo beamed, shuffling through the stack of papers on her desk. "His references are stellar. Ten years in the industry. Managed some of the biggest conventions in the Midwest. Karen Taylor at GlobalCon says he's a miracle worker. Nancy Swanson, CEO of Conventional Planning in LA, says the same."

The coffee cup made it back to the saucer on Margo's desk without spilling, which Sofie considered a minor victory. "Trevor Hoyt," she repeated, her voice carefully neutral. "From Chicago Events Network?"

"That's right." Margo looked up, finally registering Sofie's tone. "Why? Do you know him?"

Sofie's laugh came out sharp and bitter. "You could say that. You may not remember that I worked at CEN for fifteen months before coming here." She paused, weighing her words. "Margo, you can't hire him."

"Can't?" Margo's eyebrows rose. "A strong word. What happened?"

Sofie inhaled. "He's ..." She closed her eyes, memories flooding back. Late nights at the office that turned into drinks that turned into more. Trevor's magnetic confidence that had seemed so appealing at first. The way he'd made her feel special, chosen, valued. Until she realized she was just another pawn in his constant game of personal advancement. "He's not right for Prestige."

"Personal reasons or professional ones?"

Sofie met Margo's gaze and opted for full candor. "Both. We dated briefly. It ended badly. But this isn't just personal. His whole approach to event management is completely wrong for us. He wings everything, takes unnecessary risks, treats client concerns like they're mere suggestions. There was also a troubling pattern of him creating problems at events in a way that undermined colleagues. He'd then swoop in and somehow fix things, ensuring he'd always be seen favorably by higher-ups." Sofie had always worried how far he'd go to make sure that happened.

"His references—"

"Yes, I'll bet they're good. He cultivates friends in the

industry. Trust me, I've seen how he operates. He's all charm and no substance."

Margo studied her for a long moment. "You know I value your opinion, Sofie. But these ..." She tapped the pile of recommendations. "... are from friends of mine. Karen's been in this business thirty years. Same with Nancy Swanson. I know them. They're not easily fooled."

"He's very good at managing up. That's his specialty."

"Maybe." Margo's voice softened. "Look, I understand this is uncomfortable. If you'd rather not be involved in the interview process—"

"No." Sofie straightened. "I need to be there. Someone has to provide a reality check."

Margo consulted her watch. "He'll be here in twenty minutes. Would you mind meeting him in the lobby? Professional courtesy."

Sofie's protest died at Margo's expression. "Fine. But if you hire him, and this implodes? Don't say I didn't warn you."

THE ELEVATOR RIDE DOWN to the lobby felt like descending into her own personal hell. Each floor ding conjured a memory: Trevor's hand at the small of her back going into client meetings. His whispered comments that walked the line between professional and inappropriate. The way he'd convinced her to break all her own rules about office relationships, then acted surprised when she'd taken it seriously. The memories now were painful reminders of how she'd mistaken manipulation for intimacy.

The revolving door at the front of the lobby whooshed as it swept a tall man into the building, its exhalation of warm air carrying the scent of the street—bus exhaust, sun-baked concrete, and something crisp that might have been expensive cologne—cedar and bergamot. His posture was exactly as Sofie remembered—regal, confident, infuriating. An aura of absolute self-assurance filled the space around him like an invisible force.

"Sofie Chen," he said, smiling that precise smile calibrated to disarm. "Still luminous, I see."

The back of her neck prickled. His presence always had that effect—like standing too close to a power line.

He stopped in front of her.

"Trevor." She kept her voice professional, distant. "I'll show you to the conference room."

He fell into step close to her. Too close. She could feel the heat of him like a hazard light.

"You look good, Sof. New York life suits you."

"It's Sofie," she corrected. "Only my friends get to call me Sof. And this isn't CEN. We behave differently here."

"Oh, do you?" His voice dropped lower. "Not less kinky, I hope."

The elevator arrived with a soft chime that seemed to echo louder than usual in the sudden tension. Sofie stepped in, the cool metal of the handrail under her palm grounding her as she positioned herself firmly in the corner opposite from him. "It's more professional."

“Always so serious.” He leaned against the wall, studying her. “Remember Vegas? The fire alarm, mid-panel? Six hundred people evacuated?”

“You mean when you ignored the fire marshal and almost got us cited? Yes, I remember.”

His laugh was rich and warm, exactly the way she remembered—a sound that used to make her pulse quicken and now just made her teeth clench. “But we pulled it off. You and me. We made magic happen.” He shaded that last phrase with plenty of innuendo.

“That’s not how I remember it,” she said, her tone as cold as she could make it.

The elevator stopped at their floor. Trevor gestured for her to exit first, his hand hovering near but not quite touching her back.

“Maybe we should get coffee sometime. Talk about old times.”

“That won’t be happening.” She led him toward the glass-walled conference room, where Ryan was already arranging water glasses with geometric precision. “We’re both professionals. Let’s keep it that way.”

“Always so proper.” His voice held that edge of amusement that used to make her want to either kiss him or strangle him. “But I seem to remember some decidedly unprofessional moments ...”

She stopped short. “Trevor. Whatever fantasy you’re nursing, let it go. This isn’t Chicago. I know who you are now, and I really hope you don’t get this job.”

His smile didn’t waver. “We’ll see.”

Inside the conference room, Ryan assessed Trevor like he'd encountered a data anomaly. But he extended his hand. "Ryan Porter."

"Trevor Hoyt."

Sofie noticed that the handshake was aggressive—alpha-coded. Ryan's fingers twitched afterward.

"I've heard great things," Trevor said smoothly.

Ryan's frown indicated he was probably wondering exactly what Trevor could possibly have heard, and from whom, and whether those data points were statistically significant.

Margo swept in then, all warmth and professional charm. "Trevor! So glad you could come in today." She gestured to the chairs. "Please, make yourself comfortable."

Sofie took a seat directly across from him. A tactical error. Now she had to spend the entire interview looking at that face. So smug. Arrogant. Treacherous. But also hard to ignore the way the afternoon light from the windows caught the gold flecks in his eyes and highlighted the elegant line of his throat above his crisp collar. *Focus, Sofie,* she told herself. *Don't be stupid. Don't forget.*

Margo began. "We've reviewed your resume. We know the basics. So, let's dive right in: walk us through your most recent experience with a large-scale event."

Trevor leaned back—not enough to seem casual, but just enough to project ease and confidence. The leather creaked softly under his weight as he settled into what Sofie recognized as his 'I'm completely in control' posture.

"The Midwest Healthcare Summit. Nine hundred attendees, four days, sixty-eight breakout sessions." He smiled. "We leveraged best practices to maximize stakeholder satisfaction. There were zero complaints."

"Zero?" Ryan asked, without looking up from his notepad. "Reaching even an 88 percent satisfaction benchmark is rare. Zero complaints is statistically implausible."

Trevor's smile didn't waver. "Then I guess I'm just that good."

Sofie felt a flutter of irritation, her pulse quickening despite her best efforts, like her body was betraying every rational thought her mind was trying to maintain.

"What would you say is your greatest professional weakness?" Margo asked, and she seemed genuinely curious about his answer.

Trevor leaned forward slightly. "Honestly? It's probably caring too much. I've been known to stay at venues until 3 AM, making sure every detail is exactly right. I believe in going above and beyond to deliver value-added experiences that exceed client expectations."

Here, his eyes locked with Sofie's and he added, "I make sure everyone is satisfied. *Fully satisfied*." His tone was heavy with implication.

Sofie spotted a little gold stud in his ear. It seemed to wink at her.

Trevor shifted his gaze back to Margo and completed his answer. "So yeah, I guess my professional flaw is that sometimes I care too much about getting things perfect."

Oh, please, Sofie thought. *That line had expired with shoulder pads and power ties.*

“And how do you handle unexpected crises?” Margo pressed. “For instance, if your keynote speaker cancels an hour before their presentation?”

“That actually happened to me once,” Trevor said. “Remember, Sof? The tech CEO I pulled in last-minute?” He shrugged. “It’s about having backups for your backup plans.”

Sofie noticed Ryan’s pen stop moving. That was the kind of precise planning that would appeal to him. But then Trevor added, “Plus, you know, sometimes you just have to wing it and trust your instincts.”

Ryan’s pen started scratching again, more forcefully this time.

For Sofie, the rest of the interview passed in a blur. Trevor was exactly as she remembered—slick, vague, expertly rehearsed. He had an answer for everything, each response calculated to impress while revealing absolutely nothing of substance.

What bothered her most was how good he still was at it. How his practiced charm worked even on people who should know better—like Margo, who seemed swayed by his stories of crisis management and client satisfaction. And even a little dazzled. A bit smitten with him.

Sofie was pleased to see that Ryan was falling for none of it. His scribbles grew more agitated with every vague anecdote, every improbable claim. When Trevor started talking about his “intuitive approach to spatial management,” Ryan’s brow furrowed so deeply she thought he might combust.

After Trevor left—throwing her one last knowing look

that made her want to scream—the three of them sat in silence.

"Initial impressions?" Margo asked.

"His claimed success metrics require additional verification," Ryan said immediately. "And his crisis responses rely too heavily on improvisation."

Margo tapped her pen. "Confident, definitely. Maybe too confident. But he's experienced, knows the industry." She turned to Sofie. "What do you think?"

The words swarmed Sofie's mind. *Dangerous. Manipulative. Duplicitous. A saboteur in a bespoke suit.* She took a breath. "He's ... competent. But his style doesn't align with how we operate here. I don't see how he'd possibly mesh with our current team dynamic."

"His references are excellent," Margo said. "And we do need the help. We're slammed."

Pulling up a diagram on his tablet, Ryan said, "Actually, if we streamline existing workflows, we could avoid—"

"Ryan," Margo said, "We're overloaded. I'm hiring another person. Period. The question is whether that person should be Trevor."

Sofie stayed quiet. She knew better than to push. Margo clearly had secured approval for an additional hire. And it seemed equally clear she'd already made up her mind: she wanted Trevor Hoyt. Resisting this would only burn goodwill that Sofie might need later.

So she sat with her unease: a churn of legitimate professional doubts tangled with sharp personal memories. The way Trevor used to look at her across conference rooms—

and across pillows. The way he'd spun every lie with just enough truth to make it believable. The way part of her, even now, still responded to the charm like a bruise aching under pressure.

"I'll review all this again and speak with his references personally," Margo said briskly. "We'll revisit this tomorrow."

As they filed out of the conference room, Sofie caught Ryan watching her—not his usual analytical assessment, but something close to concern. She straightened her blazer, shoving the memories down deep. Time to compartmentalize. Again. Nothing to see here. Nothing worth revisiting.

"Right," Sofie said briskly. "Who's ready for the planning meeting about the urologists' convention?"

Ryan practically leapt at the subject change, visibly relieved.

But as Sofie followed him down the hall, she glanced back toward the elevators where Trevor had disappeared, the specter of him still unsettling her.

Chapter Thirteen

Small Talk, Big Steps

The Brooklyn Safehouse bar was dim and noisy. The place smelled faintly of spilled beer and secondhand bravado—hardly Ryan's natural habitat. Sticky floors tugged at the soles of his shoes. Bass pulsed through his sternum like a miscalibrated subwoofer. He paused just inside the door, mentally reviewing his list of conversation openers. He didn't want to be here, but he understood that workplace social bonds required periodic reinforcement through non-work interactions.

Megan from Accounting had invited everyone to Thursday happy hour. *"Gothic dive bar in Greenpoint. Cheap drinks"* was how she'd pitched it in the memo. Normally, Ryan would've declined, preferring to spend his evening updating behavioral observation logs. But tonight, he was determined to practice his social skills. *Field research*, he told himself.

The Prestige Events crew occupied a corner booth, their voices mixing with the clatter of pool balls and the clamor of twenty-somethings vying for the bartenders' attention. Ryan spotted Sofie immediately—hair down, eyes bright, laughing at something Todd had just said. The warm amber lighting softened her to a vision quite different from the crisp, professional Sofie he was used to seeing. He adjusted his collar. Pointless. It was already perfectly straight.

He approached the group, mentally queuing up safe conversation topics: shared experiences, light observational humor, minor self-deprecation. He stopped just short of the table, not wanting to interrupt Megan mid-story. She was telling the others of her plans for the three-day weekend ahead.

"A staycation," she said. "Just me, Netflix, and my couch."

Ryan cleared his throat lightly. "That sounds ... efficient," he offered, aiming for friendly. "Strategic recharging. No travel delays, no reentry fatigue."

Megan blinked—then grinned. "Exactly! Someone gets it."

The tension in his chest loosened slightly.

"Glad you came, Ryan," she said, raising her glass. "We were taking bets."

He decided honesty was safest. "I almost didn't, but then realized I need to work on my social-calibration blind spot."

The group laughed—not *at* him, but with genuine amusement.

"Welcome to calibration hour," Todd said, tapping glasses with Megan.

Sofie looked up at Ryan with an encouraging, almost proud smile. He felt a flicker of something absurdly close to happiness. She scooted farther into the booth, making room on the edge for him and patting the seat beside her.

"What took you so long?" she asked.

"I was finalizing a new exhibit plan for the taxidermists' convention. Based on species classification and average specimen size. The new layout should improve traffic flow by about twenty-three percent."

There was a beat of silence.

"Maybe we skip work talk for tonight?" Megan suggested gently. "You know—balance."

"Good god, yes," Todd groaned. "Someone get this man a shot before he starts graphing the bathroom line."

Ryan felt a flush crawl up his neck. Another misstep. Wrong tone, wrong topic.

A server appeared at his elbow. "What can I get you?"

"I require—" Ryan caught himself, recalling how Sofie always urged him to use more casual language. "I mean, uh … I'll have … something normal?" Then he remembered: margaritas. Sofie had introduced him to them that night of the meteorological fiasco. "A margarita, please."

Sofie leaned in. "Smart choice."

The conversation drifted from weekend plans to Netflix recs to a heated debate about the most addictive Trader Joe's snacks. Ryan listened, fascinated by the way topics passed between people like electricity through a wire—no clear initiator, no agenda. Just energy and timing.

When the server returned with his drink, Ryan took a cautious sip, the salt on the rim sharp against his lips. Citrus, sugar, then the tequila burning slightly as it went down.

"The sweet-to-sour ratio suggests—" he began.

Sofie gave the subtlest shake of her head.

He stopped. "It's good."

Sofie's smile widened. Progress.

Todd returned, clapping his hands. He waved them up from their seats. "Okay. Pool time. Everybody up."

At the billiards table, Jenny chalked a cue with theatrical flair, blue dust drifting in the bar's amber lighting, then took her break shot, scattering the racked balls. Ryan perched nearby on a tall stool, instinctively calculating shot angles, friction, force vectors. The math and physics that unspooled effortlessly in his mind delighted him.

Jenny's next shot veered wide. She laughed, unbothered, and lined up again.

Ryan shifted, his hands twitching slightly, his brain whirring with suppressed advice.

After her third miss, he couldn't contain it. "If you shift your stance and adjust your aim about twelve degrees counterclockwise, your odds of success improve significantly."

Jenny arched an eyebrow. "Appreciate it, Professor."

Just then, Sofie appeared at his elbow. She rested her hand lightly on his arm. The warmth of her fingers seeped through his sleeve like heat through insulation, short-circuiting his cognitive process for a beat.

"Come try darts," she said. "I bet you're incredible at calculating the release angles."

He recognized the tone—teasing, warm, with a hint of intervention. He followed her.

At the dartboard, she handed him three darts, their metal weight cool and precise in his palm—a comfort in the midst of all this social uncertainty.

"You know," she said quietly, "sometimes people just want to play without thinking about the math."

"But the math makes it better," he said earnestly. "More accurate. Jenny could increase her sink rate if she just—"

"Some people like figuring it out for themselves," Sofie said, smiling. "Even if it's less efficient."

Ryan considered this. "A book I'm reading says offering helpful suggestions is a good rapport-building technique."

"Book?"

"*Small Talk: A Scientific Approach to Social Connection.* I've been studying it. To improve my ... social protocols."

Sofie's expression softened. "Oh, Ryan. You don't need a book. Just ... be you."

He hesitated. "Historically, that's produced mixed results."

She smiled. "Previous data didn't include me," she said. And for once, he had no counterargument.

She tapped a dart against his shoulder. "Now—show me how to hit a bullseye."

He felt something stir in his chest—unquantifiable but

real. He started explaining: wrist angle, release speed, vector connections. Sofie nodded along, eyes twinkling, but when she finally threw her dart, it missed the board entirely and bounced off the wall.

"You're supposed to tell me that was close," she said, mock-offended.

"Technically," Ryan replied, "it wasn't." He paused. "But your follow-through was excellent."

She laughed, bumping her shoulder into his. "That's the spirit."

He took aim, released. The dart hit just inside the bullseye.

"Whoa," Sofie said. "That was kind of hot."

Ryan blinked. "It was?"

She didn't answer—just smiled, then reached for her next dart.

The noise of the bar faded, the smell of lime and salt sharp in the air, her laughter still echoing in his ears. Just for a moment, Ryan felt perfectly calibrated.

Chapter Fourteen

Trevor, Unfiltered

Sofie couldn't help it. Trevor Hoyt's mere presence annoyed her. Something about the way he lounged in an office chair—like it was a throne, and he was some kind of corporate Alexander the Great—made every smug look ten times more irritating than it would be on others. It was the same posture he'd assumed back at Chicago Events Network. And it worked on her nerves like a splinter.

His latest arrogant monologue was entering minute five. "Superhero fans. Celebrity impersonators. Political zealots. Nazi memorabilia collectors. All wackos!" He laughed—an effortless, maddening sound that somehow managed to be both amused and deeply condescending.

"That's not a fair characterization," Sofie said, her voice carefully even. The problem with Trevor was that he was exactly as handsome as he thought he was, which made it difficult to stay properly irritated. That small scar above his right eyebrow kept catching her eye—the one he got rock climbing in Wisconsin during that weekend she had vowed never to think about again. He'd been showing off, of course. Trevor Hoyt was always performing.

"Come on, Sof," he said, spreading his hands wide. "You handled the My Little Pony convention. You can't tell me those people aren't a few unicorns short of a stable."

"They're people with interests that others might not understand." She was proud of how professional that sounded, even as she noticed the way his shirt clung across his chest. *Focus, Sofie—remember how this ends.* "And it ill behooves us to mock our own client base."

Trevor arched a brow. "'Ill behooves?' Still with the SAT words, Princess? Some things never change."

The old nickname stung—more than it should've. He'd started calling her that at CEN, after she'd corrected his grammar on a memo. Back then, it had been almost affectionate. Now it just felt weaponized—a reminder of how easily he turned things against others.

She pivoted. "Let's talk about you. What are your interests these days?"

"Are we talking kinks, Sof?" The familiar suggestive tone in his voice made her want to hurl a stapler. "Because as I recall, you used to be quite interested in those."

"Your pastimes, Trevor. Your diversions. And don't call me Sof."

He leaned forward, and that cologne she used to love hit

her all at once. "I'll tell you mine if you tell me yours. Though I remember discovering quite a few of your ... preferences back in Chicago."

The innuendo made her stomach flip—and not in a good way.

"Let's get back to work," she said, gesturing at the pile of papers between them. "The reptile breeders' convention isn't going to plan itself."

Honestly, she was starting to envy snakes—their ability to unhinge their jaws and swallow things whole.

"No dodging. You first," he insisted. "What's your latest peculiarity?" The way he drew out that word was probably illegal in at least three states. "I'm sure you've picked up a few new ones since we last ... worked well together."

"I solve puzzles. All kinds," she said, her response crisp and clean. "And I still collect matchbooks and Playbills."

"Oh, thrilling," he said. "Want to hear about mine?" He didn't wait. "I still collect hotel 'Do Not Disturb' signs."

She'd remembered. He used to make it seem charming. Rebellious, even, in a boyish way. Now it just seemed pathetic and ... gross. A way of recording his conquests, no less repugnant than notches on a bedpost.

"Of course, you do. How charming."

"Oh, and I've started collecting PEZ dispensers." His eyes lit up with that dangerous sparkle she remembered too well. "There's something erotic about plucking those little candies out with your teeth. Don't you think?" He snapped his front teeth together, and she winced at the visceral memory it triggered.

“Do you ever stop?” She meant it to sound sharp. It came out tired instead.

“Not if I can help it.” He stretched—deliberate, slow, theatrical. His shirt lifted just enough to reveal a line of skin. She hated herself for noticing.

“The difference between me and the wackos? I don’t join clubs. No National PEZ Guild. Don’t go to conventions. No meetups. No swaps. I keep my eccentricities private.” He grinned. “Though if you come over for dinner, I’ll show you my newest acquisitions.”

“I’m not coming to your place for dinner.” Not again. Never again.

He ignored her and bulldozed ahead, exactly as he had back then, exactly as men like him always did. “Take those Mustache Institute guys,” he said, referring to attendees at an event that Sofie and Ryan had coordinated earlier that week. “Their whole existence revolves around facial hair—growing it, grooming it, defending its honor. They attend conventions. Pay dues, give awards. It’s like a support group for people whose lives peaked during Movember.”

He waited for a laugh. Didn’t get one.

“You don’t think that’s wacko? It’s like founding an organization of people obsessed with collecting belly-button lint. Holding conferences. Giving prizes for the biggest ball of navel fluff. It’s taking a perfectly normal thing and turning it into an obsession.”

Sofie crossed her arms and frowned. “Without ‘wackos,’ as you so charmingly term them, our industry would have far fewer clients. So maybe have some gratitude that they're out there?"

"Aye aye, captain!" He threw her a salute that somehow managed to be both crisp and deeply sarcastic. Just like the one he'd given her the day she told him she was leaving CEN. The sarcasm hadn't aged well.

The rest of the meeting devolved the way these meetings always did—Trevor being deliberately provocative, Sofie trying to stay professional while battling the weird cocktail of irritation, memory, and lingering attraction. When he called her "Martha" (his go-to jab at her organizational tendencies), she gathered her papers and left before she said something regrettable.

Out in the hallway, she pressed her back against the wall and tried to slow her breathing. What was it about him that still got under her skin so easily? The constant innuendo? The smug grin? The maddening self-certainty? Sure. All that. But also ... the fact that he actually noticed things about her—her temper, her perfectionism, her unironic appreciation for Martha Stewart.

He saw her. And that was what made him so dangerous. He'd won her over by knowing how to make her feel seen—not just for her looks or her networking charm, but for her mind, her drive, her work.

Which was infuriating precisely because she still badly wanted, needed, to be seen. Just not by him.

Chapter Fifteen

Reboot in Progress

The smell hit Ryan before he even unlocked his apartment door—musty, metallic, unmistakably damp. Like wet dog crossed with rusted pipe. He paused in the hallway, key suspended midair, trying to categorize the odor.

When he opened the door, his world tilted. Humid air rushed out to meet him, carrying the thick scent of soaked wood and mildew. Water. Everywhere. A slick sheen across the hardwood floor reflected the hallway light. Dark rivulets seeped from under the bathroom door. A bulging pustule in the ceiling released a slow drip-drip-drip that landed squarely on his arranged bookshelf.

"No," he whispered, the single syllable containing multitudes of horror. Then louder: "No, no, no."

He dropped his bag and lunged like a firefighter into triage mode. But it was too late. The bookshelf was a disaster. His taxonomy project, binders, charts, printouts, his annotated copy of *Freakonomics*—all soaked through, warped and bleeding ink. His color-coded storage containers, organized by function and emotional significance, had swollen and slumped like fallen pastry, the cardboard soft and pulpy under his fingertips. One box labeled *Early Modeling Projects* had collapsed completely, its contents bobbing in puddles like paper boats in a storm-wrecked marina. Years of work, of structure, of certainty, dissolving before his eyes.

The bathroom was worse. His socks squelched as he stepped inside. Water trailed down one wall, the sound of dripping echoing off the tile, taunting him in an irregular, maddening rhythm. He backed out slowly. It felt like a crime scene. The victim: order itself.

Ryan stood in the center of his apartment, chest rising in shallow bursts. He'd built his entire life around predictable systems—repeatable, reliable, rational. This wasn't a minor deviation, a small glitch. This was a full system collapse. Chaos incarnate, flooding into every corner of his sanctuary. The one place where variables stayed fixed, where he controlled the environment, where uncertainty remained safely outside the door. But no longer. Instead, the universe had sent him a cruel reminder, raw and unfiltered, that his attempts at perfect order were inadequate.

He sank onto the one dry corner of the couch and stared at the stream of water weaving across his floor. His heart raced, but he couldn't move, couldn't calculate, couldn't plan. For the first time since childhood, Ryan Porter had no algorithm to save him.

By 11:32 p.m., the plumber had come and gone. ("This building's a ticking time bomb, buddy. Galvanized pipes? They're basically medieval.") The culprit had been a burst pipe in the apartment above Ryan's. Two industrial fans now whirred in the corners like giant, miserable insects, vibrating through the floorboards and into his bones. They stirred humid air that was thick with the smell of damp wood and surrender.

Ryan had spent three hours cataloging the damage. He'd started a spreadsheet but abandoned it halfway through. Too many variables. Too much loss. He picked up the first taxonomy he ever created—age nine, Arctic fox den behaviors, laminated by his father—now a blur of bleeding ink and peeling plastic. He dropped it onto the table with a sigh of despair.

He lay down on the couch, damp and lumpy beneath him, eyes fixed on the ceiling. He tried counting breaths. Tracking heart rate. Mapping condensation patterns. None of it worked. The numbers slipped away before he could grasp them, scattering like startled birds.

What terrified him most wasn't the damage. It was the feeling of groundlessness—of having no solid structure to stand on, no reliable system to navigate by. Was this how other people felt all the time? This ... adrift?

At 2:12 a.m., Ryan sent a text to Sofie:

Are you awake?

His finger hovered. He felt vulnerable in a way he'd never before allowed himself to be. Then he added:

I know it's late. My apartment flooded. Everything's soaked. I can't seem to get my brain to reboot.

He stared at the words. Then added:

I know this isn't an emergency by normal standards, but it feels like one. I'm not good at this kind of chaos. I don't know what I'm supposed to do.

He hit send before he could talk himself out of it, then immediately regretted the nakedness of his admission. She'd think less of him now. She would see the truth: that he wasn't a system, or a savant. Just a scared man sitting in a wet apartment, coming apart.

Her reply came four minutes later.

Still awake. Want me to come over? Or call? Or just text quietly about something unrelated until your brain feels less scrambled?

He exhaled, something in his chest unclenching at the

simple acceptance in her message. No judgment. No surprise at his weakness. Just ... presence. The relief hit harder than he expected.

Could we just talk?

She called immediately. "Hey. I'm here."

He closed his eyes. Her voice—calm, low, real—did more to steady him than a hundred carefully tracked metrics ever could. A beat passed. Then another. "I know it's just a flood," he said finally, hating the slight tremor in his voice. "But I feel ... off-map."

"Of course you do," she said, and the validation in her tone made something tighten in his throat. "Your sanctuary got flipped upside down. You don't have to downplay that or apologize for being rattled."

He didn't answer. Couldn't.

"Ryan?"

"I didn't know I could feel this disoriented. Over furniture. Over paper." He swallowed. "It's irrational."

"It's not about the furniture or the paper." She didn't elaborate. She didn't need to.

Her quiet presence filled the silence like scaffolding. He listened to the soft rhythm of her breath through the line, the subtle human metronome he hadn't realized he'd needed all along—more grounding than any system he'd ever created.

"I keep thinking about my parents," he said. "When I was ten, a winter storm hit the research station. It tore off half the roof. Years of samples, expensive equipment—everything was at risk. I froze. I was trying to create a triage system, prioritize what to save." He paused. "My dad found me standing there with a clipboard, making a list. He snatched the clipboard from my hands and said, 'No time for systems, Ryan. Just grab what matters.'"

Sofie's voice was gentle. "Wise man."

Finally, he whispered, almost inaudibly, "Thank you. For ... answering."

"Anytime," she whispered back.

THE NEXT MORNING, Sofie showed up at his door—a canvas tote in one hand, coffee in the other. The aroma hit him first—warm, rich, normal. The opposite of the persistent smell of damp rot, burnt ozone, and machine oil that had settled into every corner of his space.

"Before you say anything," she said, brushing past him, "this isn't a rescue mission. This is a casual visit from someone bearing caffeine and friendship."

He blinked. He looked like hell. Rumpled clothes. Damp socks. Hair sticking to his forehead. One fan in the corner groaned.

"I used the intercom. You didn't answer, so I figured you were either asleep or standing in a puddle, mentally rebooting. Someone leaving the building let me in."

She handed him a coffee. "I figured you'd need this. ... You okay?" she asked, her eyes finding his.

He opened his mouth. Closed it. The automatic *I'm fine*

died before it reached his lips. Then, with startling honesty: "No. But I think I will be."

"Admitting you're not okay is progress. Statistically significant progress, even."

He gestured at the ruin of his bookshelf. "I keep thinking ... if I'd just gotten home earlier ..."

"Nope. Entropy doesn't care about your schedule. Or your color-coded filing system." She tilted her head, studying him. "That's the hardest part, isn't it? Not the stuff. But the cruel reminder that control is an illusion."

He wasn't sure when Sofie had learned to read him so precisely, but her accuracy was both unsettling and strangely comforting. He nodded. He took a sip of coffee. It was hotter than optimal, bitter at the edges and slightly acidic. He didn't care. For once, the imperfection felt appropriate.

She tossed the canvas tote onto the one remaining dry chair. "I brought plastic bags, paper towels, and backup socks."

He looked at the bag like it was a life raft. "You're extremely well prepared."

She grinned, warmth spreading across her face. "I work with a guy who's made me better at contingency planning."

He smiled. Despite everything. "I don't know how to deal with this," he admitted.

"That's okay," Sofie said, handing him a roll of paper towels. "We'll figure it out. Together."

Chapter Sixteen

Murphy's Law in Action

Trevor didn't believe in overthinking things. Never had. Not at Chicago Events Network, not during his brief but intense relationship with Sofie, and certainly not now at Prestige Events. Conventions, in his view, were self-regulating organisms—wind them up, let them go, stand back, and watch them run themselves. His recent string of successes only reinforced that belief, making Ryan's meticulous planning spreadsheets and Sofie's careful timelines seem like overkill to him.

But Murphy's Law, like karma, has impeccable timing.

The Reptile Breeders' Expo started off without a hitch. The exhibition hall buzzed with activity, a maze of glass and metal terrariums alive with scales, heat lamps, and the pungent blend of animal musk and capitalistic ambition.

Trevor, riding high, decided to escape the greenhouse funk and get some fresh air. Just before stepping outside, he fired off a text to Sofie:

```
Sorry about your fish crisis.
All smooth sailing here!
```

The message was part sympathy, part gloat. He knew she was wrestling with a catering emergency. The delivery of the fish for that evening's entrée was late. That she'd chosen to serve fish to reptile enthusiasts was, in his view, peak Sofie—theatrical, even in menu planning.

The first indication that his day was about to implode came when he hurried to the loading dock in response to an alert. The scene alarmed him: a splintered wooden crate, four panicked handlers with sweat beading on their foreheads despite the cool morning air, and a clipboard-wielding man whose hands trembled as he recited an inventory that made Trevor's blood run cold.

"Three Mexican Beaded Lizards, six Green Iguanas, and four Savannah Monitor Lizards. All ... currently unaccounted for."

Trevor's mind raced through the implications. Thirteen escaped reptiles, at least three of them venomous and dangerous. No immediate containment plan. And inside the building, hundreds of exhibitors and ticket-buyers.

"How long have they been loose?" Trevor demanded.

"About forty minutes," one handler admitted. "The driver of that Penske truck hit the crate as he was backing up to the loading dock. Didn't see it. He's over there, still in shock."

Trevor spotted the driver, slumped on the curb, mumbling about "mini-monsters" scattering in all directions. He indeed looked like a man who'd seen Godzilla's extended family.

Maintaining his composure—or at least the appearance of it—Trevor took charge. "Okay. We need to contain this situation. I'll get security and some experienced handlers—"

The universe, apparently deciding that escaped reptiles weren't enough of a challenge, chose that moment to plunge the entire convention center into darkness. The ventilation system groaned to a stop with an asthmatic wheeze, leaving the air thick and still, heavy with the smell of hundreds of scaly animals. From every direction came the sounds of panic: startled yelps, crashing displays, glass and metal fracturing, and the distinctive noise of reptile enthusiasts trying to protect their precious specimens—and themselves—in the dark. Cell phones soon lit the room with flickering beams, casting lizard-shaped shadows across the walls. The exhibition hall had transformed instantly from a controlled environment into something that felt like the scary raptor-in-the-kitchen scene from *Jurassic Park.*

Trevor's phone buzzed again. A text from Sofie:

```
Fish finally arrived!
Everything on track there?
```

He didn't have time to answer. A flashlight beam sliced through the dark. A security guard appeared at his elbow.

"Sir? This blackout? Seems one of the escaped iguanas found its way into the emergency generator. Fried it. So, both the main system and emergency power are down."

Trevor swore.

The next hour passed in a blur of flashlight beams. Reptile wranglers crawled on hands and knees. Increasingly creative expletives and terrified squeals filled the air. A reptile-loving influencer live-streamed the whole debacle under the hashtag *#lizardgeddon.*

The darkness, at least, helped mask the growing horror on Trevor's face as he realized just how thoroughly Murphy's Law had caught up with him.

By the time Margo corralled him for a tongue lashing the next morning, Trevor's carefully cultivated aura of effortless competence had taken a beating. The glassed-in conference room felt smaller than usual, the sun streaming through the windows making the space uncomfortably warm as he watched Margo pace like a caged tiger, her heels clicking against the polished floor with military precision.

Outside the glass walls, Sofie was at her desk, pretending not to watch. She had that look Trevor remembered from Chicago, the one that said *I told you so.* Even Ryan had paused his eternal spreadsheet-updating to watch the unfolding carnage, eyes narrowed with anthropological curiosity.

Margo pounced. "What is Rule Number One?" Her voice was like a loaded trap.

Trevor straightened his collar, buying time. "Ensure the safety of everyone attending and working an event," Trevor recited.

"And how," Margo continued, her voice dropping to a dangerous whisper, "do we ensure safety?"

"Through ... careful risk assessment." The words tasted bitter. "But Margo, nobody could have anticipated—"

"*Nobody?*" She planted her hands on the table, leaning forward. "Really? Because I have here—" She held up a familiar-looking document. "—Ryan's original proposal for the Reptile Breeders' Convention. 'Section 4.3: Potential Emergency Scenarios.' Would you like to know what's listed as scenario twelve? Care to guess?"

Trevor's stomach dropped. "I'd rather not."

"'Risk of specimen escape during loading or unloading,'" she read aloud, "'requiring containment protocols and backup power systems specifically isolated from areas accessible to escaped reptiles.'" She let the paper fall. "It's even double color-coded. Orange for high probability. And red for severe impact."

Trevor winced. Outside the glass, Sofie's expression was a perfect mix of vindication and restrained glee. Even Ryan's normally unreadable face showed the tiniest glimmer of smug.

"No one was injured," Margo said. "That's the good news. The bad news? Let's recap. Loose reptiles. Power failure. Reptile urine and feces everywhere. Angry client. Frightened ticket-buyers. Guest appearance from animal control. ... Should I go on?"

"Margo, I—"

She silenced him with a look. "Let me be clear," Margo said, walking to the door so she could address those outside the conference room as well as the person currently imprisoned in it. "This company has a reputation for handling complicated events with precision and care. We are not—" her eyes fixed on Trevor "—in the business of 'winging it.'"

SOFIE COULDN'T QUITE STOP SMILING all afternoon. Any guilt about her feeling of schadenfreude was minimal—after all, she'd warned him. Repeatedly. And he'd smirked at her whenever she suggested he do more prep.

When she walked into the break room later, the familiar smell of burned coffee and the hum of the refrigerator greeted her. She was surprised to find Trevor lounging there. She thought he'd be at his desk, at least pretending to be hard at work. But there he was, in one of the plastic chairs, his head and shoulders bent over his phone, completely at ease despite his recent professional humiliation. It looked like he was playing a game.

"Oh, hi there, Sof."

"Still limping after that spanking you got from Margo?"

Trevor looked up from his device, his usual confidence dimmed but not extinguished. He raked a hand through that artfully tousled hair. "Yeah. That was brutal. But come on—you know it wasn't entirely my fault."

She did know, which was the annoying part. The whole

thing had been a perfect storm of unlikely events—the kind of chaos that would have Ryan reaching for his probability matrices. But there was something about Trevor's refusal to accept any responsibility that needled her. It was exactly like him, this inclination to slide away from consequences while maintaining that infuriating charm. Still, she couldn't help but feel a little bit bad for him.

"Bosses love to assign blame," she said with a shrug, measuring out just enough sympathy to be collegial but not enough to encourage him. "It's part of their job."

His eyes lit up at this small concession. "Exactly! Sometimes shit just happens, right?"

Before she could respond, Jenny and Todd entered the room, both wide-eyed.

"You two look like you just saw a train wreck," Sofie said. "What's up?"

"Funny you should ask," Todd said. "Remember how we only booked half the Javits Center for The International Ventriloquists' Association?"

The tone in his voice gave Sofie pause. She nodded slowly. "Please tell me the other half is still empty."

Jenny made a noise—half giggle, half snort. "Nope. Certainly isn't. The International Mime Festival just signed a contract for the other half."

Silence.

Sofie blinked. "You're kidding."

"Nope," Jenny said. "We'll have mimes in one half, where the lineup will include 'Advanced Box Technique' and a showcase called 'Pantomime Through the Ages.' And—"

Todd cut in. "Ventriloquists in the other half, with seminars like 'Making Your Dummy's Voice Distinct From Your Own.'"

"Oh my God." Sofie's laughter bubbled up before she could stop it. "It's like the setup for a sitcom episode. Silent performers crossing paths with people who make their living throwing their voices."

Now Jenny was in full giggle mode. "Can you imagine? 'Excuse me, is this the workshop on 'The Invisible Wall' or the masterclass on 'Ventriloquism Without Moving Your Lips?'"

"The invisible rope demonstration could get confused with the puppet string workshop," Trevor suggested, and Sofie hated that this made her laugh. She finally managed to get words out. "Stop, you guys. This is serious. We need to figure out how to handle this."

"Ryan's going to have an aneurysm trying to create a spreadsheet for this," Jenny said, wiping tears from her eyes. "What is the risk probability of a scary ventriloquist dummy causing a mime actually to scream aloud in fright?"

The mention of Ryan sobered Sofie. Jenny was right: he was going to need sedation. "Has anyone told Margo yet?" she asked, already knowing the answer from their guilty expressions.

"I should probably be the one to tell her," Trevor said. "Show her I can handle the tough stuff."

Sofie watched him go, unsure if he was finally maturing —or just staging another well-timed performance.

Chapter Seventeen

Feel the Space

Now that it was underway, Sofie couldn't quite remember what madness had possessed her to suggest that the four of them spend Saturday evening bowling, followed by axe throwing.

But here they were. The Gutter buzzed with activity—the crash of pins, the rumble of balls, the low hum of friendly heckling.

Ryan had pulled out a notebook before they'd even laced their shoes. "Did you know that lane oil patterns affect ball trajectory in complex, nonlinear ways?" he asked, flipping to a page dense with diagrams. "I've been modeling it. There's a substantial effect on the optimal angle of release."

Val gave Sofie a look that could only be described as gleefully horrified. She leaned in. “Sweet baby Jesus! You weren’t kidding when you said he was intense.”

“Please don’t encourage him,” Sofie whispered.

“Please don’t stop him,” Val whispered back. “This is fascinating.”

Trevor bent over the scoring console, entering their names with the relaxed confidence Sofie always found infuriating—like he assumed everything would just work out. She looked away.

Ryan was still explaining rotational momentum. “... and if you account for the coefficient of friction, then the ideal angle of release—”

“Let’s each take a practice roll. You first, Ryan,” Trevor called out with the breezy impatience of someone who valued doing over thinking.

Ryan stepped up, released the ball, and watched it curve neatly into ... two pins ... with a disappointing clatter that echoed down the lane. He stared at the result like the lane had betrayed him. “That’s not possible,” he said, flipping his notebook open. “The angular velocity should’ve—”

“Look,” Val interrupted, moving closer to inspect his diagrams. “Sofie’s told me a bit about you—your systems, models, the whole quantitative thing. So I get how you’re approaching this.”

Ryan blinked, surprised. “You ... do?”

“Hell yes. I direct actors across stages. Spatial relationships are everything in my world, too. Just with people instead of bowling balls.”

Trevor grabbed his own ball and muscled past them.

"You're both overthinking it. You just have to go with your gut." His form was terrible—too much arm, zero alignment—but he hurled the ball down the lane like a cannon, knocking down seven pins with a satisfying crash. He turned, arms raised in triumph.

Ryan hadn't noticed. He was still pointing out arc vectors to Val.

"Okay, but look," Val said, tracing a line on one of his diagrams. "You're assuming the lane is uniform. But in theater, we know every stage has a different personality—dead spots, sweet spots, places where the acoustics are weird. Maybe lanes do, too."

Ryan's eyes lit up. "Environmental variables that can't be quantified in advance."

"Exactly! So maybe your math gets you close, but then you have to ... feel the space."

On his first real turn, Ryan got a spare. He turned back to Val and Sofie, offering his own version of Trevor's victory stance—somewhere between scientific pride and cautious optimism.

"Bravo! Bravo!" Val cheered.

Two hours later, four rumpled figures walked the three short blocks along Wythe Street to the NY Axe Throwing Range, the cool evening air scented faintly with the East River and the sound of music spilling from nearby bars. Ryan had, astonishingly, abandoned his calculations and managed to bowl a decent game—with Val coaching him to "read the lane's energy" in a way that somehow made sense to him.

"I need beer," Val said, falling into step beside Sofie. "And to understand why you're not jumping that man's bones immediately."

"What're you talking about?" Sofie whispered. "We're just four people out for a fun Saturday."

"Mmm-hmm." Val's tone could've stripped varnish. "Ryan's got that look—like you're a math problem he wants to solve. With his mouth. And you keep pretending not to notice. Meanwhile, Mr. Slick over there is basically performing a one-man show called 'Watch Me Be Charming.'"

"I need you to stop analyzing everything."

"Honey, I'm in theater. Analyzing subtext is literally my job."

Inside the axe-throwing bar, the air smelled like beer and sawdust. The rhythmic thunk of axes hitting wood targets mixed with cheers and the occasional clang of someone ringing the bullseye bell.

Val offered to get the first round. She turned to Ryan. "Want to come with? I'm curious about your take on the optimal beer-to-body-weight ratio for axe throwing."

Ryan brightened. "Actually, alcohol consumption does affect fine motor control in measurable ways ..."

They headed to the bar together, leaving Sofie alone with Trevor.

"Interesting," Trevor murmured, settling beside her. "Your friend's got good instincts."

Sofie watched Val and Ryan at the bar, laughing. Real

laughter, not Val's polite theater laugh. Ryan chuckled and gestured with unusual animation.

"She's just being nice," Sofie said, but something uncomfortable twisted in her stomach.

"Is she?" Trevor followed her gaze. "Because from here, it looks like she's genuinely interested. Smart move, actually. Most women try to change guys like Ryan. Your friend's just ... listening, trying to understand him. Unless, of course, she's trying to make a move on him."

When they returned with drinks, Val claimed the seat next to Ryan. Soon, Sofie heard her voice cut across the table: "So, Ryan—completely hypothetical question—are you into women or men?"

Ryan blinked. "I, uh ... women."

"Good to know."

Sofie noticed her move an inch closer to him, her smile warm, genuine.

"Any luck dating in New York?" Val asked.

Ryan glanced briefly at Sofie, then down at his drink. "Not really. Work keeps me busy."

"I've seen that show before! Our friend Sofie here puts the 'no' in work-life balance. But you don't have to be like her. ... You should try online dating," Val said brightly.

Ryan blinked, like a startled owl. "Online dating? I wouldn't even know where to begin."

"It's actually perfect for someone like you," Val said. "You get to present all your best qualities upfront—your intelligence, your interests, your ... unique lens on life. No pressure to make small talk with strangers at bars."

Sofie felt an unexpected pang watching Val work to put Ryan at ease, to make him feel valued rather than weird. If that's what she was doing.

"Plus," Val continued, "you'd probably create the most statistically optimized profile in history. Turn your analytical mind into an advantage."

"I ... hadn't considered that application," Ryan said slowly.

"Okay," Val suddenly announced, standing. "Time for axes. I call the human calculator as my partner. Let's combine theater intuition with mathematical precision."

"Guess that leaves you and me, partner," Trevor said to Sofie, picking up an axe with unnecessary flair. "Like old times."

"We never threw axes in Chicago."

"No, but we had other kinds of fun." His voice had dropped—just enough to hit a nerve. Not predatory, though. Almost ... wistful?

The group gathered for the mandatory safety instructions and quick lesson in technique. Ryan watched intently—then promptly discarded the suggestions in favor of his own calculated approach. His first throw was perfect in form but utterly ineffective. The axe bounced off the board with a sad thunk, clattering to the floor.

"You're overthinking again," Val said gently. "Here, watch me." She stepped up and nailed a bullseye—flair and all. "Trust your instincts."

"That's what I keep saying," Trevor muttered, managing a decent throw of his own.

Ryan stepped up again. “The rotational velocity suggests—”

“Hey,” Val said gently. “Remember what we talked about with the bowling? Feel the space first. Then apply the math.”

To everyone’s surprise, Ryan paused, took a deep breath, and let the axe fly. It stuck with a clean, sharp sound. Not dead center, but solid.

“See?” Val beamed. “Trust your gut, then use your brain to fine-tune.”

“My gut lacks a reliable data set,” Ryan muttered—then surprised himself by smiling anyway.

Val was laughing, Ryan was glowing, Trevor was sharpening his charm.

And Sofie?

She wasn’t sure if she was the lead, the understudy, or the girl who exits stage left while everyone else falls in love.

Chapter Eighteen

Eau de Pretentiousness

Ryan stood in the grand foyer of Atlanta's Kimpton Sylvan Hotel, clipboard in hand. The air conditioning hummed softly overhead, an ornamental fountain burbled nearby, and conversations about mineral content and pH levels drifted gently through the cool air. The FineWaters Summit—as the Global Premium Water Conference insisted on branding itself—buzzed with the soft clink of crystal glasses and the occasional satisfied *ahh* from attendees sampling their liquid obsessions.

Although the entire conference defied logical classification in his mental taxonomy of events, Ryan took satisfaction in knowing his scheduling matrices for this one were elegant in their precision. As he scanned the room and saw everything proceeding exactly as planned, a small thrill passed through him.

It fascinated him that humans could develop such specific passions. By his count, there were eight distinct behavioral subtypes among the attendees—ranging from "The Mineral Absolutist" (who refused to acknowledge waters with fewer than three trace elements) to "The Origin Fundamentalist" (who asked each distributor about the geological age of their source before even considering a sip).

His favorite—not that he would admit to such bias in his data collection—was the "Terroir Purist," identifiable by their habit of sniffing samples like fine wine and using sommelier terminology to describe what was, fundamentally, two hydrogen atoms and one oxygen atom bonded together.

"Things are going well," Sofie said, appearing at his side.

"Yes," Ryan said. "The event is flowing smoothly." He allowed himself the pun. His mother had once said wordplay was a sign of cognitive agility, and he'd been consciously exercising that particular muscle.

"Attendance is 9.3 percent above projections," he added, "and we've had zero reportable incidents—unless you count the Icelandic water distributor who nearly fainted when someone asked if his product contained fluoride."

"Which you're not counting because ...?" Sofie's voice lifted slightly—the pitch he now recognized as a cue for playful banter.

"Statistical anomaly. Plus, he recovered quickly once we

assured him no one had introduced municipal contaminants into his precious glacier runoff."

Six months ago, Ryan would've filed an incident report. Now he understood that some things, while technically incidents, didn't require formal protocols. He'd mentally filed this one under "unnecessary paperwork." The shift felt almost liberating.

Sofie grinned. "The water sommeliers are ready for the afternoon tasting panel," she said. "Though there's some tension between the Spanish and French contingents about proper minerality descriptors."

Ryan had anticipated this conflict. The Franco-Swiss and Iberian water schools had long-standing lexical differences, even for identical taste profiles. "I prepared a bilingual terminology concordance," he said, pulling a laminated chart from his portfolio. "It establishes equivalencies between the Franco-Swiss and Iberian mineral-water lexicons."

Sofie blinked. "You made a translation guide for ... water adjectives?"

"It seemed efficient. And wise caution. The previous SUMMIT devolved into a sixty-minute debate over whether the Slovenian entry was 'crisp' or 'brisk.'"

She laughed. "Well, no point repeating that diplomatic incident."

"Agreed. This entire conference is a fascinating study in perceived value—how humans assign prestige to something as elemental as water, purely through context and story. The scientist in me finds it irrational. The emerging student of human behavior finds it ... remarkable. And, frankly, a bit repugnant."

"You think?" Sofie gestured toward a nearby tasting station, where a woman in a lab coat was carefully pipetting drops onto the tongues of enraptured attendees. "That's Tasmanian rainwater. Forty dollars a droplet. Gathered from nets hung in a rainforest. They say it 'never touched Earth.'"

Ryan frowned. "That's physically impossible. Even collected directly from clouds, water molecules would've participated in the hydrologic cycle, meaning they've—" He caught her expression.

"Marketing hyperbole, my friend. 'Perceived value,' remember?"

He felt his face flush. "Ah, of course."

She patted his arm. He registered the contact, but didn't flinch. Further progress.

"Come on," she said, "we need to check the setup for the Water Experience Dinner. They're pairing Wagyu beef with water from an Antarctic crevasse that's been sealed for ten thousand years."

"That's excessive." Ryan couldn't help calculating the carbon footprint of importing ice from Antarctica purely for palate cleansing.

"Worse than excessive. It's obscene. Two hundred dollars for a six-pack of 'pre-industrial purity,' while half the world can't get clean tap water. And here they are swirling it in crystal like it's vintage Bordeaux."

Ryan was quiet for a beat. Then: "And we're helping orchestrate this absurd theater of exclusivity, enabling them in their illusion that they're connoisseurs because they can distinguish between Dolomitic limestone and Icelandic lava filtration."

That stopped her. She turned, saw something new in his expression. A flicker of disillusionment—subtle, but unmistakable. She'd known it would surface eventually. It always did when you worked absurd, excessive events like this. She thought about this past year alone. Gift bags stuffed with luxury watches or diamond bracelets. Keynote speakers arriving by helicopter. Clients who referred to their assistants as "supporting cast." Sooner or later, even the most data-driven coordinators felt the churn. She tucked the moment away. A conversation for another day.

A frantic server jogged up to them, slightly out of breath, sweat beading on his forehead despite the air conditioning. "Mr. Porter, we have a crisis. Madame Beauvoir insists she can taste 'modernity' in the Peruvian snowmelt."

"Socosani or Andea?" he asked, already narrowing the variables.

"Socosani. She says the volcanic filtration has been compromised!"

"Impossible." Ryan's tone was calm, steady. "That water was bottled at source in temperature-controlled containers. Any perceived changes would be psychosomatic." He paused, then said, "Please take us to her."

They followed the server to a tasting station where a stern Frenchwoman held a glass aloft like evidence in a trial.

"This water," she intoned in a thick French accent, "has lost its primordial essence."

Ryan took the glass, cool and smooth against his palm, examined it, and then mimicked the mannerisms of a sommelier. He sipped. The water was unremarkable—clean, tasteless, exactly what water should be. He closed his eyes briefly, feigning deep concentration. He considered the most effective response. A technical rebuttal would fail. A deferential validation of her expertise with a gentle redirection was statistically more likely to succeed.

"Madame Beauvoir," he said solemnly, "I believe you're experiencing flavor transfer from the Himalayan sample you tasted previously. The high mineral content of the 5100 Tibet water is known to leave residual sensory impressions that can affect subsequent tastings for up to twelve minutes."

The woman's eyes widened. "Mon Dieu! How could I have been so careless?" She placed a hand dramatically over her heart, her French accent thickening with emotion. "I have violated the palate-cleansing protocol!"

"A simple oversight," Ryan assured her gently. "I recommend a seven-minute rest before returning to the Peruvian selections."

As they walked away, Sofie whispered, "That was masterful. Did you actually taste a difference?"

"It's water, Sofie. Just water." But privately, he took some pride in how he'd handled the situation. The challenge of human interactions of this sort was becoming less daunting to him, more like a complex equation that could be solved with the right approach.

"You've developed quite the poker face."

"My analysis shows that 69 percent of client concerns are

psychological rather than factual. So, I've begun validating the concern while redirecting the underlying anxiety. It's more efficient."

She raised an eyebrow. "So ... you're saying you've learned to BS professionally?"

He considered. "I prefer to call it applied human psychology with strategic factual deployment."

"Fancy way of saying BS."

"Perhaps," he conceded, allowing himself the faintest smile.

As the evening wound down and attendees moved to the networking reception, Ryan found a quiet corner, away from the clink of glasses and murmur of conversations, where he could update his event logs. This was his favorite part of any event—the quiet documentation of successes and learnings, the transformation of chaotic human activity into clean, ordered data. But lately, he'd also appreciated the chaos itself a little more.

He sensed Sofie's approach before she spoke—the particular cadence of her footsteps had lodged in his brain, a rhythm he didn't know he knew.

"You look pleased with yourself," she observed.

"The event has exceeded efficiency projections by 12 percent. And preliminary survey responses suggest an 89 percent satisfaction rating."

Sofie smiled warmly. "For what it's worth, I think you handled this event perfectly. Even the water fanatics are impressed—and they're not happy unless their spring is tapped by virgin monks under a full moon."

That made him smile—genuinely, not the practiced version he'd once studied in a mirror. "The virgin monks are scheduled for tomorrow's specialty-sourcing panel."

"Of course they are." She nudged him lightly. "Let's go make sure the after-party doesn't devolve into water-flinging. Though if it does, at least it's just water."

"Premium water," Ryan corrected, falling into step beside her. "With terroir."

"Heaven forbid we forget the terroir."

Chapter Nineteen

Like Snowflakes

From: Ryan.Porter@gmail.com

To: Drs.Porter@nordvik.uaf.edu

Subject: Update from NYC

Date: August 11, 2024

Dear Mom and Dad,

I'm writing this from the exhibition hall of the North American Window and Door Manufacturers Association's convention. It's 1:21 AM (EST), and except for Jeff the security guard, I have the place to myself. Jeff makes his rounds every 47 to 50 minutes. He thinks I should be heading home instead of sitting here, fine-tuning tomorrow's breakout sessions on my spreadsheet.

You asked for more details about my life at Prestige Events. I've drafted a reply full of metrics and performance summaries. I assume that's what you're actually requesting. I'll send it separately.

But in the interest of writing about "the human side of things," as Sofie, my team leader, would say, I'll attempt something less structured here. It's fair to say I remain suboptimal in this realm. But as you always said about methodology: the only thing that matters is that we work toward improvement.

You also said that good science starts with honesty—especially with yourself. So here's my honest assessment: the job, the city, the constant proximity to other people—it's changing me. Not drastically. I still categorize, analyze, track patterns, and find comfort in numbers. But something's different.

I'm more interested in people. Sofie, for instance. I spend a lot of time observing her behavioral patterns. According to our colleague Todd, that sometimes leaves me "verklempt." (I told him that's a meaningless data point. Impersonating Mel Brooks, he said, "Too bad. It's still a fact: you get verklempt when you're around Sofie.")

Imprecise, but not inaccurate. I could tell you my productivity drops 23 percent when she wears her hair down. And that I've documented nine distinct variations of her laugh. But what matters more is this: I want to be the reason for that laugh. Especially the one that makes three small creases appear at the corners of her eyes—what I originally labeled Laugh Variation #4, though lately I've just been thinking of it as my favorite.

Mom, I'm fairly certain you're smiling as you read this,

probably thinking about your sea lion pair-bonding research. And yes, I see the parallels. But this feels more complex than any behavioral pattern I've ever studied. Sometimes, when Sofie touches my arm—her standard cue for "maybe dial back the statistics"—I forget what I was calculating in the first place. Todd says that's further proof of my verklemptness.

But Sofie's teaching me things I never knew I needed to learn. Like how to interpret the micro-signals in a crowd—the shift in a murmur's pitch when people get restless; the way bodies cluster near coffee stations, signaling that the pacing is off; or when a group needs an unscheduled break so the whole schedule doesn't implode.

It's like learning a new dialect of human. I'm not fluent, but I'm starting to pick up key phrases. Last week, at the American Academy of Actuaries convention, I correctly diagnosed what Sofie calls "critical restlessness" before the afternoon breakout sessions. Instead of consulting my optimization flowchart, I improvised—authorizing an emergency deployment of the backup pastry reserves intended for the following morning.

Sofie high-fived me for that. The impact of her palm against mine triggered a flutter in my peripheral nervous system that I've been meaning to document. I suspect it's another example of verklempt syndrome.

I'm beginning to understand that human behavior, like weather patterns, is chaotic but not random. There are patterns and systems in the mess, but you have to know how to look for them. Sometimes, like snowflakes, the most beautiful structures emerge when a system allows for just enough chaos. I should probably add that to my taxonomy spreadsheet—once I figure out how to quantify beautiful.

Overall, my taxonomies are evolving. What used to be a neat kingdom/phylum structure now feels more like a nuanced field guide—strange outliers, delightful exceptions, hybrid types that refuse easy classification. Sofie seems to appreciate this. She finally admitted last week that I was hired because I'm "differently wired." Her words. She immediately looked worried she'd offended me. I told her that accurate categorization is never offensive.

The clients never fail to surprise me. Take the American Pyrotechnics Association conference Sofie and I handled a while back. I discovered that pyrotechnicians are precision-chaos artists. They combine mathematical calculations with an almost poetic reverence for what they call the perfect boom. During a keynote dinner, I had a long, unexpectedly emotional conversation with Dr. Mieko Takahashi about the specific shade of blue produced by copper chloride at optimal temperature. She teared up, just talking about it. (Like you get, Dad, when talking about ice-core clarity.) Later, Sofie told me I should've seen my own face during that conversation. Apparently, I "lit up like a grand-finale sequence." I'm still parsing the simile, but I think it's complimentary.

It's 2:13 AM now. Jeff just walked by and said, "Normal people don't smile while working at this hour." I tried to explain that normalcy is a statistical construct dependent on sample size. He shook his head and called me "a sick puppy."

I genuinely don't understand what canine illness has to do with any of this.

Sometimes I miss the clarity of Arctic data. Whale songs and ice formations follow rules. But I'm beginning to see that human variables, though messier, have their own kind of structure. Like snowflakes—unique, ephemeral, and shaped by invisible principles.

Will call soon.

—Ryan

Chapter Twenty

Protocols and Pillows

Sofie prided herself on never missing work. Even during last year's flu outbreak, when half the office was down for the count, she'd powered through on a rotating cocktail of over-the-counter meds and sheer willpower. Being reliable was her thing. The person others could count on, no matter what.

Which made the text she sent Ryan at 6:11 AM all the more frustrating to write:

```
Caught some kind of plague.
Can't come in. Sorry to leave
you solo with the paper-doll
expo. 💀💀💀
```

She collapsed back into bed. Her head throbbed with a dull, persistent ache. Her throat felt like she'd swallowed glass shards. And a bone-deep chill made her teeth chatter, even under three blankets. Whatever this virus was, it had ambushed her around 3 AM with the ruthless efficiency of a special ops team. Now her entire body ached like it had been trampled by stampeding horses.

Ryan's response arrived 29 seconds later:

> `Noted. Feel better.`

Typical Ryan brevity. She managed a weak smile, picturing him already recalibrating assignments for the event. Guilt flickered—briefly—but another wave of chills pushed it away. She burrowed deeper under the covers, resigned to a day of miserable solitude.

Which is why the knock on her door at 7:32 AM seemed like a fever-induced hallucination.

She ignored it at first, pulling the pillow over her throbbing head. Then it came again—three precise raps that echoed through her foggy brain. She knew that knock.

"Ryan?" she croaked, struggling to untangle herself from the nest of blankets.

"Yes," came his muffled voice. "Please open when you're able. I'm holding perishable items."

Sofie staggered to the door, not bothering with her appearance. Ryan had seen her in plenty of unflattering states—late-night setup disasters, post-convention exhaustion, one very unfortunate wedding-cake collapse. She was beyond caring anyway. She unlocked the door and pulled it open to find Ryan holding three shopping bags and a drink carrier.

"You're sick," he said, matter-of-factly, eyeing her disheveled hair, flushed cheeks, and the way she clung to the doorframe for support. Then he stepped past her, bringing in with him the crisp scent of morning air.

"What are you doing here?" Sofie managed, her voice a raspy whisper. "The conference—"

"Doesn't start for two hours and sixteen minutes," Ryan finished. "Plenty of time to initiate your treatment."

"Treatment ...?" She blinked and closed the door, leaning against it, suddenly dizzy. "Ryan, seriously—you should be at the hotel. The setup—"

"Todd and Jenny are on-site. Setup is proceeding." He unpacked the bags with clinical focus. "Assuming you have the current influenza strain, early intervention will improve your recovery trajectory."

Sofie watched, dazed, as he methodically laid items on her counter. "Electrolyte solution, fever reducers, throat lozenges with a numbing agent, antiviral tea, honey, soup—both chicken noodle and vegetable."

"You didn't have to do this," she said, slumping onto the couch.

"True. But I wanted to." He handed her a bottle of water and a pair of pills. "Your recovery is important to me."

She swallowed the medication, too tired to argue. Ryan was already scanning her apartment like a battlefield medic. He cleared the bedside table, replacing the clutter with a neatly arranged row of water, tissues, lozenges, and meds. Then he disappeared into the bathroom. She heard water running, followed by the sound of something being filled. He returned with her long-forgotten humidifier.

"This was stored improperly behind your cleaning supplies," he noted, placing it on her dresser and plugging it in, a soft whir soon sending out a gentle mist. "Elevated humidity will improve respiratory comfort and accelerate recovery."

She watched in fevered awe as he adjusted the blinds ("optimal light for rest"), rearranged pillows ("elevated head reduces sinus congestion"), and transformed her living room into what could only be described as a boutique recovery ward.

"How do you know all this?" she asked.

"I did research. After last year's outbreak, your extended illness was ... upsetting to me. I wanted to be better prepared. I hope to avoid a repeat of that outcome."

"You researched flu-treatment protocols ... because of me?"

"Yes. This should reduce your recovery time by 30 to 45 percent."

"That's very ... efficient of you."

He handed her tea—something herbal and soothing that steamed gently in the ceramic mug, its warmth seeping through to her cold fingers. "We'll monitor your temperature every ninety minutes."

"We?" Sofie raised an eyebrow, accepting the tea. "Aren't you going to the hotel?"

"I'll join at 10:45 for keynote prep. Until then, I can establish your care system."

The matter-of-fact way he said it made something catch in Sofie's throat. He'd re-arranged his meticulous schedule for her. Without hesitation.

"You're staring at me," he said. "Are you disoriented? Confusion can be a sign of a fever."

"I'm just ... surprised. I didn't expect this. You. Here. Doing all this. Taking care of me. Most people don't create personalized treatment plans for their sick coworkers."

"You're not just any coworker," Ryan said simply, as if this explained everything.

"What does that mean?"

He paused, choosing his words. "I don't like it when you're sick. It disrupts my mental equilibrium. It ... affects me differently from when other coworkers are unwell."

From anyone else, it might've sounded clinical. From Ryan, it landed like a love sonnet.

"You worry about me?" she translated, a smile spreading despite her misery.

"Concern is a natural response to a valued colleague's incapacitation," he said, but the way he fluffed her pillows betrayed something at work beyond professional regard.

"Of course," Sofie agreed, not pushing further. "Well, I appreciate the concern. And the tea. And the ... well, everything."

He moved quietly through her space, tidying, checking the humidifier, adjusting a blanket like a backstage manager prepping an actress for a big scene. Most people brought sympathy and canned soup. Ryan brought protocols, precision, and an uncanny ability to make her feel seen, understood.

"Ryan," she murmured softly. He looked up. "Thank you. Really."

A flicker passed over his face, a softening around the eyes. Subtle, but genuine. "You're welcome."

As the medication kicked in, Sofie drifted toward sleep, comforted by the sounds of Ryan moving through her apartment, setting everything in quiet, perfect order. Her last conscious thought before sleep claimed her was that she'd never felt quite so well-cared for while feeling so completely awful.

When she woke two hours later, Ryan was gone—off to the conference as planned. But evidence of his presence remained everywhere: the humidifier gently misting the air with a soft, rhythm; the row of medications neatly labeled with sticky notes in his small, steady handwriting, indicating exact times for each dose; the containers of soup in her fridge, organized by temperature tolerance and salt content.

And on her phone, a series of carefully timed reminders had been programmed, each with specific instructions. The 11:30 AM reminder read simply: "Medication. Hydration. Rest."

Sofie smiled. She felt marginally better—not just from the medication, but from the lingering sense that she'd been cared for. Fully, precisely, and unmistakably. In the most Ryan way imaginable.

Chapter Twenty-One

Fault Lines

Ryan arrived at the conference room exactly seven minutes before the scheduled presentation to the planning committee of the American Association of Marriage and Family Therapy. Trevor strolled in with thirty seconds to spare, his smile as white as Arctic snow—but lacking its honest clarity.

Six weeks into Trevor's time at Prestige Events, and something about his presence still triggered Ryan's internal warning system. Maybe it was the clothing. Or the predatory smile. Or the way Trevor's gaze lingered too long on Sofie whenever she passed by. Ryan had learned in Alaska to recognize early signs of threat. A polar bear's subtle shift in weight before an attack. An Arctic fox's too-casual meander toward the food cache.

Trevor exhibited the same patterns—just with better tailoring.

Ryan had also noticed how Sofie tensed slightly whenever Trevor entered a room. Her movements, usually fluid, became deliberate. Controlled. Like a deer adjusting its stance in tall grass.

Now, as Sofie stepped into the conference room, voice pitched higher than usual—a tone he had begun tracking as a stress indicator—he watched her scan the space quickly.

She said, "Remember now, guys, the planning committee wants two distinct workshop models for the couples' sessions. Margo's counting on us to wow them."

Trevor moved a few steps toward her. Ryan noticed how Sofie shifted her weight—almost imperceptibly—away. A small move. Subtle. But he took note.

"I think both your approaches have merit," Sofie said, tension rising in the room. "They're just ... different philosophies."

Ryan stepped between them without thinking.

"'Different philosophies,'" Trevor repeated. His eyes fixed on Sofie like a wolf remembering the taste of previous prey. "That's diplomatic of you, Sof. But we all know which one they're going to prefer."

When Trevor said her name, Ryan saw a flicker at Sofie's pulse point. A flutter. Whether it was anger or something more complex, he wasn't sure. He still lacked good descriptions of the expressions that crossed her face when Trevor spoke to her directly.

The committee members began arriving then, filtering

into the room in familiar patterns—early birds claiming corners, social clusters forming and reforming like cloud systems. Ryan logged their entrance behaviors only as background noise—because Trevor was leaning close to Sofie, whispering something that made her cheeks flush. She stepped away quickly, busying herself with papers, but Ryan caught the slight tremor in her hands.

"Shall we begin?" Dr. Eleanor Franklin, the conference chair, adjusted her glasses and arranged her papers at the head of the table. "We're particularly interested in your thoughts on the workshop environment for our Breaking Through Communication Barriers sessions."

"Of course," Sofie said brightly. "We've got some excellent options for you. Let's start with Ryan Porter, who's done some fascinating work on optimal space deployment for couples workshops—"

But before Ryan could step forward, Trevor was already at the front, holding his palm-size presentation remote like a magician's prop.

"Actually, Sofie," he said smoothly, "I'll go first, if you don't mind." He turned to the group. "Ladies and gentlemen, I'm Trevor Hoyt, and I'm here to show you how we can leverage synergistic solutions to revolutionize your workshop environment through dynamic space utilization ..."

What followed was twenty-three minutes of what Ryan's mother would call "aggressively uninformative data visualization." Slides full of upward-trending arrows and context-free percentages. Stock photos of implausibly happy couples

—including two that looked suspiciously like Tony Robbins ads.

"And with this arrangement," Trevor concluded, "we can optimize our footprint to accommodate 35 percent more concurrent sessions. It's all about maximizing our value proposition."

Sofie said, "Thank you. And now, we'll hear from Ryan Porter, whose analysis reveals some interesting patterns in how physical space affects workshop outcomes."

Ryan started. "Traditional conference-room layouts create hierarchical power dynamics that can impede effective discussion of topics such as therapeutic progress. By implementing a modified circular arrangement with adjustable proximity zones—"

He caught Sofie's subtle head tilt, and he remembered her advice: *be clear, simple, direct.*

He recalibrated. "If you use my approach, the chairs will be comfortably positioned so that people won't have to lean to the side to see the speaker. I'm concerned that Trevor's approach puts too many people too close together. Not only would that make it hard for them to see the speaker, but they may not be able to exit the room safely in an emergency."

The air shifted with a slight hum of tension. Dr. Franklin tilted her head—a gesture Ryan associated with heightened attention.

Trevor gave a condescending smile. "Ryan, not everyone appreciates your ... unique approach to space dynamics."

"Efficiency and safety require optimal spacing," Ryan replied, pulling up a new slide. "There are strong correlations between giving people sufficient personal space and achieving workshop satisfaction and personal security."

Dr. Franklin leaned forward. "That's exactly the kind of detailed thinking we need." She then turned back to Trevor and changed topic. "Mr. Hoyt, what's your view on breakout session spacing?"

Trevor smiled and launched into what he called a "people-first approach to stakeholder engagement," which seemed to consist primarily of vague statements about "organic flow," "natural energy," and "best-in-class user experiences." Slogging through the business-buzzword blizzard, Ryan identified six logical fallacies in the first two minutes of Trevor's spiel.

Sofie's hand found Ryan's arm as Trevor presented room layouts that violated at least four fire-safety regulations.

"Breathe," she whispered, her voice barely audible above the hum of the projector.

"Of course," Trevor was saying, "I could also pivot and be agile with timing when required. Unlike some approaches that are a bit more ... rigid and siloed."

"'Rigid?'" Ryan echoed, his voice spiking half an octave. His hands clenched unconsciously into fists. And before he could run his next thought through his social-interaction filter, he said, "You mean like having actual plans, instead of just winging it? That didn't work too well for you at the Reptile Breeders' Conference."

Sofie stepped forward, addressing the committee. "Perhaps," she said smoothly, "this discussion itself demonstrates exactly why your couples workshops matter.

Different approaches to the same goal can create ... interesting dynamics."

Dr. Franklin smiled. "Well ... this has been fascinating. Gentlemen, you've given us much to consider. And, Ms. Chen, permit me to say: your facilitation of this conversation is a perfect example of the principles we teach. You're a talented mediator. I believe we made the right choice with Prestige Events. Thank you all."

A flush crept up Sofie's neck, blooming across her cheeks. Ryan watched it with fascination—and delight. His heart rate ticked up by twenty percent.

After the committee left, Trevor lingered, the leather of his expensive shoes creaking softly as he moved closer. His voice dropped to that slow, syrupy register that made the air in the room feel thicker.

"Impressive performance, Ryan. Very ... detailed." His smile reminded Ryan of the way Arctic foxes grinned at seabird nests—all teeth and predatory calculation. "But not everyone appreciates having every variable measured. Life's messy. You can't spreadsheet your way out of it."

"Calculation isn't about gaining appreciation," Ryan said. "It's about accuracy."

"Is it?" Trevor's gaze slid to Sofie. "Or is it about control? About making the messy world fit into your tidy little systems? Maybe that worked at your research station. Or when you were writing your very important master's thesis. But here in the real world ..." He shrugged, letting the implication linger.

When Trevor finally left, the tension drained from the

room like air from a deflating balloon. Sofie exhaled audibly, her shoulders visibly relaxing.

"You know he's just trying to upstage you, right? Get under your skin?" she asked.

"He's a snake-oil salesman," Ryan said.

Sofie gave a quiet laugh. "God, yes."

Her tone held more weight than he expected. Laced with memory. Experience. He realized there was a whole complicated story here that he may never be allowed to understand.

Chapter Twenty-Two

Business Buzzword Bingo

The break room smelled faintly of burned bagel and mutiny. The overhead fluorescent light buzzed with low-grade menace, casting everything in an unflattering migraine glow.

Sofie leaned against the counter, arms crossed, voice low and urgent. "Okay. I know I can't be the only one who thinks Trevor's buzzword addiction is getting … intolerable and unmanageable."

"Oh, my god!" Jenny leapt off the counter where she'd been perched, nearly upending her half-empty energy drink. Her sneakers squeaked on the linoleum as she landed. "Yesterday, I asked what else we needed on the snack re-order list, and he said we should 'deep-dive to leverage our core competencies for maximum synergy.' I'd merely been wondering what else to add besides granola bars and trail mix."

"I asked him if the ballroom A/V was set up," Todd said. "He told me he'd 'circle back once he'd drilled down on KPIs.'"

Ryan gave a slow nod. "He told me my data audit lacked 'narrative propulsion.'"

Sofie raised an eyebrow. "Was that ... feedback or a screenplay critique?"

"Unclear," Ryan said. "But he used 'granular' four times in one sentence and invented the phrase 'dashboard-forward storytelling.'"

They all paused for a moment of silent mourning for the English language.

"I actually brought it up with Margo," Sofie said, lowering her voice. "Told her the team was struggling with Trevor's nonstop buzz-speak. She said—and I'm not kidding—'I don't see a problem as long as he continues to leverage high-impact phrasing to drive ideation across verticals. He's one of our client-facing thought leaders.'"

Todd choked on his coffee. "No."

"She did. I blacked out halfway through, but I'm 90 percent sure she called him a 'synergy asset.'"

Jenny buried her face in her hands. "We're living in hell. A brightly branded, onboarding-heavy, acronym-laden hell."

"Exactly," Sofie said. "And since Margo's reaction means formal intervention is off the table, our only path to survival is mockery. So, last night, I created ... a game!" She pulled multiple sheets of paper from her tote with dramatic flair. "We'll print these on card stock."

Jenny uncrumpled it. "'Buzzword Bingo'?"

Sofie beamed. "Every time Trevor uses one of these corporate nonsense phrases, you mark a square. Win a row, you shout 'Bingo.' Win the full card, you get naming rights for the office's new espresso machine."

"What?" Todd cried. "Margo's replacing Sir Steams-A-Lot?"

"Yep. He's hissed his last hiss."

Ryan was still squinting at the grid. "Is ... is 'pain point' really that common?"

"We have a meeting in an hour," Jenny muttered, reaching for the thermostat. "You'll have Bingo by lunchtime."

THE CONFERENCE ROOM was unusually quiet—the only sounds the soft scratch of pens on paper and the barely audible hum of the overhead projector.

Trevor stood at the front, radiating confidence and PowerPoint illumination, while the team sat at the table, hyper-attentive, pens poised, water bottles discreetly shielding their Bingo cards.

"... And if we don't push the envelope," Trevor intoned, "we'll never optimize our low-hanging wins. This is really about activating cross-functional collaboration in real time, you know?"

Jenny marked a square with the silent glee of an assassin notching a kill.

Trevor clicked to the next slide. "We need to think outside the box and curate a frictionless value experience. Otherwise, we risk losing narrative cohesion."

Todd snorted so violently he had to fake a coughing fit, the sound ricocheting off the glass walls as he took an overlong sip of water to cover his reaction.

Unfazed, Trevor pressed on. "Let's not silo our ideation streams. We need to drill down on ecosystem alignment until we find the core DNA of the—"

"Bingo!" Ryan called out, his voice clear, excited.

The room froze.

Trevor blinked. "'Bingo'?"

Ryan didn't look up. "Sorry," he murmured, jotting something on his notepad. "Just ... thinking."

Trevor paused, then nodded like he'd witnessed a profound breakthrough. "Right. Bingo. Great synergy, Ryan. Love the energy. Keep it going, team. That spirit is scalable!"

Jenny clapped twice. Softly. Into her lap.

Todd took another long, expressionless sip and stared at the ceiling like he was trying to astrally project.

Sofie didn't dare make eye contact with anyone.

Trevor, glowing with confidence, forged ahead. "Now, let me pivot to the next value proposition ..."

Behind her notebook, Jenny quietly marked another square.

Chapter Twenty-Three

Future Imperfect

The Shoreham Hotel in Washington, D.C., with its art-deco elegance and old-world grandeur, had hosted presidents, diplomats, and celebrities throughout its storied history. This week, however, its marble corridors echoed with a different kind of guest: professional prophets and predictors, visionaries and doomsayers—the assembled members of the American Futurologists Society.

Ryan took a deep breath as he surveyed the controlled chaos unfolding before him. When Margo, pleased with his handling of the FineWater Summit, had assigned him this AFS convention, he'd been cautiously optimistic. Futurologists were systematic thinkers, after all—people who analyzed trends and then projected outcomes. That should align well with his methodical approach. Sofie had been assigned to handle the personalities, which seemed like an optimal pairing. But when Todd—who was supposed to help with logistics—came down with food poisoning, Margo sent Trevor in his place.

Not ideal. Ryan filed this under "unpredictable variables requiring adaptation."

Even before Trevor's arrival, Ryan had understood that handling this convention would present unique challenges. Where most professional associations operated with clear hierarchies and defined agendas, the AFS was a chaotic stew. Its annual meeting was part academic conference, part sci-fi convention, part doomsday-prepper summit.

The schedule was a fascinating study in contradictions and competing prophecies: panels ranged from "Quantum Computing: The End of Privacy?" to "Insect Protein: Humanity's Salvation," to "Preparing Your Bunker for the Coming AI Apocalypse."

The exhibitor hall presented an equally intriguing dataset of technological optimism and dystopian preparation, featuring everything from humming weather-control devices to cryonic preservation booths that emitted a distinctive chemical signature—a combination of ozone and antiseptic that made Ryan's nose wrinkle. He automatically catalogued the odor for future reference.

"I'm creating a taxonomy of attendee types," Ryan announced, showing Sofie his tablet with barely contained excitement. "So far I've documented Tech Optimists, Neo-Luddites, Apocalypse Entrepreneurs, Aquatic Adaptationists, Mars-or-Bust Enthusiasts, and Insect Protein Evangelists, among others. The behavioral patterns are fascinating—each group exhibits distinct clustering behaviors and communication protocols."

"Impressive," Sofie said, her gaze landing on Trevor trying to charm a woman whose jumpsuit appeared to be made entirely from emergency thermal blankets. Every crinkle caught the overhead lights like a disco ball.

Ryan consulted his notes. "The Insect Protein Evangelists have submitted a unique catering request for their afternoon breakout session on *Entomophagy: The Future of Food.* They've specifically requested live mealworms and black soldier fly larvae as snack options."

A look of disgust crossed Sofie's face. "Apart from being gross, is that problematic?"

"From a supply chain perspective, yes. Quite challenging," Ryan explained. "While live mealworms present minimal logistical difficulties, *Hermetia illucens*—the black soldier fly larvae—require precise temperature and humidity control during transport. Our original FedEx shipment experienced a preservation failure."

Trevor appeared beside them with perfect timing, his expression triumphant. "Actually, I've already solved that particular crisis. I found a specialty reptile-supply store twelve minutes from here that stocks fresh feeder insects. I arranged for delivery exactly thirty minutes before the *Entomophagy* session. Maximum freshness guaranteed."

Sofie blinked, processing this development.

Ryan lowered his tablet. "You successfully sourced replacement larvae? Within optimal timeframe parameters?"

Trevor smiled like a man who'd just hit a backdoor flush. Sofie glanced at Ryan, who was clearly recalculating everything he thought he knew about Trevor Hoyt.

"That," Ryan murmured, "was ... resourceful."

And all too familiar, Sofie thought, remembering times back in Chicago when things had gone wrong at events and Trevor had swooped in to save the day. But there was no time to dwell on that now.

She said, "The panel on 'Competitive Futurism' is starting soon. We should get over there to make sure it doesn't devolve into a fistfight."

The panel featured four of the Society's most intellectually combative members, each convinced they alone saw the future clearly. Sofie, Ryan, and Trevor arrived just as the opening statements began.

Dr. Isaac Kurzweil (only an "intellectual relative" of the more famous Ray, he often told people) had set up an impressive array of pulsing electronics that cast rhythmic blue patterns across the panel table. "The future is entirely digital!" he proclaimed, adjusting his bow tie. "All human cognitive processes will be reducible to binary code!"

Adjacent to him, Dr. Harvey Bracken—whose rail-thin frame and unsettlingly intense gaze suggested someone who'd spent considerable time studying very small creatures—was methodically arranging specimen jars filled with preserved insects, the smell of formaldehyde somehow escaping the sealed lids. "Completely incorrect," Bracken hissed. "Silicon is finite. Insect biomass is nearly infinite! The six-legged inheritors of Earth hold the key to humanity's survival—or its doom!"

The third panelist, a serene woman in flowing robes who'd introduced herself only as "Gaia's Voice," was lighting incense in direct violation of the hotel's fire-safety regulations. Sweet, cloying smoke drifted across the panel area as attendees in the front row began discreet coughing. "Both those perspectives demonstrate fundamental misconceptions," she intoned with mystical authority. "The future transcends technology and biology alike. The coming consciousness revolution will render your machines and bugs equally irrelevant."

Completing the quartet was Colonel Westbrook (retired), whose rigid military bearing and clenched jaw suggested deep skepticism regarding his fellow panelists' credentials. "EMP attack," he stated grimly, arranging tactical equipment across his section of the table. "Solar flare. Complete grid collapse. The future requires preparation for inevitable technological regression to pre-industrial baselines."

As Kurzweil and Bracken began arguing loudly about whether artificial intelligence or evolved insects would dominate the post-human world, Ryan felt the tension escalate beyond optimal parameters. He started calculating intervention probabilities.

Sofie leaned closer to him. "This is deteriorating rapidly. Someone needs to redirect their focus before all hell breaks loose."

"Standard mediation protocols suggest—" Ryan began, but stopped. His reserve protocols included nothing to deal with this level of ideological chaos. Then he remembered something his mother once told him about her dealings with the Arctic research team: "Sometimes, when multiple expert perspectives conflict, the solution isn't choosing sides, but finding a framework that accommodates all valid hypotheses."

"Would you mind if I try something unconventional?" he said quietly to Sofie.

Unconventional? Ryan? She looked at him with a mix of surprise and confusion. "If you have an idea, go for it."

Ryan nodded and approached the moderator's podium, his heart rate accelerating to approximately 95 BPM.

"Distinguished futurists," he said, his voice carrying the calm precision he'd learned from years of presenting research findings. "Forgive me for intruding. May I propose a thought experiment?"

All four panelists turned toward him, their arguments suspended by this unexpected interruption. The audience quieted.

"What if," Ryan continued, feeling his confidence stabilize, "each of your predictions is correct ... just in different timelines?" He gestured toward the whiteboard behind the panel table. "The multiverse theory in quantum mechanics suggests infinite parallel futures. So, isn't it possible that Dr. Kurzweil's digital ascension occurs in one probable timeline, Colonel Westbrook's technological regression in another, Dr. Bracken's insect revolution and Gaia's Voice's consciousness evolution in still others? Couldn't they all be equally valid futures, each unfolding along separate branches of possibility?"

The panelists exchanged glances, their hostility temporarily replaced by intellectual curiosity.

Seeing their reaction, Ryan pressed the point: "Rather than competing for singular predictive accuracy, perhaps your models complement each other across the spectrum of probable futures."

He watched as the transformation occurred: suspicion gave way to cautious agreement. By the session's end, all four panelists were huddled around the whiteboard, sketching a crude diagram of timeline convergence, their earlier hostilities suspended in favor of cross-dimensional probabilities.

"That was ... extraordinary," Sofie whispered to Ryan, as the session concluded to enthusiastic applause. "You just turned an ideological battlefield into a collaborative workshop."

Ryan felt the unusual warmth of satisfaction. "I hypothesized that each of them is motivated by a need for intellectual validation rather than competitive dominance. By reframing the scenario to allow multiple correct answers, I removed the zero-sum dynamic."

Sofie beamed at him. "You were so flexible. Improvisational. You really shined, Ryan!"

For that evening's "Foods of the Future" dinner, Ryan had created an elaborate seating chart that segregated attendees with contradictory food ideologies: lab-grown meat advocates were stationed far from the Ancient Agriculture Alliance, while Dr. Bracken and his entomophagists were tucked in a back corner where their insect hors d'oeuvres and caterpillar consommé wouldn't disturb other diners.

The carefully calculated arrangement lasted approximately eight minutes.

Trevor had begun circulating with champagne, casually suggesting attendees "mix things up a bit," "explore cross-pollination opportunities," and "challenge your own echo chambers."

"What are you doing?" Sofie hissed, as she watched the careful seating arrangement dissolve into free-form mingling. "Ryan spent hours optimizing that seating chart!"

"Exactly!" Trevor replied with characteristic confidence. "It was too perfect. These people imagine chaos for a living—they need it. Look—now the underwater-city designers are talking to the vertical-farming engineers. Connections are happening!"

And, Ryan had to admit, the chaos seemed to be working. Conversations sparked. Napkin diagrams bloomed. Even the insect advocates found new allies. The networking outcomes emerging from the chaos seemed optimal.

But then ...

The dining disruption created a new problem: the food itself became a weapon. Trevor's well-intentioned mixing had triggered cascading ideological warfare.

It started with the lab-grown meat samples somehow migrating to the Ancient Agriculture table, where they were being examined with the disgusted fascination typically reserved for biological warfare specimens.

"Is this lab-grown meat?" a woman in hemp attire demanded, holding a protein cube with tweezers. "This is cellular blasphemy! An abomination!"

"It's cleaner than methane-spewing beef," snapped a man wearing what appeared to be a vest made entirely of sprouted seeds.

Soon, the insect-protein evangelists, emboldened by Trevor's suggestion they "cross-pollinate," began hawking their wares with militant enthusiasm. Dr. Bracken himself moved from table to table, pressing samples of crickets and mealworms on increasingly horrified attendees.

A pale woman from the oceanic nutrition faction made the tactical error of suggesting that Bracken's insects were "nutritionally inferior to properly harvested seaweed."

Bracken's response was immediate and unfortunate. "Inferior?" he hissed, his entomologist's pride thoroughly wounded. "I'll show you superior protein efficiency!" He grabbed a handful of live mealworms from his plate and flung them directly at the oceanic nutrition table.

The mealworms scattered across the white tablecloth in all directions, several landing in wine glasses and at least one disappearing down the front of someone's dress, triggering a scream that could've summoned emergency services from three states away.

"Get those ... things ... away from me!" the woman

shrieked, knocking over her water glass in her haste to escape.

What followed was not technically a food fight in the traditional sense. Ryan himself would later describe it in his report as a "weaponized nutritional ideology conflict." The Ancient Agriculture Alliance began hurling organic vegetables with the precision of trained warriors. The synthetic nutrition faction responded with lab-grown protein cubes that, due to their enhanced density, achieved remarkable ballistic properties.

"EVERYONE STOP!" Ryan shouted, his systematic mind struggling to process the complete breakdown of all social order. But his voice was lost in the chaos as the underwater city designers used their architectural training to construct defensive barriers using overturned tables. The Mars colonization group responded by implementing what they called "hostile-environment survival tactics."

A clump of kelp hit Sofie in the arm, clinging to her blazer like an octopus seeking safety.

"Trevor," she hissed, grabbing his arm as a cricket landed in his hair, "your 'cross-pollination' just created a nutritional civil war!"

Trevor's confident expression finally cracked as he ducked a flying protein cube. "This is ... not what I anticipated," he admitted.

"Clear the room!" Ryan ordered, emergency protocols kicking in. "Sofie, get security. Trevor, assist with evacuation routes!"

It took hotel security, the local fire department, and what

Ryan later learned was a specialized hazmat team (called in when someone reported "biological contaminants being weaponized in the ballroom") to finally restore order.

The aftermath was devastating. The dining room looked like the site of a nutritional apocalypse, with organic vegetables, synthetic proteins, various insects, and kelp formations scattered across every surface. Three attendees required medical attention.

"The health department wants a full incident report," Sofie said grimly, returning from her conversation with the officials. She pulled out a chair next to Ryan. "Also, the hotel is charging us for complete carpet replacement, wall cleaning, and something called 'biological decontamination services.'"

Surrounded by the wreckage of his carefully planned event, Ryan heard her, but was focused on Trevor, who was trying to charm the increasingly unimpressed hotel manager.

"I understand your concerns," Trevor was saying, his usual smoothness sounding strained. "But if you consider the ... passionate engagement our event generated ..."

The hotel manager's expression suggested she was considering exactly one thing: the fastest way to ban them from the premises forever.

"It's his superpower," Sofie said quietly, watching Trevor fail spectacularly at damage control. "He becomes exactly who people want him to be. But apparently, nobody wants someone who accidentally triggers nutritional warfare."

Chapter Twenty-Four

Fault Lines

Sofie often felt a strange sense of possibility in Margo's office. Something about the way morning light streamed through the tall windows and warmed the polished desk reminded her of a theater just before the house opened—quiet, charged, expectant, vibrating with nerves and anticipation.

For her two-year performance review, Sofie'd chosen to wear one of her "power blazers"—the deep aubergine one that made her feel like she could handle anything, its structured shoulders bolstering her with extra confidence.

"Two years," Margo said, settling into her chair. "Hard to believe, isn't it?"

"Sometimes it feels like two decades," Sofie said, smiling.

"Do I look older? Because I feel having Trevor on the team has aged me."

Margo offered an indulgent grin in return, but her eyes were cold. "Ah yes, well ... let's talk about your team. How do you think the dynamics are working? Why don't you start with Todd and Jenny. How are they developing?"

"They're both exceeding expectations," Sofie said, her tone bright. "Todd's client management has really matured—he's got this steady, reassuring presence that works particularly well with nervous first-time convention chairs. And Jenny's become our quality-control specialist. She caught three potential catering disasters last month before they went nuclear."

"Excellent. Any concerns with either of them?"

"None. They're reliable, collaborative, and fully invested. Todd and Jenny make the team stronger."

Margo made a note. "Good to hear. Especially with the other dynamics in play. I'm referring, of course, to Ryan and Trevor."

Sofie considered her reply carefully. "Yes, it's complicated. Two very different approaches that can complement each other when the stars align. I spend a lot of time trying to bring about that alignment."

"Elaborate, please."

"Ryan's all systems and precision—which we desperately needed. He's brilliant at finding patterns and creating frameworks that actually improve our events. His data don't lie, even if his delivery sometimes needs, let's say, subtitles."

She grinned. "And he's usually right, which is helpful ... and only occasionally irritating." Another grin.

"And Trevor?"

Sofie felt the familiar knot. She chose her words carefully. "Trevor is ... gifted with people. When he wants to be. He can read a room instantly and adapt his approach. But his planning and preparation are ... not strong. I'm thinking of the reptile expo, for example. And he relies too heavily on improvisation and what he thinks of as an unerring instinct for what will work in the moment. The dinner fiasco at the futurologists' convention is a perfect instance of that. He knew about Ryan's careful arrangement of those dinner groupings, and he just decided he knew better. What a disaster."

Margo remained silent, apparently waiting for more.

"But, when everything's going his way, Trevor's effective. And, as I say, charming. It's when things go sideways that you see the real person."

"And where do you fit into this dynamic?"

Glad to be moving on from the topic of Trevor, Sofie said, "I'm the translator. The stage manager. I can take Ryan's beautiful but complex systems and make them accessible to clients. And I usually can channel Trevor's improvisational energy into something that won't blow up in our faces." She straightened. "Plus, I know them both well enough to predict their failure modes."

"That's quite a management challenge."

"It keeps things interesting." Sofie's smile was wry.

"Though, if I had to choose, I'd take Ryan's methodical intensity over Trevor's improv roulette any day."

"Speaking of Ryan ..." Margo's tone shifted. "You two seem to have developed quite a partnership."

Sofie felt heat rise in her cheeks. "He's not what I expected. When he first started, I thought he was just this analytical machine. But he sees patterns in everything—not just data, but people, emotions, timing, the way things connect." Sofie realized how animated she'd become. She dialed it back. "He's genuine. What you see is what you get, which is ... rare."

"Mmm-hmm," Margo said, with a raised eyebrow. She paused, then pulled out a folder. "Your client satisfaction scores are excellent. The Orthotics and Prosthetics convention was particularly well-executed. Walk me through how you and your team managed that one."

Sofie relaxed into familiar territory. "It was a classic study in contrasts. Trevor treated it like a networking opportunity—within twenty-four hours he was best friends with the keynote speaker and had talked his way into a VIP whiskey tasting. He called it relationship building. I called it shameless opportunism."

Margo frowned. "And Ryan?"

"He spent the first day analyzing foot-traffic flow patterns and assessing the efficiency of the exhibit-hall layout. One vendor came back from lunch to find their booth relocated to prime real estate because Ryan had determined they were suffering from 'suboptimal positioning algorithms.'" Sofie grinned.

Margo consulted notes in the open folder. "I understand there was an incident at the ... prosthetic running blade demonstration? Fill me in on that."

"Ah, yes. Well, Trevor, ever the opportunist, saw an opening for a viral marketing moment and convinced the event photographer to snap him 'testing' a blade. Let's just say the resulting image belongs in an ad titled *Man Deeply Regrets Choice.* By the end of the convention, Trevor had charmed half the industry and pocketed several high-end swag bags, while Ryan submitted a proposal for a more efficient convention layout that could cut next year's footprint by a third."

Margo closed the folder and crossed her hands over it, regarding Sofie closely before saying, "Sofie, your tone when discussing the two of them is noticeably different. You're far more negative about Trevor. I know you didn't want me to hire him. But I did, and, unlike you, I'm not displeased with his work. But I'm concerned that if you can't overcome this ... animus you harbor toward him, it may compromise your leadership. Damage the work of your team."

Sofie felt her heartbeat race, the rapid pulse echoing in her ears as she realized Trevor already had Margo in his pocket, which was going to make managing this team in the future all the more difficult.

"This is a relationship business," Margo continued. "How you manage them affects everything else."

Sofie bristled at Margo's presumption to coach her on the primacy of relationships. Her hands clenched involuntarily in her lap as she seethed but remained silent. She kept her expression composed.

Margo leaned forward. “For what it’s worth, I believe your instincts about Trevor are wrong. You’ve got history with him that’s coloring your judgment. And you’ve clearly developed feelings of some sort for Ryan. It’s all over your face when you talk about him.”

Sofie was about to push back then stopped. “Fine. Yes, working with Trevor is complicated because I know exactly what sort of deceptive behavior he’s capable of when his performance is underwater.” She paused. “And yes, Ryan ...” She trailed off, uncertain how to continue.

“Ryan what?”

After another long pause, Sofie said, “Nothing. I’ve said all I have to say about Ryan.”

Margo stood. “Sofie, your two years here have been strong. Positive. You’ll get the raise you deserve. But you’re managing competing tensions—old baggage with Trevor, and ... something with Ryan, all stuffed into compartments. Resolving those tensions, even just acknowledging them, could make your work—and your life—a lot easier.”

Sofie rose, the review having reached its final, pointed note. “I’ll take that under advisement.”

“I’m sure you will.” Margo’s smile was unreadable.

As Sofie walked back to her office, her heels clicking on the polished floor, her thoughts tumbled over each other like dice in a cup. The ground she’d spent years mapping—between professionalism and emotion, between past and possibility—no longer felt like neutral territory. It felt like a fault line waiting to crack.

Chapter Twenty-Five

Trivial Pursuits

The dimly lit interior of Brooklyn Brewery hummed and thrummed to the sounds of clinking glasses, animated conversations, and occasional, overenthusiastic shouts from the corner where the Knicks game played on muted screens. Ten minutes until Tuesday Trivia Night kicked into gear.

Their table—squeezed between the dartboard area and a column blanketed in decades of stickers—forced them all into what Sofie, channeling Ryan, considered "uncomfortably intimate proximity."

"I still can't believe we got Ryan to come out on a weeknight," Jenny whispered, sliding into the booth with a pitcher of beer. "Does he know there's no spreadsheet category in bar trivia?"

“I told him it’s a perfect petri dish for observation, for research,” Sofie said, grinning. “He’s developing a taxonomy of competitive group behaviors.”

Todd snorted. In a Bela Lugosi voice, he said, “Of course he is.”

Trevor arrived, all charisma and Banana Republic swagger. “Who’s developing what now?”

“Ryan’s cataloguing trivia dynamics,” Jenny explained.

“Is he?” Trevor’s smile widened as he spotted Ryan approaching with Val. “Our very own David Attenborough, studying the natives!”

Sofie rolled her eyes. “Be nice.”

“I’m always nice,” Trevor said.

Ryan came back from his utensil-hunting mission, which the others told him was unlikely to be successful. “It’s mostly finger food here, Ryan,” Jenny had said. But like Indiana Jones with a tray of ancient relics, Ryan returned with napkin-wrapped utensils. He gave the table a wary once-over. “Bar tables like this one harbor almost half again as many bacteria as the average toilet seat.”

“Charming,” Trevor said, grabbing a mozzarella stick with his fingers.

“Who’s played before?” Val asked brightly.

“College champ three years running,” Trevor boasted, leaning back with infuriating confidence. “Mostly carried my team, if I’m being honest.”

“Which you rarely are,” Sofie muttered under her breath.

“What’s that, Short Fuse?” Trevor’s use of another of his old nicknames for her made her cheeks warm with irritation.

“Nothing. Just remembering your creative interpretation of ‘team effort’ back in Chicago.”

Before Trevor could retort, the trivia host’s voice crackled through the speakers. “Alright, quiz-heads! Get your team names on the scorecards. Five rounds, six questions each. Winners get bragging rights and fifty dollars off their bar tab!”

“Team name ideas?” Jenny asked, pencil poised.

“Event Horizon,” Todd offered. “We’re from Prestige Events.” He absently peeled the damp edges of a beer mat, its fibers coming apart beneath his restless fingers.

Val raised a brow. “We’re not all from Prestige. And that’s boring. How about ‘The Spreadsheet Supremacy’?” She nudged Ryan, who was sanitizing his portion of the table with clinical precision.

“Statistically, team names containing puns win 23 percent more often,” Ryan noted.

Trevor leaned forward. “How about ‘Trevor’s Angels’?”

“Not in this lifetime,” Sofie shot back.

They settled on “The Convention Misfits,” a name Ryan approved.

“Its mild self-deprecation makes us appear less of a threat to other teams,” he said.

Jenny said, “Ah, I like it. Wolves in sheep’s clothing.”

Or in Banana Republic’s, Sofie thought.

The first round—pop culture, sports, geography—was a slow burn. Trevor got three right with the smug assurance of a man who’d memorized every *Esquire* listicle. Sofie and

Jenny snagged one each. Todd guessed the previous year's Super Bowl MVP. Ryan said nothing.

"You good, Calculator?" Trevor smirked. "This game not your forte?"

Ryan tilted his head slightly. "I'm observing the optimal strategic approach before contributing."

Then came the History round. The host had barely finished the question—"Which Roman emperor completed the Colosseum?"—when Ryan's hand shot up, nearly toppling a pint glass.

"Titus Flavius Vespasianus inaugurated the structure in 80 CE with 100 days of games, including gladiator combats and wild animal fights."

Trevor's fingers tightened on his glass.

Jenny, recording responses, deadpanned, "Next time, just 'Titus' is fine." She leaned toward Sofie and whispered, "If he starts listing decimals of pi, I'm getting another pitcher just for myself—maybe two."

When Ryan rattled off the Treaty of Versailles' signing date—"June 28, 1919"—and cited three key clauses, Trevor muttered, "Lucky guess." By the end of the round, Trevor's smile had tightened to something closer to a grimace.

"You didn't say he was a history buff," he whispered to Sofie as they waited for round three.

"Ryan's an ... everything buff."

The Science round made things worse. Trevor—who claimed to be "second only to Bill Nye" in science expertise—missed basic questions. Ryan rattled off the 27 bones of the hand and identified a star's gas composition without blinking.

The Literature round finally broke Trevor. When Ryan not only cited an obscure quote but named the page number from the first edition, Trevor got up and stalked to the bar. Sofie knew that he hated being outshone. In any setting.

"Maybe dial it back?" Sofie suggested quietly to Ryan.

Ryan looked genuinely confused. "Isn't accuracy the objective?"

"The objective is drinking beer and showing off just enough to feel smart without making everyone else feel dumb," Val explained, patting his arm. "It's a delicate balance."

"Should I introduce an error rate? Maybe 25 percent?"

Sofie laughed. "Maybe just skip a question now and then?"

The air was thick with fryer grease and yeasty beer as Trevor returned with fresh drinks and a smile reinstalled.

"Ryan, my man," he said, sliding over a beer. "You've been holding out on us. Where'd you learn all that random stuff?"

"Learning isn't random," Ryan explained, placing his pint glass on a fresh coaster. "During polar winters at the Arctic research station, I had access to the digital library. With eighteen hours of darkness, reading was a statistically significant use of time."

"So you just ... memorized entire books?" Jenny asked.

"Only the ones with useful data sets," Ryan replied, as if that clarified anything.

Trevor's smile had taken on that calculated edge Sofie remembered too well from Chicago—the look he got when assessing a potential rival. "Well, you're full of surprises, Calculator. Wouldn't have pegged you for a trivia guy."

"This is my first formalized competition in recreational knowledge. Though my father did test my recall abilities using similar formats during ice-drilling expeditions."

Val shot Sofie another wide-eyed look. *You weren't kidding about the childhood either.*

The final round—"Potent Potables"—was their last hope. But Ryan, it turned out, had also memorized cocktail recipes, brewing methods, and the history of distillation and fermentation.

"The process of distilling whiskey likely came to Ireland via monks in the 11th century. The term 'whiskey' derives from the Gaelic *uisce beatha*—'water of life'—first recorded in the year—"

Jenny cut him off with an exaggerated sigh. "Ryan, that's the fourth time you've given us an etymology lesson. Next time, just A, B, C, or D. Okay?"

When the Convention Misfits were declared runaway winners, the host half-jokingly accused them of cheating. "Nobody knows that much random crap."

"Actually—" Ryan began.

"We'll take our bar tab now," Sofie said, cutting him off, her voice bright enough to forestall further discussion.

As the team celebrated, Sofie and Val watched Ryan animatedly explain fermentation processes to Todd, who stared at the ceiling fan, clearly overstimulated.

"He's a walking encyclopedia," Val whispered to Sofie. "You told me, but wow."

"He's unique," Sofie agreed, not bothering to hide the affection in her voice.

Trevor caught it. Leaning closer, his voice smooth and taunting, he murmured, "Well, well. Does our Sofie have a thing for the human calculator?"

Sofie stiffened. "Don't be ridiculous," she snapped. "We're colleagues."

"If you say so," Trevor replied, his familiar, knowing smirk firmly in place. "But I've seen that look before, Short Fuse—it used to be directed at me."

Later, Ryan announced, "I've analyzed our performance metrics. Trevor contributed most in pop culture—66.7 percent accuracy. Sofie excelled in questions requiring intuitive leaps rather than factual recall. The group's most interesting dynamic was during answer deliberation—"

"Ryan," Sofie interrupted gently. "Maybe save the analysis for tomorrow? Tonight's just for having fun."

Later, as they walked toward the subway, Trevor gestured expansively beneath the glow of street lamps, Ryan listening with intense focus.

"They seem to be getting along," Val observed.

"For now," Sofie replied. She couldn't shake the feeling Trevor was gathering data of his own. He hated being outshone—and Ryan hadn't just outshone him.

The game had just changed. And Sofie knew one thing for sure about Trevor Hoyt: he never played fair.

Chapter Twenty-Six

The Saboteur's Martini

Trevor believed in two things: his own charm and the power of last-minute improvisation. He could feel that charm working even now as he straightened his collar and checked his reflection in the lobby's mirrored wall. To Trevor, event planning was like jazz—improvised, charming, and never the same twice. A little rhythm, a lot of ego, and plenty of behind-the-scenes fixes nobody saw coming.

The problem was, the attendees at the International Gathering of Psychic Intuitives & Mystical Practitioners (IGIMP) believed in approximately eight thousand things—including the power of planetary alignments, the restorative effects of crystal energies, and the cosmic significance of proper event scheduling. And they were in no mood for Trevor's jazz.

The universe sent its first warning Tuesday morning when Trevor arrived at the Grand Meridian Hotel's registration desk and found himself facing a coven of displeased astrologers. Oblivious as always, he greeted them with his usual bonhomie and most winning smile. "Good morning, my mystical friends! Feeling the vibrations?"

They turned on him as one, jewelry jangling like wind chimes in a hurricane. The scent of patchouli and barely contained fury hung heavy in the air. The eldest—silver-haired, eight rings per hand, eyes sharp as obsidian—stepped forward and jabbed an accusatory finger into his chest. Trevor recognized her as Madame Celeste, the head of the Astrological Planning Committee.

"You," she hissed, voice low and ominous, "have committed an act of cosmic negligence."

Trevor blinked. "I—I what? I'm sorry? What seems to be the—"

A second astrologer, draped in a shawl patterned with planetary symbols, snarled. "You scheduled the Grand Banquet during the Void of Course Moon!"

Trevor's smile faltered. He remembered seeing their ten-page memo on planetary timing. He'd skimmed it—skimming was his thing. He'd assumed their fixation on celestial timing was more suggestion than necessity. A vibe. Like feng shui—decorative, optional. He was suddenly realizing that wasn't the case.

"The thing is," he tried, smoothing his blazer's lapel, "sometimes we have to work within logistical constraints—"

"Constraints?" barked a bearded man in a vest covered in

star charts. "You ignored the Grand Conjunction of Jupiter and Saturn—a moment of cosmic power and infinite possibility! By ignoring our request on scheduling the banquet, you've now consigned the entire event to the Abyss of Misfortune and Lost Vibrations."

Trevor frowned. "That sounds like a goth metal band."

"This is not a joke!" shrieked a woman clutching a crystal ball. "You've cursed the convention!"

"I ... okay, just so I understand—are we talking, like, low attendance, bad vibes, food poisoning?"

"Worse!" gasped another, clutching her amethyst pendant. "A banquet held during the Void of Course Moon is doomed. Utterly doomed."

Trevor exhaled and pinched the bridge of his nose. "Okay, folks, let's not panic. Take a deep breath. I'm sure we can, uh, counteract this. Maybe we can open the banquet with a quick cleansing ritual? Sage? Chanting? Whatever it takes."

The suggestion backfired immediately.

Within the hour, the entire hotel lobby had become a metaphysical triage center. Tarot readers were dealing cards in a frenzy. Mediums linked hands in emergency séance circles, channeling spirit guides for advice. Three psychics live-streamed doom-laden predictions, and one commandeered the hotel PA system to apologize to "the spirits" on behalf of the convention.

Trevor was trying to convince a group of crystal healers that realigning the banquet tables might offset the disharmony when someone nearby chanted "Cleanse the space!" A heartbeat later, the fire alarm shrieked. Sprinkler systems hissed to life, sending mystical practitioners scrambling for cover. Chaos erupted.

Trevor spun to see smoke billowing from a makeshift bonfire on a glass coffee table. "Who," he asked of no one in particular, "thought burning sage indoors was a good idea?"

"The spirits demanded it!" declared a woman in a turquoise head wrap, brandishing a smoldering bundle as hotel security closed in.

By the time the fire department arrived, *#cosmicdisaster* was trending across three social-media platforms. The hotel manager looked ready to commit violence. Somewhere across town, Margo's phone was no doubt lighting up like a solar flare.

It wasn't even noon, but Trevor had already retreated to the hotel bar, nursing something the convention menu called a 'Mystic Martini'—vodka with edible glitter that swirled like tiny galaxies. The cold vodka burned slightly going down. He stared into the drink as it glimmered ominously. Somewhere behind him, a psychic was still chanting.

Ryan Porter, he thought bitterly. Ryan Porter would've read every word of that memo. Would've calculated moon phases, cross-referenced planetary alignments, and created a color-coded matrix for the salad course.

Trevor caught sight of himself in the bar mirror—hair disheveled, collar askew, eyes red with nerves. He looked like the before photo in a career rehab brochure. How had it come to this? He used to be the rising star. The improviser. The charmer. He was too experienced to be second-guessing himself every time Ryan Porter pulled out another fancy spreadsheet. And the way Sofie looked at Ryan lately, like he was some kind of adorable puzzle to be solved—that wasn't helping either. She used to look at Trevor that way, back when *he* was the office golden boy.

Something had to change—he was too good at this job to keep being overshadowed.

He needed to prove himself. To show everyone—especially Margo—that his way of doing things was better. More organic. More human. But every major project seemed to end up in Ryan Porter's hands, while Trevor got stuck with the smaller events, the ones nobody cared about.

Unless ...

If the universe wasn't going to align for him, he'd twist it himself.

An idea settled into his mind like sediment in wine. He didn't need to wait for his opportunity. He could make one.

He opened his phone and scrolled through the events calendar. The Jane Austen Conference. Two weeks away. Eight hundred attendees. Ryan's project. Three days of lectures and panels. Plenty of things could go wrong. Equipment failures. Vendor mix-ups. A few key details shuffled just enough to throw off the whole thing.

Trevor swirled the glitter in his glass like it held the future. Behind him, the woman in the turquoise head wrap was now predicting his "dark future" to anyone within earshot—something about betrayal and karmic retribution. What did she know? She couldn't even predict a smoke detector would object to a sage bonfire.

Trevor drained his martini, the last of the glitter sliding down the glass like a constellation coming undone. He smiled at his reflection one more time. He told himself it wouldn't really be sabotage. Or betrayal. Just a course correction. A touch of chaos. A reminder to Ryan and Sofie that perfection is fragile.

Chapter Twenty-Seven

Systems of the Heart

"I can't find my keys. Again."

Sofie's voice crackled through Ryan's phone as he sat down to breakfast—steel-cut oats still steaming in the ceramic bowl, fresh blueberries arranged in precise concentric circles, coffee cooling to its optimal drinking temperature of 140 degrees.

"Where did you last see them?" he asked, aligning his spoon parallel to the bowl.

"If I knew that," she snapped, "I wouldn't be calling you at 7:30 in the morning, would I?" A crash followed, along with what sounded like cushions being thrown. "I've looked everywhere. Under the couch. In the fridge—don't laugh, I found them there once—in every jacket pocket, on every surface. They've vanished into the void."

"This is the third time this month you've lost your keys," Ryan noted.

"Thanks for the quantitative update," Sofie muttered. "Very helpful."

"It wasn't meant as criticism," Ryan said, his tone neutral. "I'm establishing a pattern frequency to determine the optimal intervention."

Another crash. More swearing. A particularly colorful vocabulary he wasn't used to hearing from Sofie.

"The optimal intervention would be a fucking time machine so I can start the day over and not knock my purse off the counter while reaching for coffee."

"That technology remains theoretical." Ryan took a precise spoonful of oatmeal. "Have you checked inside your shoes?"

A pause. "Why would my—wait." More shuffling. Then: "Oh my god! They're in my running shoe. How did you—?"

"You said, last Tuesday, and I quote, 'At least I'll know where to look next time.' That was after your keys fell out of your jacket when you kicked off your shoes."

Another pause. "I have absolutely no memory of that."

"I do." He glanced at his watch. "If you leave in the next twelve minutes, you'll arrive at your meeting with the pharma folks with 6 minutes to spare."

"You're a lifesaver," she said. "Seriously, Ryan. Thank you."

After they hung up, Ryan finished breakfast, cleaned the dishes, and packed for work. But a thought kept circling: Sofie's disorder wasn't random. During flu week—when she'd fallen asleep on the couch and he'd quietly observed her apartment—what he saw wasn't actually chaos. It was unstructured logic.

And logic, he understood.

THAT EVENING, Ryan called her. "I need to confess something."

"Oh no," she said. "What did you do?"

"Remember the morning I brought you medicine? While you were asleep, I studied your apartment. Your organizational patterns."

"You mean my mess."

"No. Your system." Ryan's tone was firm. "You have a system, Sofie. It's just not optimized for efficiency."

Sofie was quiet for a moment. "Okay, I'll bite. What kind of system do I have?"

"You organize things by how they make you feel, not by what they are. It's actually quite elegant. But you need better storage solutions."

There was a pause. "Are you offering to help me organize my apartment?"

"Yes."

"Will you judge my chaos?"

"It's not chaos," Ryan said immediately. "It's a different ordering principle. And no, I won't judge it. I'd like to help you enhance it."

Sofie laughed, surprising him. "You know what? Why

not. I'll provide the wine and pizza. You provide the Porter Method."

"The what?"

"Your systematic approach to everything. I'm calling it the Porter Method."

Ryan considered this. "The methodology would be collaborative. A synthesis of your associative patterns and my optimization protocols."

"Fine. The Collaborative Porter Method. When do we start?"

"Saturday morning would be optimal. We'll need approximately six to eight hours, depending on implementation complexity."

"Six to eight—right. Of course we will. Saturday it is."

SATURDAY MORNING, at precisely 9:00 a.m., Sofie opened the door in pajama pants and an oversized T-shirt, coffee in hand. Ryan stood in the hallway with several shopping bags rustling with purpose.

"You brought supplies," she said.

"Preliminary assessment indicated specific storage-solution requirements," Ryan replied, stepping inside. "I came prepared for multiple organizational scenarios."

Sofie eyed the bags: bins in graduated sizes, a brand-new label maker, and a stack of laminated index cards covered in his handwriting.

"This feels very ... Broadway-level systematic. Like you're staging a revival."

“All effective systems are systematic by definition,” Ryan said, already unpacking.

“Show me what you’re thinking,” she said, sitting cross-legged on the floor.

Ryan pulled out a laminated card covered in notes and small sketches. “Okay. You keep theater tickets and programs together not because they're both paper items, but because they represent cherished experiences you shared with other people.”

Sofie leaned over to examine the card, surprised. “You noticed that?”

He nodded. “Yes. You group items by emotional association. Even books.” He ran his finger along the spines—worn paperbacks that had been read multiple times. “Your books aren't alphabetized or shelved by genre. They're arranged by how they made you feel when you read them. Comfort reads are together. Challenging reads are together. Books that made you cry—together.”

Sofie blinked. “That's exactly how I think about them. But I thought it was just ... random.”

“Not at all random. It's a consistent pattern.” Ryan held up another card. “Even your kitchen tools are arranged by emotional context. 'Comfort cooking' tools are in the most accessible drawer.”

Sofie felt something warm bloom in her chest. “You actually understand how my brain works!”

“I find it fascinating,” Ryan admitted. “My systems are linear, designed to eliminate variance. Yours embrace it, create space for emotional resonance and unexpected connections." He looked up from his cards. "I can't create systems like that. But I can enhance them."

"Okay," Sofie said, grinning. "Let's do this."

They started with her theater memorabilia. Ryan had brought clear bins. "You want to maintain visual access because your system depends on seeing connections," he explained. Together, they sorted programs, tickets, and photos.

"This goes with the Shakespeare stuff," Sofie said, holding up a Stratford Festival program.

"Because it's Shakespeare, or because of how it made you feel?"

She thought. "Because ... I cried. Like during that Puccini opera." She pointed to a program from *La Bohème.* Excited, she said, "They should go together, shouldn't they?"

"According to your organizational logic, yes." Ryan handed her a bin. "What would you call that category?"

"'Things that wrecked me emotionally'?" Sofie laughed. "No, that's too dramatic. How about ... 'Beautiful Devastation'?"

Ryan wrote it on a label. "Perfect."

They moved through her apartment like curators of memory, Sofie explaining her associative logic, Ryan creating infrastructure to support it. He'd brought different types of storage solutions—clear bins for visual collections, closed containers for private items, shallow trays for things she liked to spread out and examine.

"I observe that you like to *see* your possessions—probably because visual access reduces your search anxiety. You want to be able to see your ... I almost said 'tchotchkes.' But that's not right. For you, these things are anchors."

"Anchors," Sofie repeated softly. "Yeah. That's exactly what they are."

The afternoon brought more revelations. Ryan had noticed that she kept certain items in multiple locations—phone chargers, pens, hair ties—not because she was disorganized, but because she used them in different contexts throughout her day.

"Instead of consolidating them, we'll create strategic distribution points," he explained, setting up charging stations in three different areas.

"Most people tell me I have too much stuff," Sofie said. "They say things like, 'you've got to get rid of a lot of this crap.' Like they want me to strike the entire set and start over."

"I repeat: most people don't understand your system." Ryan's tone was matter-of-fact. "Your possessions serve specific emotional and practical functions. Removing them would damage the ecosystem of your living space. Your instinct is correct. The solution isn't fewer items—it's better placement."

By early evening, they'd transformed her apartment. But it still felt like Sofie. Her memories were intact. Her emotions had space. Ryan's infrastructure simply gave it all form.

"This is incredible," Sofie said, walking through her transformed space. "I can find everything, but it still feels like me."

"Because it *is* you," Ryan replied, packing up his unused

supplies. “I didn't change your story—I just ‘gave it better staging,’ as you might say.” He gave her that sweet smile she was growing fond of.

Sofie looked at him, warmth rising in her chest. “You’re going to make me cry, and we just sorted the ‘Beautiful Devastation’ bin.”

Around them, the apartment glowed with golden light and quiet satisfaction. They sat on the couch, surrounded by the evidence that her chaos and his order weren't so incompatible after all. Her heart. His systems.

Somehow, together, it all worked.

Chapter Twenty-Eight

Pride and Pitfalls

The first sign that something was wrong came at 8:11 a.m., when Ms. Harriet Tilney, president of the Jane Austen Society of North America, burst into the conference control room in full Regency fury. Her silk petticoats swished with authority, her fan snapped open like a dueling pistol, and the scent of rosewater and outrage filled the air.

"Mr. Porter," she announced, voice trembling with barely suppressed rage, "perhaps you can explain why Dr. Pruitt is talking about Feminist Undertones in *Pride and Prejudice* in a ballroom where people are queueing up for a workshop on The Art of the Regency Country Dance?"

Ryan's fingers flew to his tablet. "That's not possible. The dance workshop is scheduled for Ballroom A, and Dr. Pruitt's address is in—" He stopped. Both events had been assigned to the same room.

He would never do that. His entire organizational system was based on strict adherence to the plan. This wasn't just an error—it was impossible. His schedule had been checked. Triple-verified. Then locked.

Trevor appeared in the doorway, eyebrows knit with feigned concern. "Heard there's a mix-up. Everything alright?"

Ryan didn't respond. Ms. Tilney was fanning herself so vigorously it looked like she might take flight.

"We have three hundred people discussing feminist theory in a ballroom set up for quadrilles, galopades, and polonaises," she said. "Dr. Pruitt is trying her best, but the fiddlers are right outside the door, tuning up. She's having to shout over them."

Ryan's heart rate accelerated. He had triple-checked every detail of this conference. The room assignments had been perfect, each space optimized for its intended purpose. The dance workshop had specific square footage requirements for the expected number of participants, while the feminist-theory discussion needed theater-style seating with optimal sight lines for PowerPoint visibility.

"There must've been some kind of error," he said to Ms. Tilney, trying to maintain his professional tone despite the growing chaos in his mind. "I'll resolve this immediately."

But the problems were just beginning.

Young Janeites were given *Mature Reader* badges. Earl

Grey tea was delivered with the coffee service instead of English Breakfast. ("A grave insult to authenticity," according to one particularly agitated professor of Regency social customs.) Crates of antique porcelain teacups—sourced from three different historical societies—were mistakenly offloaded to the coding bootcamp across the hall, while swag boxes full of Red Bull koozies and foam fingers that read *My Other Finger Writes Python* ended up at the Austen registration table.

Ryan turned to his fail-safes. This was why he had backups. This was why he planned.

He opened his device—only to find his spreadsheet frozen. Then it crashed. Then it restarted with red text bleeding across the screen like a wound:

ERROR: CLOUD SYNC VALIDATION FAILURE. RESTORE POINTS CORRUPTED.

A cold sensation spread through his chest. His cloud storage had hit a sync error overnight. The live backups hadn't run. He reached for his local storage—nothing.

A cascade of alerts began pinging from the event app: mixed-up speaker bios, misprinted name badges, overlapping schedules, broken links.

None of this should be happening. He'd accounted for technical failures with redundant systems. He'd created fail-safes for his failsafes.

"Server trouble?" Trevor asked, peering over his shoulder. "Brutal timing, buddy. You'd think these systems would have better redundancy."

Ryan didn't answer. Trevor's sympathy was too polished,

his tone just a beat too smooth—like what a funeral director might offer. All surface concern with something calculating underneath.

Everything about his demeanor reminded Ryan of *Pride and Prejudice*'s untrustworthy George Wickham.

Ryan looked at Trevor and thought, *This man is Wickham.*

But before Ryan could confront him about this mess, a new wave of attendees surged into the room—bonnets bristling, fans snapping, the rustle of taffeta and indignation filling the air. Their volley of complaints rained on Ryan like musket fire during the Napoleonic Wars.

—"I'm listed as a fanfic reader. I'll have you know I am the panel chair on 'Feminist Discourse in Regency Literature'!"

—"My name badge says *Darcy cosplay semi-finalist.* I'm the keynote on Austen's economic theory!"

—"The tech conference across the hall is blaring EDM! We're trying to discuss *Persuasion*!"

—"This says my panel on letters in Austen's novels is at the same time as my own lecture on matrimonial law! I can't be in two places at once!"

Ryan felt his heart rate accelerate. Ninety-two BPM. Ninety-eight. One-oh-five. His palms dampened. His throat tightened.

But he had prepared for this, too. He pivoted to his fall-back: a comprehensive set of tailored scripts designed to defuse attendee frustration based on personality type, complaint category, and emotional intensity.

He launched into Protocol 3C: sincere-meets-calm-under-pressure.

"Thank you for your feedback," he said, his voice modulated to the precise tone his research indicated conveyed both authority and empathy. "Your concern has been escalated to Tier One Reconciliation. Let me offer you commemorative fans as a restorative token."

The group stared at him in angry silence, some accepting the token, some not.

One woman in a perfectly recreated Regency gown—empire waist, seed pearls, the works—crumpled the fan between her opera-gloved hands with a sound like breaking bones and thrust it in Ryan's face, close enough that he could smell the lavender sachets tucked into her reticule.

"You're offering me a paper fan while my cosplay judging panel is unattended?" she snapped. "I drove up from Baltimore for this, buster!"

"Correction: it's a silk-screened fan," Ryan said weakly, feeling the situation slipping away from him. "High thread count. Era-appropriate motif."

She hurled it to the floor.

Then came the sound—a metallic rattling that built to a spectacular crash from the hallway. A wheel had snapped off the replacement tea cart. It lurched sideways, flinging cucumber sandwiches and miniature scones across the burgundy carpet like confetti. China cracked. Cream pooled. Guests gasped.

There was a horrified silence, followed immediately by a rising murmur of discontent.

Ryan froze. Every system he'd built was collapsing, every contingency failing simultaneously. His breath shortened, each inhale hitting a wall in his chest. The room pulsed at the edges with each thudding heartbeat while fluorescent lights buzzed too loudly overhead. The mingled scents of Earl Grey and panic sweat made his stomach clench.

His throat closed.

There was no algorithm for this. No pattern to follow. No structure to cling to when structure itself was breaking down.

What would Sofie do?

What advice would she give him right now? She'd tell him to stop mentally scanning for a structure and start connecting. She'd tell him just to be here with these people. Talk to them—not as variables, but as people who loved Jane Austen and were deeply disappointed in how their cherished annual event was going.

He turned to the still-fuming cosplayer. She was holding her shoe, which had somehow gotten frosting on it.

"I'm so sorry," he said.

He had no script. He had to just rely on truth, raw and unfiltered. "You're right. This is a mess. I can't fix everything. But may I start by getting you a clean pair of slippers and fresh scones?"

Something shifted. The woman's expression didn't soften—but she paused. And that was enough.

From there, it began to turn. Ryan stopped managing and started relating. He recruited volunteers to reprint badges. He escorted a panicked Colonel Brandon re-enactor to the correct breakout room with a joke about "dueling schedules."

At one point, he ended up on his knees in a service corridor that smelled of industrial cleaning supplies, helping a tearful graduate student salvage her water-damaged presentation printouts. The pages were soft and wrinkled as tissue paper, her careful annotations running together in watercolor streaks.

"It's ruined," she said, holding soggy pages of her analysis of female friendship in *Emma*. "My first major conference presentation, and it's—"

"No. It's not ruined," Ryan said, consoling her and carefully separating the pages. "Just damp. Imperfect. There's a difference." He looked up at her. "I'm learning that myself, actually."

By mid-afternoon, something remarkable had happened.

The errors hadn't disappeared, but they'd transformed. The scheduling conflicts had become impromptu joint sessions that attendees were calling "inspired programming." The mixed-up name badges had become conversation starters. Even the collapsed tea cart had evolved into a "Regency picnic" on borrowed hotel blankets.

At 4:52 p.m., an elderly woman in a lace cap approached him.

"Young man," she said, "that was one of the most delightful Jane Austen events I've attended in thirty years."

Ryan blinked, uncomprehending. "But ... very little went according to plan."

She patted his arm with a gloved hand that smelled faintly of violets and old books.

"My dear, Jane herself would have loved the irony. Her stories always remind us: real joy begins after the best-laid plans fall apart."

Chapter Twenty-Nine

Adorably Nerdy

Sunday mornings in Ryan's apartment followed a precise choreography. The familiar sounds were soothing: the quiet hiss of his coffee maker, the gentle spray of filtered water on succulent leaves, the clink of measuring spoons against a ceramic bowl. He portioned his breakfast for optimal nutritional balance, then updated his weekly log of urban bird behavior, noting an uptick in the territorial disputes between pigeons and sparrows on the ledge.

The laundry timer chimed—his calculated interval between wash and dry, engineered to minimize wrinkle formation. He gathered his basket and headed to the basement. The laundry room air was thick with the humid warmth of running machines and the clean, chemical comfort of detergent. Ryan fed quarters into the dryer slot, each coin dropping with a satisfying metallic ping. As he transferred his clothes—shaking each item for optimal airflow—he heard the door open with a groan.

"Oh good, machines are free!"

He turned to look. A woman about his age entered, balancing an overfull laundry basket and a half-eaten everything bagel. Her curls were pulled into a messy bun, and her sweatshirt—Carnegie Mellon—was splattered with coffee.

"Hi! You're 4B, right? I'm Sarah from 7C." She grinned and dropped her basket.

"Yes. I'm Ryan Porter." He hesitated. "I know who you are. From my resident database."

Her eyes widened. "You have a resident database? Okay, that's either deeply creepy or kind of adorable. I'm choosing adorable."

This conversation wasn't following Ryan's familiar patterns for laundry room interactions, which typically consisted of silent nods or brief comments on machine availability.

"It's for efficiency," he said, loading a second dryer. "Understanding traffic patterns helps optimize use of shared resources."

Sarah leaned against a washer, watching him with an expression he couldn't quite categorize. "You know what? I bet you're really good at your job—whatever it is."

"I coordinate conventions and other large events. It requires significant attention to detail and—"

"Spreadsheets?" she guessed. "Lots and lots of spreadsheets?"

He nodded. For some reason, this made her smile even more.

"I've seen you in the elevator," she said. "You're always so focused on your tablet."

Ryan blinked. He assumed no one ever noticed him. "I was likely modeling elevator loading patterns based on stop frequency and passenger distribution."

She laughed—a genuine, delighted sound that startled him with its warmth. Not the awkward laugh of someone unsure what to do with his data-talk, but a hearty guffaw.

"I love that. I'm a data scientist at Google. I get why someone would model elevator loading. That's adorably nerdy."

Adorably nerdy. He filed the phrase away for further analysis.

"The current system is inefficient," he said, encouraged. "If we implemented a modified queuing algorithm—"

"Let me guess," she said, eyes lighting up, "you're factoring both temporal and spatial variables?"

He paused. "Yes."

"My master's thesis was on multi-dimensional optimization problems," she said.

He blinked. This was the most interesting laundry-room conversation he'd had since leaving Caltech.

"I've got a fresh pot of coffee upstairs," Sarah said, tossing her last armful of clothes into the washer. "It's good coffee. I measure water temp and everything. Want a cup while these machines do their thing?"

Ryan's social-interaction flowcharts had no algorithm

for: *attractive neighbor invites you for coffee after referencing queuing theory.* His pulse spiked.

"I ..." he froze.

"I even measure bloom time," she added gently, as if speaking his native dialect might tip his decision.

"Yes," he managed. "That sounds ... ideal. I appreciate precise coffee preparation." Then, more cautiously, "Though I should wait for my laundry to—"

"Great." She glanced at his dryer readout. "Come up in ... forty-four minutes?" Her smile widened.

"Precise timing. I like that."

After she left, Ryan stared at the dryer, trying to recalibrate. He'd created models for most social situations, but this felt like trying to forecast atmospheric pressure during a geomagnetic storm.

Forty-eight minutes later—he'd taken an extra minute to realign his shirt hem—he stood outside 7C, second-guessing his decision. But his mother had always said: *"If you commit to something socially, follow through. Even if it feels like calculating pi without any known digits."*

Sarah's apartment mirrored his in layout but not in style. Where his was ordered, hers was comfortably cluttered. Sunlight filtered through pothos vines and book stacks that climbed toward the ceiling. A whiteboard bore looping machine-learning equations. A shelf of vintage cameras lined the wall.

"Sorry about the mess," she said, heading into the kitchen. "I was mid-code when inspiration hit and ... well, there's the aftermath." She gestured toward the whiteboard. "You know how it goes."

He did. He'd papered his own walls with statistical models more than once.

"Make yourself comfortable," she called over her shoulder. "And by that I mean: if anything's spatially bothering you, feel free to fix it. I saw you side-eye that crooked picture frame."

It was four degrees off level.

"You take photographs?" he asked, gesturing to the cameras.

"Since high school. There's something satisfying about capturing a moment at its peak."

He nodded. "I tracked Arctic weather systems for the same reason."

She poked her head out of the kitchen. "Wait—Arctic?"

"I grew up on a research station. It was isolated. But fascinating. I learned to track weather patterns and whale migrations."

Sarah stared at him. "Yeah ... that explains a lot," she said, but not unkindly. "Come on, make yourself useful. Grab this for me."

She handed him a tray with two mugs and a small plate of danishes.

The coffee was, in fact, excellent—precisely the right temperature, grind consistency spot-on. They talked easily—about code, patterns, behavioral math. She understood his references, finished his sentences, and offered insights sharp enough to surprise him.

Ryan asked about her background—her childhood in Denver, how she'd ended up at Google, what she loved most about coding. She made conversation feel like a puzzle where all the pieces clicked into place without effort.

"The thing I love about coding," she said, curling her legs under her on the couch, "is that it's creative within structure. There are rules—but infinite ways to solve a problem."

"Like convention planning," he said. "Everyone thinks it's just logistics—schedules and room assignments. But really, it's about human patterns."

"Tell me about it," she said, leaning in. "I bet you have some amazing stories."

So he told her. About indoor lightning storms. Rival Lincolns. Austen fans Regency-cosplaying in silk petticoats. About Sofie.

"Sofie?" she said. "Your girlfriend?"

"No." He paused. "I wish she were, but I don't think that's ever going to happen. Still, she's a good colleague. The best. She helps me interpret social cues I don't always catch. My social interactions until fairly recently have been ... somewhat limited."

"They don't have to be," she said, leaning forward. "You should try online dating. It's a low-friction way to meet people."

Val had said the same thing. Maybe there was merit to the idea.

Sarah tilted her head, smiling. "You're like this perfect

mix of brilliant and completely oblivious. It's refreshing. If I didn't already have a boyfriend, we'd make a great match." She gave him a quick, warm smile. "But we'll make great friends, too. Want to analyze some datasets together sometime?"

An hour later, back in his apartment, Ryan sat at his desk, still stunned. He'd had a full conversation—about algorithms, coffee, and chaos—with someone who got him. Who laughed at his analyses and didn't blink at his eccentricities. She'd called him cute. And adorably nerdy.

He pulled out the scrap of paper she'd used to give him her number—a Melitta #4 cone filter—and slipped it into a protective sleeve.

And then he opened the dating app.

Now it was nearly 9:00 p.m., and the app blinked at him from his laptop, full of empty boxes and chipper prompts that seemed designed by people who'd never experienced social anxiety. The cursor blinked mockingly in the first field, waiting for some authenticity he wasn't sure how to manufacture.

Tell us about yourself! (Be creative and fun!)

Ryan had spent the last hour building a structured approach to this prompt.

Attempt one: Detail-oriented professional with extensive experience in data analysis and convention coordination.

Too bland.

Attempt two: Arctic-raised researchers' son seeking compatible partner for mutual life optimization.

Somehow worse.

He opened his spreadsheet: Dating_Profile_Metrics_v3.xlsx. His analysis of 50 high-performing profiles was not reassuring. The words *spontaneous, adventurous,* and *fun-loving* appeared with alarming frequency. Ryan was none of those. And pretending to be felt unethical.

He tried again.

Methodical event coordinator (26M) seeks romantic partner. Strong organizational skills. Excellent crowd-flow intuition. Experience with arctic wildlife may be relevant.

Delete. Delete. Delete.

What's your idea of a perfect date?

He opened a new tab: Optimal-Date_Parameters.xlsx.

Eventually, he typed: *Prefer quiet venues with low ambient noise and moderate temperature settings. Will happily calculate optimal seating arrangements. Strong opinions on coffee preparation.*

Still too weird?

Delete. Re-type. Delete again.

What are you passionate about?

At last—an honest, straightforward question.

He typed confidently: *Efficiency optimization, data analytics, and identification of behavioral pattern clusters. Enjoy applying Fibonacci sequencing to three-day event schedules.*

Pause. Delete. (Though it was true.)

By the second hour, Ryan's shoulders were tight. He repeatedly changed his monitor angle, then his chair height, then the position of his coffee cup—small calibrations that usually brought improved physical comfort but now felt futile. His typing had devolved from measured pecking to aggressive stabbing at keys, each deleted attempt making his jaw clench tighter. He'd arranged and rearranged his pens by length, then by ink color, then back to length again.

By the third hour, Ryan had something that resembled a dating profile.

It was awkward. Honest. Certainly not perfect. But it was his.

Chapter Thirty

Sabotage, Served Neat

The Chicago Marriott Marquis gleamed in the late afternoon sun, its glass façade reflecting the downtown skyline in fractured, golden panels. Inside, the lobby buzzed with the polished chaos of a major event—rolling suitcases across marble floors, the soft ding of elevators, and the roasted aroma of espresso from the café.

Near the main reception area, Sofie watched Ryan, tablet in hand, methodically checking each element of his carefully orchestrated setup for the Distilled Spirits Council's annual conference. She knew better than anyone that Ryan didn't normally congratulate himself on a job well done. But she also knew he was feeling confident about this event.

As usual, he'd planned every detail meticulously. He had spreadsheets, backup plans, and contingency protocols for every possible scenario. He'd left nothing to chance. He'd booked the best bartenders in the country for the Mixologist Showcase. Assembled an all-star keynote panel on the future of craft distilling. And his planning for the VIP cocktail reception? Flawless. He'd met every metric he could think of.

Checking off the last item on his list, he turned to Sofie. "Care to inspect our *pièce de résistance?*"

"Let's do it," Sofie said, grinning.

They headed to the Grand Ballroom, where a custom bourbon fountain stood at center stage—Woodford Reserve bourbon cascading over crystal tiers in amber ribbons that caught the light like liquid gold. The gentle splash of bourbon against glass created a hypnotic rhythm, while rich caramel and vanilla aromatics perfumed the air. Guests filled their tasting glasses directly from the flow. It was theatrical. Luxurious. Exactly the kind of touch that got people talking —and signing contracts.

"It's gorgeous," Sofie said. "I'm so glad we did this."

"I am, too," Ryan replied, as they watched Jenny adjust the dramatic uplighting behind the Brown-Forman logo. "But it took significant calibration to achieve optimal flow without splash."

"Good thing we had an applied-math expert on staff."

Trevor appeared at Sofie's side, too casual. "Very impressive, Porter. Though I hope you've accounted for the inebriation variable. Drunk people and flowing liquor can be ... unpredictable. People get sloppy ... fall over, bump into things. Disasters occur."

"Statistical analysis of similar events indicates minimal

risk when proper crowd-control protocols are implemented," Ryan said, not looking up.

Trevor's smile was indulgent. "Sure. But someone needs to handle the human element. I'll go work the room."

As he glided away, Sofie felt that familiar knot of unease. Trevor had been unusually helpful—volunteering for tasks, making suggestions, acting almost ... accommodating. In her experience, a cooperative Trevor meant a calculating Trevor.

DAY ONE RAN FLAWLESSLY.

Ryan's systems hummed along like clockwork—registration was smooth, panels ran on time, and the bourbon fountain drew admiring crowds.

"Young Mr. Porter is a revelation," Susan McKenna, the Council's events director, gushed to Sofie over lunch, her voice carrying the relief of someone who'd finally found competent help. "Our last two coordinators ... well, let's just say they enjoyed the product a bit too much. This level of precision is exactly what we needed."

Trevor, overhearing, said, "Ryan's definitely brought some fresh thinking to our approach. Very systematic."

Sofie glanced at him, noting the tonal dissonance between his words and his expression.

Day two began to unravel minutes before the keynote luncheon.

Sofie was reviewing final details with Ryan when Jenny rushed over, breathless. “The bourbon fountain—it’s gone haywire.”

They rushed to the ballroom.

Chaos.

Instead of a graceful, controlled cascade, the fountain now sprayed bourbon in wild, pressurized arcs, like a golden firehose. Streams of liquor hit linens, soaked carpets, drenched loudspeakers. The air filled with the overwhelming sweetness of wasted premium bourbon, the sharp tang of alcohol, and the panicked sounds of guests scrambling to save their phones and designer clothes from the boozy deluge.

“Emergency shutdown protocol,” Ryan said, rushing to the control panel. He toggled the switches. Nothing happened. “The manual override isn’t responding.”

Trevor appeared—too quickly, too conveniently. “Let me take a look.” He lifted the cloth on the table supporting the fountain and dove under, his voice muffled as he called out diagnostics. “Ah, the pressure regulator’s calibration is off. Something must’ve bumped it.” When he emerged again, he dusted off his sleeves. “These things happen. Good thing I’ve worked with one of these before. Tricky little mechanisms.”

Soon, not only had he restored the fountain and helped mop up the damage, he’d even fed the keynote speaker a clever line about *“spirits too eager for their debut.”*

“I’m just glad I could help avoid disaster,” he said,

modest and glowing as Susan McKenna thanked him profusely.

Ryan pulled Sofie aside and pointed to a chart on his tablet. Quietly, he said, "The pressure readings showed everything to be fine, stable, until 44 minutes ago. Then this spike. No 'bump to the regulator' caused this," he added, his voice tight with anger. "Someone would've had to crawl under that table and deliberately change multiple settings to create the exact malfunction we witnessed. ... Trevor. He did this."

Sofie's heart rate began to accelerate as she processed his statement, her chest tightening with the familiar sensation of pieces clicking into place. The sweet bourbon smell that had seemed inviting moments before now felt cloying, almost nauseating. She thought of the fly larvae, the Jane Austen chaos, all of Trevor's perfectly timed rescues.

Ryan was right. Trevor was behind this.

They both knew it.

But there was no time to talk about it now. The luncheon had to go on.

Later that afternoon, during the Craft Distillery Showcase, another glitch.

The specialty lighting—meticulously designed by Ryan to highlight exhibitor booths—began strobing erratically. Harsh white flashes pierced the amber glow, slicing through the space like lightning. Guests winced, shielding their eyes as light bounced off crystalware and polished metal in disorienting bursts.

"The control system's corrupted," Ryan said, baffled. "This shouldn't be possible with the safeguards I put in place."

Trevor appeared. Again. "I might know someone who can help," he said, already pulling out his phone. "There's a lighting tech I worked with here who owes me a favor. I called him this morning—just in case."

Thirty minutes later, the tech arrived. Lights were stabilized. Guests applauded.

Susan McKenna beamed. "You're a lifesaver, Trevor," she said. "I don't know what we'd have done without you."

After the final guests trickled out, Sofie cornered Trevor in the now-empty Grand Ballroom. The fountain burbled innocently nearby, as if it hadn't sprayed top-shelf bourbon across half a ballroom six hours earlier.

"Convenient how you were ready with solutions for each crisis," she said, her voice even.

Trevor's smile was smooth, innocent. "Just good preparation, Sof. Ryan's systems are impressive, but sometimes you need someone who can think on their feet when technology fails."

"Funny thing about technology," Sofie replied. "In my experience, it usually works exactly as designed. Unless someone interferes with it."

Trevor's expression faltered. His practiced smile froze at the corners, his eyes narrowed with the cold calculation of someone doing rapid risk assessment. In that split second, Sofie could almost hear the gears turning as he weighed options.

Then the smile returned, brighter than ever. "I'm sure I don't know what you mean," he said. "Just glad we could pull together as a team to make the client happy."

He turned and walked away.

Sofie felt that familiar chill of recognition. She'd seen this play before. Right here in Chicago. The sabotage. The spotlight-stealing. The hero act. The collateral damage.

But this time, the target wasn't some other colleague she didn't really know. It was Ryan. And that changed everything.

Chapter Thirty-One

The Pattern

That night, Sofie stared at the ceiling of her hotel room, the faint hum of the heating system doing nothing to quiet her racing thoughts. Sleep remained just out of reach, despite the exhaustion that tugged at her bones.

Her confrontation with Trevor had stirred memories she'd carefully packed away. Chicago. Three and a half years ago. A different time. A different city. A different Sofie.

And a Trevor she had, for a time, believed in.

Chicago, Three and a Half Years Earlier

"The problem with most event managers," Trevor said across the small bistro table, "is that they think this job is about logistics. It's not. It's about moments."

Warm lighting caught the amber flecks in his eyes.

Sofie leaned in, curious despite herself. Nine months into her role at Chicago Events, she'd already developed a healthy radar for charm-disguised opportunism. But Trevor felt different—conviction instead of charisma.

"What do you mean by moments?" she asked.

"Think about it," Trevor replied, gesturing with his wine glass. "Nobody remembers if the room was exactly 68 degrees or if the lunch service was on time. They remember how they felt. The moment a speaker changed their perspective. The unexpected connection with a stranger in the coffee line."

There was a softness to the way he said it, a gravity that didn't feel rehearsed. It drew her in.

"So logistics don't matter?" she teased.

He laughed, and it wasn't performative—it was easy. "Oh, God. That's not what I'm saying. Of course, they matter. Logistics are the skeleton. The supporting structure. But they're not the soul." He studied her. "You understand systems surprisingly well for someone new. That logistics report you prepped for the Illinois Medical Association? Very impressive."

The compliment caught her off guard. It was specific, informed, and about her work. Not the vague flattery or flirtatious comments she'd grown used to deflecting from others. She blinked. "You read my logistics report?"

"Of course. We're working the conference together, aren't we? You have a gift—spotting the weak points before anyone else sees them."

Something warm unfurled in her chest. This wasn't flattery—it was recognition. In a world full of smooth talkers, someone had finally noticed her mind. It was like finding water in a desert.

"I've always been able to see how pieces fit," she admitted, "and think about what could go wrong. It's like blocking a scene in a play—you try to spot where the collapse could start."

"That's exactly what I need," Trevor said. "Someone to handle the invisible structure so the on-stage talent can shine. We'd make an incredible team."

"Well, then," she said, lifting her wine glass with a small smile, "to getting things right."

Trevor's answering smile seemed to transform his entire face.

"To getting things right. Together."

When their glasses clinked, she didn't yet know she was stepping into the most elaborate production of her professional life—written, directed, and starring Trevor Hoyt.

Two Months Later

The professional partnership had been intoxicating at first. Electric. Trevor sought her insight, listened, gave her real credit.

When late-night work sessions turned into late-night drinks, she told herself it was networking. When he kissed her in a dark conference room after they saved the Midwest Innovation Summit, she told herself it was inevitable.

Trevor had made her feel valued, not just useful. Like her perfectionist tendencies weren't neurotic quirks, but essential skills that made their events better.

"You see what no one else sees," he'd whispered against her ear that night, his hands tangled in her hair. "I've never had someone who works in sync with me like this."

For three months, Sofie believed she'd found someone who both admired her professionally and wanted her personally. He made her feel competent in meetings and adored when they were alone. It was a heady combination—and the perfect formula for getting her to let her guard down completely.

One Month Later

"I don't understand why we need to totally revamp the registration process two days before the conference," Sofie said, frowning at Trevor across his office desk. "The current system works perfectly well."

"It works," Trevor agreed, leaning back in his chair with that easy confidence that had once charmed her but now increasingly frustrated her. "But it doesn't *wow.* Eventscape's platform is cutting-edge. This is an opportunity for us to showcase it."

"But it's still in beta. It's never handled traffic at this scale."

"Which is precisely why this is such an opportunity," Trevor countered smoothly. "We'll be the first to implement it at a major conference. Think of the publicity."

"Think of the risk," Sofie pushed back. "If it fails, three thousand attendees will be stuck in registration limbo."

Trevor's expression tightened almost imperceptibly. "There are benefits beyond the technical. Relationships that matter to the company."

"What relationships?" Sofie asked, her suspicion growing.

Trevor hesitated, then sighed as if reluctantly sharing a confidence. "Michael Weber—Eventscape's CEO—plays golf with ours every month. He specifically requested that we showcase their platform at this conference."

It was a reasonable explanation. A common reality in their industry. Yet something in Trevor's delivery felt rehearsed, as if he'd prepared this justification in advance.

"May I see that directive?"

Trevor's smile didn't falter, but something in his eyes hardened slightly. "It came in a verbal conversation, not an email. But I assure you, the message was clear."

Three months earlier, she'd have accepted that. But patterns were forming. Crises that just happened to showcase Trevor's strengths. Decisions that bypassed process and conveniently elevated him. Supposed connections and relationships that always seemed to position him as indispensable.

"I'd be more comfortable if we kept the existing system as a backup," she said. "Just in case there are issues with the new platform."

"That would send the message that we don't trust

Eventscape's technology," Trevor replied, his tone reasonable but firm.

"No," Sofie said. "It would signal our responsible planning."

She felt a familiar tension building—the conflict between her instinct for caution and Trevor's push for impact. It wasn't the first time they'd disagreed, but something about this particular decision felt different. More calculated. Less about the conference's success and more about ... something else she couldn't quite identify.

He must have seen the conflict in her eyes. He reached for her hand. Once, that gesture had been intimate. Now it felt like a lever.

"Sofie, you know I value your input more than anyone's. But sometimes you have to trust the bigger picture."

That line—*you know I value your input*—had become his standard response whenever she questioned his decisions. He always delivered it with just enough affection to cloud her objections.

It was the same voice he used when they were alone together, when his breath was warm against her neck and her defenses were completely down. Now that voice felt like a tool he deployed whenever her professional judgment conflicted with his plans.

"Besides," he added gently, "when have I ever steered you wrong? We make a good team, Sof. In every way."

"Trevor," she said slowly, choosing her words carefully, "in the months we've worked together, how many times have we made last-minute changes to accommodate relationships or opportunities that suddenly emerged?"

He shrugged, apparently unconcerned by the question. "That's the nature of this business. Adaptability is key."

"Is it adaptability, though?" Sofie pressed, watching him closely. "Or is it a pattern where stable plans get upended last minute—only for you to save the day?"

Something flickered across his face—surprise, quickly replaced by studied confusion. "What are you suggesting?"

"Nothing. I'm just ... noticing a pattern."

For a brief moment, Trevor's carefully maintained façade cracked. The mask slipped. "You think I'm manufacturing crises?" he asked, his voice unusually quiet.

Sofie held his gaze. "I think you try to ensure you're always seen as essential. And I don't know what you're willing to do to maintain that."

Silence.

Then, just like that, he pivoted. His mask slid back into place, smooth and impenetrable. "I get your concerns about the registration system," he said, as if their deeper conversation hadn't happened at all. "But the decision's made. Eventscape goes live tomorrow." It was a clear dismissal—of her technical concerns and of her more unsettling questions.

Sofie stood, feeling the line between personal and professional snap into clarity. "I'll make it work," she said, because professionally, she had no other choice. "But I'm documenting my concerns."

"Of course," Trevor agreed amicably, already turning his

attention to his computer screen. “That’s what makes you so valuable, Sofie. Your attention to detail.”

The Eventscape registration system failed spectacularly. Chaos at check-in. Angry attendees. Frantic troubleshooting.

And Trevor? He spun the narrative, solved the crisis, and walked away with praise he hadn’t earned.

It was the first time Sofie saw the full script. The compliments that roped her in. The late-night work sessions. The perfectly timed technical failures. The way her expertise had been deployed to enable his successes. All of it suddenly visible—like words appearing in invisible ink. And all of it a polished performance, with the spotlight always landing on Trevor, as she and others scrambled behind the scenes to make him look good.

The worst part wasn’t the betrayal or the sabotage. It was realizing that even his vulnerability had been calculated. The breathless declarations, the admiring glances when she problem-solved, the whispered *I’m falling for you.* Just another part of his performance—carefully calibrated to extract from her the emotional investment and work effort he needed. All tools. All strategy.

Two weeks later, she applied for a position at Prestige Events. When Trevor asked why, she gave the safest answer: “New challenges.”

The flash of regret in his eyes almost fooled her. Almost.

Present Day

Sofie opened her eyes, the hotel room coming back into focus as she went over the pattern—how Trevor had weaponized affirmation, leveraged intimacy, and made her feel indispensable until he no longer needed her.

She'd learned the hard way that the most dangerous colleagues weren't the obvious ones who used intimidation to get compliance. It was the manipulators. The ones who made you feel special, seen, chosen—until you realized you'd been performing a script you didn't write, for an audience of one.

This time, though, she wouldn't just up and leave. Wouldn't exit the stage. She was going to rewrite the ending.

Chapter Thirty-Two

Proof by Execution

"The Joint Mathematics Meetings," Margo had said, standing at the head of the conference table, "is one of the most complex events we handle. Over five thousand attendees, nearly four thousand presentations, and a schedule so dense it makes quantum physics look like kindergarten arithmetic."

Sofie had watched Ryan's posture shift—his spine straightened, his eyes sharpened, and his fingers inched toward his tablet. Classic Ryan: alert, engaged, already strategizing.

"That's why," Margo continued, "Ryan will be taking the lead on this one."

Trevor's coffee cup hit the table with a sharp click. He didn't speak right away, but tension radiated from his suddenly rigid frame. "With all due respect, Margo," he said finally, his voice carefully level, "my recent track record has been … flawless. The Medical Device Expo was a knockout. Excellent stakeholder engagement, best-in-class metrics across all key performance indicators—"

"Exactly," Margo replied smoothly. "Which is why I'm sending you to New Orleans. The Interior Design Show needs your touch. It's the same week as JMM—and just as important."

Trevor's expression flickered—equal parts pride, frustration, calculation. Sofie saw it in his eyes. He was weighing his options. Trevor didn't usually lobby this hard for specific assignments unless he had an angle. She suspected he couldn't think of a way to sabotage Ryan's handling of JMM if he was stuck all the way in New Orleans.

"And, Sofie," Margo continued, turning toward her, "you'll stay in New York and work with Ryan at JMM. I know your plate is full with prep for the Healthcare Forum. That's why I'm not sending you to lead in New Orleans."

"Of course," Sofie nodded.

As the team filed out, Ryan was already absorbed in his tablet, undoubtedly constructing a model for optimal mathematician-traffic flow.

In the weeks leading up to the event, Sofie didn't mind the chaos. Not this time. Ryan approached the project with a joy she hadn't seen in months. His step was lighter, his voice animated when he discussed scheduling structures and behavioral modeling. He'd found his people.

One evening, he showed her a complex grid. "Mathematicians often lose track of time when discussing especially compelling theorems," he explained. "So I built in temporal buffer zones. The P vs. NP debate could easily run into overtime. And I've scheduled cooling-off periods after the 'Ontological Status of Imaginary Numbers' panel. That topic tends to get people heated."

"I have no idea what any of that means," Sofie admitted, "but you look really happy."

His smile was unguarded. "I get these people, Sofie. They understand the beauty in patterns."

THE OPENING DAY of the conference buzzed with intellectual energy. Sofie watched with fascination as the mathematical tribes assembled and collided in the convention center's soaring atrium. The Pure Mathematics Purists had claimed the east wing, disdainfully eyeing the Applied Mathematics Alliance across the lobby. The Constructivists had set up camp near the registration desk, loudly questioning whether the conference badges even provably existed.

"Who are those people?" she asked Ryan, nodding toward a group in a conspiratorial huddle.

"That's the Finite Field faction," he said. "They're in a blood feud with the Cantorians." He pointed toward a group clustered around a display of specialized chalk. "They believe

Georg Cantor's work on infinite sets is the foundation of all mathematics."

Sofie nodded slowly. "Naturally. And those guys counting ceiling tiles?"

"Combinatorics people. They can't help themselves." Ryan's tone was affectionate.

The vendor hall was its own ecosystem of mathematical madness. The Mathematical Anxiety Support Group had set up a counseling station next to the Number Theory Conspiracy Theorists, who were distributing pamphlets claiming prime numbers were government surveillance codes.

Ryan consulted his schedule. "The MIT professor's talk on the topology of coffee-cup handles is about to end. Next up is *'Why Zero Isn't a Natural Number: A Philosophical Manifesto.'* I've positioned security nearby. I'm told that last year, a similar panel ended in a food fight. Donut holes everywhere."

Later, the Computational Complexity Death Match drew a large and boisterous crowd to watch colleagues competing to prove their problems were the most difficult to solve. Researchers hurled impossibility proofs like weapons across whiteboards, the air thick with excitement and marker fumes.

Meanwhile, Sofie's phone buzzed with updates from Jenny in New Orleans. The lighting designer had quit after a shouting match with Trevor over color temperature. Three major vendors had been double-booked for the same premium exhibit space. One text read simply:

```
Trevor is screaming about
Kelvin ratings again.
```

But here in New York, everything was humming along smoothly. Ryan had organized the vendor hall using optimal clustering theory. Watching him navigate through the space—directing, tweaking, fine-tuning—Sofie felt like she was watching a conductor lead a deeply personal symphony. His face reflected the deep contentment of someone whose natural language was finally being spoken around him.

A voice interrupted her thoughts.

"Impressive work."

She turned to see James Morton, CEO of Occasional Planning, sharply dressed and smiling like a man used to getting what he wanted.

"James! What brings you here?"

He shook her hand, letting the gesture linger. "Honestly? I came hoping things were going badly here. JMM is a plum contract, and I'd love to steal it from Prestige. But it's clear you're running a flawless event. Congratulations."

"Thank you," Sofie said, meaning it—but knowing most of the credit this time belonged to Ryan.

"Prestige is lucky to have you, Sofie. We're looking to expand our senior team, and someone with your experience, your cool under pressure ..." He trailed off as a minor commotion broke out near the escalator.

They turned to see an elderly woman down, her shoe having tangled in the treads.

Morton caught Sofie's arm before she rushed over. "Let's

talk. I'll pay you more than you're getting now. Make an appointment next week. Let's see what we can work out."

She nodded, but her mind was already elsewhere. She jogged over to help the woman. Still, Morton's offer echoed in her mind for the rest of the day. More money. A senior title. Escape from the whole Trevor situation.

But as she watched Ryan coordinate logistics with quiet joy—unburdened, clear-eyed—she realized something. Leaving would mean abandoning him to deal with Trevor alone. And she didn't think she could tolerate that.

On the final day of JMM, as the last session wrapped—*"Loops in Four-Dimensional Space: A Romantic Comedy"*—Sofie and Ryan walked side by side through a quiet section of the convention center, heading for a coffee to see them through to the finish.

"You did it," she said. "It was a fabulous event, flawlessly executed. Great job, Ryan. I still can't believe you got the combinatorics faction and the number theory crew to agree on room assignments. That's like—" She searched for the right metaphor. "Like resolving a turf war between rival jazz bands and expecting them to play the same song."

Ryan nodded. "It was primarily a matter of resource optimization and timing. And also letting Dr. Sakamoto pick which coffee station he wanted."

"You weaponized caffeine to achieve peace? Brilliant." She gave him a sidelong glance. "You know, I think this is the first time I've ever seen you *glow* on the job. You're in your element. Organized chaos. Dense schedules. Mildly combative geniuses."

His smile was introspective. "It helped that Trevor wasn't here to sabotage it. ... But you're right. It is ... deeply gratifying. Like solving a loud, spatially inefficient equation with too many variables and no known solution. Except there is one."

"And you found it." She paused. Then caught his eye, "You're kind of hot when you're triumphant."

Ryan froze mid-step. "Oh. Was that ... a flirtation?"

"Maybe." She stopped walking and turned to face him. "You gonna run a regression analysis on it, or just enjoy the moment?"

Ryan blinked, then looked at her—really looked. For once, he didn't say anything. Instead, he just stepped a little closer. Not enough to touch her, but enough that she could feel the shift in pressure, the warmth. His eyes held hers, steady and open. "I'm enjoying it," he whispered.

The silence between them wasn't awkward. It was charged. Weightless. Like standing on the edge of something very new.

Then Sofie's phone buzzed. She looked down, sighed, and shook her head. "Jenny needs me in the vendor hall. You're off the hook."

As they started walking again, Ryan said, just loud enough. "I wasn't trying to get off the hook."

Chapter Thirty-Three

High Stakes, Low Morals

Trevor Hoyt adjusted his tie, meeting his own eyes in the hotel bathroom mirror. Perfect Windsor knot, silk smooth against his throat. Perfect smile, facial muscles trained into the exact curve that conveyed confidence without arrogance. Perfect mask, polished to reflective brilliance over years of careful construction.

"Ready to dazzle?" he asked his reflection.

The Greater New York Hospital Association's quarterly mixer was exactly the kind of event where careers were made—not through the panel discussions or presentations that Ryan obsessed over, but in the margins. The hallway conversations. The bar meetups after hours. The places where the real work happened.

Trevor had learned that lesson the hard way. He straightened his cuffs, mind drifting back to his first major convention ten years ago. Twenty-six years old, armed with a meticulously researched presentation on immersive experience design that had taken months to perfect. He'd rehearsed until every word was flawless, created stunning visuals, prepared for every possible question. And then watched in the darkened auditorium as his mentor, Stephen Grayson, delivered virtually the same presentation—using Trevor's research, Trevor's slides, even Trevor's anecdotes—to thunderous applause.

"Groundbreaking," they'd called it. "Visionary."

The same presentation that had been sitting on Grayson's desk for "feedback" the week before.

Trevor had confronted him afterward, voice shaking with betrayal and rage. "That was my work. My research. My ideas."

Grayson hadn't even had the decency to look embarrassed. He just clasped Trevor's shoulder with practiced avuncular concern. "Welcome to the real world, kid. There are people who create content, and people who get credit for content. You're smart enough to figure out which group gets ahead." Then he'd leaned closer, voice dropping to a confidential whisper. "Nobody succeeds in this industry by playing it straight. The sooner you learn that, the better."

Trevor had quit the next day, determined to prove Grayson wrong. He'd taken a position with a smaller firm, worked twice as hard, played by all the rules. Watched for two years as colleagues with half his talent but better connections sailed past him. Colleagues who understood the unwritten rules that Trevor had been too naïve, too principled, to accept.

The day he'd finally embraced Grayson's lesson had been oddly anticlimactic—no dramatic moral crisis, no stormy soul-searching. Just a quiet recognition while sitting in another fluorescent-lit conference room, watching another less-qualified colleague receive credit that should have gone to Trevor. The realization had settled over him like dust, coating everything in a fine layer of cynicism that never washed off.

He'd been operating under a false paradigm. Integrity didn't matter in a system designed to reward relationships over merit. Talent meant nothing without strategic positioning.

Once he accepted that reality, everything changed. His career accelerated. His influence expanded. He developed his own system—one that prioritized perception over performance, relationship cultivation over actual competence. And if that occasionally required creating small problems that he could then heroically solve? Well, that was simply how the game was played.

The Margo situation had been perhaps his most elegant success. She'd been vulnerable when he'd arrived at Prestige Events—recently divorced, feeling overlooked by senior management despite her competence, hungry for validation from someone who seemed to truly see her worth. Trevor had read that need like a survival manual.

So, late-night strategy sessions gradually became more personal. He found ways to make her feel more like a collaborator than a boss, more like a desired woman than a recently dumped one. When she'd finally crossed that line—allowing their professional relationship to become personal—she'd handed him the ultimate insurance policy.

Now Margo wasn't just his supervisor; she was his co-conspirator, whether she fully realized it or not. The intimate relationship they'd carefully hidden from HR and others in the office—stolen moments in empty conference rooms, late dinners that carried the thrill of the clandestine, the lingering scent of her perfume on his jacket after out-of-the-way meetups—gave Trevor a layer of protection that even his most carefully cultivated references couldn't provide.

If Ryan and Sofie ever brought their suspicions to her, Margo wouldn't just be defending an employee—she'd be protecting herself. Her career, her reputation, her carefully constructed image as a consummate professional who'd never let personal feelings compromise her judgment.

Trevor's phone buzzed with a text from Margo:

> Where are you? Memorial Sloan
> Kettering people asking
> for you.

He smiled. The relationship had started as strategy, but he'd been surprised to discover he genuinely enjoyed her company. Margo was intelligent, accomplished, sophisticated in ways that made their clandestine meetings feel like more than just professional maneuvering. If she were ultimately to serve as a shield against workplace consequences, well—that would simply be a bonus to what had become a surprisingly satisfying arrangement.

He texted back:

```
On my way. Saving them the
Château Margaux 2015.
```

He was referencing the wine he'd specially imported for tonight. Another calculated investment. The MSK executives would remember the man who introduced them to a $900 bottle they couldn't find stateside, not the details of whatever project they were discussing.

As Trevor stepped out of the bathroom and into the crowded reception hall, he automatically calibrated his demeanor—shoulders relaxed, smile confident but not arrogant, pace unhurried despite Margo's implied urgency. *Never let them see you rush. Never let them see you sweat.*

He spotted Ryan across the room, huddled with a convention center tech manager over what was probably some mind-numbing logistics issue, his intense focus creating a small bubble of serious conversation in the otherwise social atmosphere. The sight triggered that familiar mix of irritation and something that might have been envy—Ryan's complete absorption in his work, the way he cared so genuinely about getting every detail right.

The man was brilliant with systems but completely blind to the real dynamics of their industry. All that meticulous work, all those careful plans—and he had no idea how irrelevant they were to actual success.

People like Ryan thought the event management world

operated on competence and systems. People like Trevor knew it ran on relationships and perception.

For a moment, Trevor felt an unexpected twinge—not quite guilt, but something adjacent to it, like the phantom pain of an amputated conscience. Ryan wasn't playing the game. He didn't even know there was a game. And there was something almost admirable in his stubborn belief that good work spoke for itself.

The thought made Trevor's chest tighten in a way he'd learned to ignore. Admirable didn't mean successful. And in Trevor's experience, being right didn't pay the bills.

His gaze shifted again, landing on Sofie as she deftly managed a conversation between two competing vendors, her hands moving in that animated way they did when she was smoothing over tensions. She caught his eye across the room, her expression cooling instantly like a door slamming shut. The warmth that had once lit her face when she saw him—back in Chicago, back when she'd looked at him like he was someone worth knowing—had been replaced by a curt professional politeness that cut away everything personal they'd once shared.

That hurt more than he cared to admit.

Chicago had been ... complicated. She'd been different—smart, perceptive, seeing through the polished version of him in ways that were both exhilarating and terrifying. For a while, he'd let himself believe he could be different with her. More honest. More himself, whoever that was beneath the layers.

But then she'd started asking questions. Noticing

patterns. Expecting explanations. Wanting the one thing he couldn't give her: authenticity.

So he'd done what he always did—he redirected, reframed, repositioned. Until she started looking at him the way she did now. Like she knew exactly what he was.

The thought sent a cold ripple through him that he quickly suppressed. He had a role to play, after all. The charming industry insider. The connected problem-solver. The indispensable asset.

He set off through the crowd with his usual ease, collecting tidbits of information, making introductions, building currency. This was what he excelled at—the human element that Ryan's systems could never capture. The subtle alchemy of influence and impression that determined who succeeded and who remained perpetually overlooked.

"Trevor!" An MSK executive waved him over. "Some of our younger guys are in a softball league. They have a game this Sunday afternoon against Tisch. Margo says you might be the ringer we need. Any chance you're free?"

"I'd be happy to help if I can," Trevor said, seamlessly joining the conversation circle. "Let me grab my phone and check."

As he pulled out his phone, he caught sight of Ryan watching him from across the room, eyes narrowed in that analytical way that meant he was trying to solve a puzzle. Trevor knew what he was looking for—evidence, patterns, proof. What Ryan didn't understand was that in this world, perception always trumped reality.

It wasn't personal, this subtle undermining of Ryan's

carefully constructed systems. The dislocation of his shipments. The mixing up of his room assignments or catering orders. It was just business. Just survival in an industry where being good wasn't enough—you had to be seen as irreplaceable.

For a brief, disorienting period earlier, Trevor had allowed himself to imagine a different approach. What if he just ... did the job? Applied his undeniable talents to making all events as successful as possible rather than selectively sabotaging Ryan, manufacturing problems to solve? What if he collaborated with Ryan's systems rather than undermined them? Reconnected with whatever version of himself had once believed good work was enough?

The thought had been so foreign it almost made him laugh. That path had closed years ago, the day Stephen Grayson had stolen his presentation and shown him the real rules of the game. There was no going back to the naïve idealist he'd been. Only forward, to increasingly elaborate strategies and ever-higher stakes.

Now, Trevor turned his attention back to the hospital executives, pushing aside the hollow feeling that sometimes crept in during quiet moments—the sense that in learning to play the game so well, he'd excavated something essential from himself, leaving behind a perfectly functioning shell where a person used to be.

But that was a thought for late nights and empty hotel rooms. Not for now. Now, he had valuable connections to cultivate, impressions to manage, a reputation to secure.

After all, that's what this was all about, wasn't it?

Being wanted. Being necessary. Being valued. Being enough.

Trevor pasted on his most engaging smile—the one that had taken years to perfect, muscles moving in precisely the right sequence to suggest spontaneous charm. He joined the group of hospital execs and launched into his spiel about what he had in mind for their next event. His voice carried just the right blend of authority and approachability, each gesture calculated to draw the executives deeper into his web of professional charisma.

If his smile didn't quite reach his eyes, if something essential remained carefully buried beneath layers of performance—well, no one would notice that.

Almost no one ever did.

Chapter Thirty-Four

Game On

The exhibit hall at the American Amusement Machine Association Convention throbbed with the discordant electronic symphony of a thousand arcade games—bleeps, bloops, synthesized explosions, the metallic ping of pinball bumpers, and the triumphant fanfares of high scores. It sounded like a mashup between Anton Bruckner and Arnold Schoenberg—if they'd composed for eight-bit synthesizers.

Somewhere in that auditory soup, Ryan detected the precise *waka-waka* rhythm of a flawless Pac-Man run. It had cadence. It had pattern.

To his left, two pinball restoration specialists were locked in an increasingly heated argument about 1970s flipper-tension specs, their voices rising over the mechanical noise of silver balls ricocheting off bumpers.

"Don't adjust that! You're killing the action!" shouted a man in a *Galaga* tee, waving like his hair was on fire. "These machines need to breathe!" His face flushed with the passion of someone defending sacred doctrine.

"The factory specs clearly state—" began his opponent, draped in seven *Space Ins* pins and brandishing a calibration tool like it was a dueling foil.

Ryan moved past them, mentally cataloging the tribes of the arcade world in their native habitats. VR developers clustered around sleek black booths like acolytes around altars, communing with invisible deities through wireless headsets. Claw-machine vendors marked their turf with a steady rhythm of whirring gears and the soft thud of lost plush-toy dreams. Vintage-game enthusiasts naturally gravitated toward the classics section, their path determined by chronological progression. E-sports competitors queued with martial discipline. Collectors of classic games murmured reverently around a pristine *Defender* cabinet, whispering about "PCBs" and "ROM dumps" as if deciphering scripture. In the tournament zone, pro gamers warmed up with elaborate finger stretches. A woman with rainbow hair performed tai chi while reciting *Donkey Kong* level sequences under her breath.

The centerpiece of the show—thirty vintage arcade cabinets, including a mint-condition *Computer Space* from 1971—was due to arrive at 8:00 a.m. sharp. Ryan had confirmed the delivery schedule, routing number, and loading-bay code.

He allowed himself a small smile. The morning sunlight streaming through the convention center's skylights caught the polished chrome of vintage cabinets, and everything was unfolding exactly as designed. The overlapping patterns of nostalgia and neon felt elegant. Predictable.

At 8:12 a.m., the first crack appeared.

"The exhibitor check-in software's glitching," Jenny said in his headset, her voice slightly distorted. "It's not reading the pre-registered badges."

Ryan adjusted his earpiece, already tapping his tablet. Minor issue. A temporary anomaly. He had contingency protocols in place for this sort of problem. He rerouted three staffers to manage manual check-in. He began running diagnostics. This was what systems were for.

At 8:18 a.m., his phone rang.

"Mr. Porter? This is Carl, from the loading dock. We've got a situation with the vintage game delivery."

Ryan's pulse jumped. "What kind of situation?"

"The machines aren't here. Delivery company says the shipment got redirected to New Jersey."

The world seemed to tilt.

"That's not possible," Ryan said. "I confirmed the delivery address yesterday. Twice."

"Yeah, well, someone changed it. Last night. You've got thirty pieces of gaming history sitting in a warehouse in Atlantic City."

Ryan's fingers flew across his tablet. The logs confirmed the original routing—delivery, code, timestamp—all correct.

Then he saw it.

A revision.

Timestamp: 11:29 p.m.

Original Delivery Location: OVERWRITTEN

New delivery coordinates

Login credentials: RPorter

His hands went cold. His breath caught. His vision tunneled, the colorful arcade lights blurring into streaks at the periphery. But the central fact burned with crystal clarity: someone had used his identity to sabotage the centerpiece of his event.

The background noise of games and conversation seemed to fade, replaced by the thunderous sound of his own heartbeat.

His eyes scanned the hall, his tablet momentarily forgotten as rage and disbelief warred in his chest. Across the room, past a row of dancing rhythm games where players stomped out electronic beats, Trevor Hoyt leaned casually against a *Medieval Madness* cabinet, laughing with a group of developers.

Relaxed. Confident. Knowing.

Fury surged through Ryan's usually methodical mind. This wasn't an accident or a mishap. Not a glitch. Not a fluke.

This was Trevor's doing.

He scanned the crowd for Sofie. She stood near the *Pac-Man Battle Royale* station, clipboard tucked under one arm, laughing at something an exhibitor had said. Around her, spectators cheered as two legendary players went head-to-head, ghost-dodging at impossible speeds.

She didn't know. Not yet.

"Sofie." His voice came out taut, clipped.

She turned, registering his intensity with the quick

assessment of someone who'd learned to read his moods. Her expression shifted in an instant—smile fading, posture bracing as if preparing for impact. She knew this tone.

"What happened?" she asked.

He told her—words coming faster than usual, emotion pressing on the edges, the careful modulation he normally maintained cracking under pressure. Then, without a word, he thrust the tablet toward her—delivery logs pulled up in stark detail.

She took it, brow furrowed as she read.

The final notes of a perfect Pac-Man run echoed behind them, the fanfare landing like mockery. He watched her, his jaw clenched so tight it ached, waiting for the moment it would click.

"I don't get it," she said slowly. "Why would you do that?"

"I didn't." His voice cracked, the words coming out sharp and raw. "Someone used my credentials. They got into the system and changed the destination." His hands balled into fists at his sides, months of suppressed frustration finally finding a target. "This is deliberate sabotage, Sofie. The timing. The method. It's meant to disrupt everything." He gestured wildly across the convention floor—where veteran game developers mingled with the next generation. "Thirty pieces of gaming history. *Computer Space*—the crown jewel of this whole show. Now sitting in a warehouse in Atlantic City because someone hijacked my identity to destroy my event!"

Sofie stood still. The implications washed over her. The

background sounds of the convention seemed to fade as she processed what he'd said. She looked from the tablet to his face. Then followed his gaze across the hall.

Trevor. Schmoozing. Laughing. Smiling that easy, effortless smile of his. Joking with Leonard "The Pinball Wizard" Watanabe, the keynote speaker—instantly recognizable in his championship-patch-covered denim jacket.

"This has to be him," Ryan said, his voice low and certain, each word like a dropped weight.

"No doubt about it."

Chapter Thirty-Five

Key Change

"Absolutely not." Ryan sat ramrod straight in the vinyl booth, looking like he'd rather explain the second law of thermodynamics to a group of toddlers using sock puppets than approach the karaoke stage. "There are no circumstances under which I will do that."

"Come on!" Val leaned across the table, giving him her best theater-kid smile—the one Sofie had seen her rehearse for countless auditions. "Everyone's terrible at karaoke. That's the point!"

The K-Town karaoke bar was packed for a Thursday night, filled with the usual mix of aspiring Broadway stars, tone-deaf enthusiasts, and people who'd had just enough alcohol to think "Sweet Caroline" was within their range.

The air was thick with beer, sticky-sweet cocktails, and what might've been burnt mozzarella sticks. A group of sales bros was onstage slaughtering "Livin' on a Prayer," while their colleagues cheered them on with the uninhibited joy of the moderately hammered.

"Actually," Ryan said, "studies show that approximately twenty-three percent of karaoke performers have some formal musical training and—"

"Nope! No statistics tonight!" Jenny snatched the song-book from his hands, nearly upending her third mojito. "Tonight is about fun! We're celebrating Sofie's job offer."

"Yes!" Todd said. "Tell us about Occasional Planning. What's it like?"

Sofie widened her eyes theatrically. "Oh, my God, you guys. Their offices? Insane. Floor-to-ceiling windows. Panoramic views of Manhattan. It's like the most expensive set design you've ever seen—everything perfectly lit and staged for maximum impact. Ergonomic everything. Fancy Japanese toilets that practically analyze your DNA before flushing. The break room has an espresso machine with a biometric scanner. It figures out who you are and just ... makes your preferred drink."

"Great!" Val said flatly. "You'll be living the dystopian dream. Louboutins, a Birkin bag, fourteen-hour days, and sobbing breakdowns in soundproof pods between strategy sessions."

Sofie looked up, surprised at the edge in Val's voice. "I haven't accepted the job. And I don't think I will." She caught the flicker of relief on Ryan's face. "But it's nice to know I have the option."

Ryan said, "Why wouldn't you take it? They have a stronger market position than we do, and a fifty percent salary increase is—"

"But they're so big! Seven hundred employees. Prestige is messy, sure, but I know everyone. It feels ... I don't know ... manageable. Like an intimate theater company where everyone knows their part. Plus, I'd miss you all too much."

A group "awww" swept across the table. When the mutual wave of affection settled, Val—now noticeably closer to Ryan than earlier—perked up. "Hey, everyone! I just booked a national TV commercial. I'm Woman Excited About Yogurt #3."

"That's ... remarkable?" Ryan said, clearly unsure of the appropriate response.

"My character has three distinct reactions to the probiotic content." She demonstrated each, her hand grazing Ryan's arm as she did. "What do you think? Too much? Not enough?"

Sofie took a too-large sip of her gin and tonic. When had Val gotten so ... handsy? Was that flirting, or was Sofie just being wildly jealous?

Another round arrived. Todd wobbled to his feet. "If no one else is going first, I will. Who's ready for some Journey?"

What followed was either "Don't Stop Believin'" or an elaborate experiment in tonal distortion. Todd's voice cracked on every high note while he gestured dramatically, one shirttail flying free, beer sloshing dangerously from his swinging pint glass. Jenny captured video of the whole thing, presumably for future blackmail purposes.

"See?" Val purred at Ryan. "If Todd can do it ..."

"His performance actually supports my position," Ryan said, his eyelids hanging a little heavier than usual. "His pitch variance is approximately—"

Val touched his arm again. "Oh, come on. Please? I bet you have a great voice. You have that whole precise, controlled thing going on. You know, I just did *Pirates of Penzance*. I could give you some pointers ..."

Something tight twisted in Sofie's chest. "Leave him alone, Val," she snapped. "If he doesn't want to—"

"Actually," Ryan said, sitting up straighter. "I was in a college a cappella group. I know quite a few songs."

"You were in what now?" Sofie asked, blinking.

"The Mathematical Harmonics. We specialized in traditional barbershop arrangements."

"That's the most on-brand thing I've ever heard," Todd declared, settling back into his seat.

Ryan stood, slightly unsteady but determined, and made his way to the stage. As he selected his song, his face glowed blue from the karaoke machine's screen. Soon, music started, the room filling with the opening bars of "Lida Rose" from *The Music Man*.

Despite the alcohol, Ryan's voice was perfect—clear, warm, precise. He even added a little soft-shoe step, and Sofie suddenly realized there was so much she didn't know about him. The bar's ambient noise faded to nothing as his voice filled the space, warm and rich and completely unexpected.

"Lida Rose, I'm home again, Rose ..."

"Holy shit," Jenny whispered.

"Okay, that's adorable," Val said. "You know, I played Marian in *The Music Man*. We could duet—"

Sofie had to physically stop herself from saying *back off*.

The bar erupted in applause when he finished. Ryan returned to their booth, a bit pink-eared but pleased.

"The acoustics in here are suboptimal," he said. "The reverberation time is approximately—"

"Ryan," Sofie cut in, "that was amazing!"

He ducked his head. "The Mathematical Harmonics had very high standards."

"I guess they did!" Val agreed, basically in his lap now. "Any other hidden talents we should know about? Maybe acting? You know, I'm teaching a workshop next—"

"Sofie's turn!" Jenny shouted, either oblivious to—or deliberately diverting—the undercurrents at the table.

"Oh no. No, no, no." Sofie held up her palms. "I know my limits. No effing way."

"Okay! Then I'll go." Jenny stood up, swaying slightly. "Who's ready for 'Total Eclipse of the Heart'?"

As Jenny launched into a deeply impassioned wail, Sofie caught Ryan's eye. He smiled—that smile, the one that meant he was actually enjoying himself.

Val raised her glass in a toast to Sofie. "To whatever comes next, and—" But Jenny's power note drowned out whatever she said next—and whatever new excuse she'd found to touch Ryan's arm.

"Turn around ..." Jenny wailed.

"Bright eyes," Todd bellowed.

SOFIE AND VAL lingered after the others left, finishing the night with just the two of them.

"Ryan truly is amazing," Val said, polishing off her drink.

Sofie couldn't hold it in any longer. She snapped. "Pretty obvious you think so. You've been all over him tonight."

Val blinked. "Excuse me?"

"I'm sorry," Sofie backpedaled. "I shouldn't have said that."

"No, please go on," Val said, setting her glass down with deliberate slowness. "Explain how I've been 'all over' him."

Sofie hesitated, then blurted, "You're practically in his lap. Every time we're all together. Tonight. The trivia night. That time we went bowling and axe-throwing. You coo and flirt and touch. You're all ..." She made a vague handsy gesture that looked like she was swatting at gnats.

Val stared for a beat. Then burst out laughing.

"I'm serious!"

"Sofie Chen," Val said through tears. "That is the most ridiculous thing you've ever said to me. And I was there when you claimed your theater professor was a vampire."

"He had weird teeth—"

"I'm not into Ryan," Val cut in. "I'm being nice to him

because I can see how much he means to you, you absolute walnut."

Sofie blinked. "But the touching. The cooing—"

"I'm drawing him out. Making him comfortable." She leaned closer. "Do you hear yourself? This is textbook romantic jealousy."

"It's not—" Sofie started, but even she didn't believe it.

"Look, I love you, but this whole 'I'm definitely not into Ryan' routine is lame and getting old. You're obviously crazy about him."

"Val, that's not—"

"You can pretend he's just your work husband all you want, but the way you look at him says otherwise."

"It's complicated," Sofie said quietly.

"It's really not." Val reached across the table and squeezed her hand. "You're in love with him, and instead of dealing with your feelings like an adult, you're projecting them onto me and making up stories about how I'm trying to seduce your non-boyfriend."

Put that way, it did sound ridiculous—like a bad rom-com where the heroine finally realizes she's been the source of her own drama all along. Sofie groaned, dropping her head into her hands, the cool metal of her rings pressing against her flushed cheeks as the full weight of her own absurdity settled over her like a hangover that hadn't waited for morning.

"I'm the worst. I'm so sorry, Val."

"Apology accepted. Now, when are you going to be honest with yourself about what's really going on?"

"I already know what's going on," Sofie said miserably. "I'm falling for a coworker. During a workplace sabotage scandal. While still technically entertaining a job offer. I'm in a phase of peak Sofie idiocy."

"Nothing wrong with falling in love," Val said gently. "And Ryan's definitely one of the good ones. But, Sof, if you don't make a serious move soon, someone else will."

Chapter Thirty-Six

Crossed Boundaries

Sofie had been looking forward to a quiet weekend—the kind where her biggest decision was Chinese or Thai takeout, and her most strenuous activity was reaching for the remote. After three back-to-back convention crises, she craved the simplicity of pajamas, couch cushions, and zero logistics. Her apartment looked as exhausted as she felt—scattered with the debris of rushed mornings and late nights.

Which is why, when she opened her laptop Saturday morning and was greeted by nineteen calendar notifications, she nearly hurled her coffee mug at the wall.

Her fingers froze over the trackpad, steam curling from her favorite ceramic mug as the screen filled with the soft blue glow of incoming alerts.

• Meeting request: Reconnect with Sandra Wu (Potential Client)

• Meeting request: Quarterly check-in with Jamal (Boston Convention Center)

• Meeting request: Coffee with Daniel C. (Event Tech Solutions)

On and on they went—networking meetings, client check-ins, professional development sessions she hadn't scheduled, with people she hadn't contacted. A completely restructured professional life... that she hadn't created.

For a few seconds, she just stared. Had she been hacked? Was this some kind of bizarre phishing stunt?

Then she saw the pattern: the precise language. The methodical spacing between appointments. The efficient categorization.

"Ryan," she whispered, realization dawning like a cold sunrise.

The coffee suddenly tasted bitter. Her pulse quickened. She clicked through more entries. Each one came with prep notes—detailed, polished, strategic.

• "Sandra Wu previously indicated interest in event management services. She was recently promoted to VP of Operations. Good time to re-engage."

• "Daniel C. has expertise in AR integration. Explore use cases for the Healthcare Forum."

The detail was impressive. The organization flawless. The presumption breathtaking.

Scrolling further, she discovered her entire contact database had been reorganized. What had once been a messy archive of evolving business connections—accumulated through years of conventions, networking events, and client work—had been transformed into a precision-engineered system of categories, metrics, relationship histories, follow-up schedules. Every interaction meticulously plotted for maximum professional efficiency.

Her messy record of human relationships now resembled a CRM dashboard, stripped of context. It felt like finding her diary rewritten by a data scientist—all the personal nuance scrubbed and sorted into sterile submission.

And she hadn't given him permission to do any of it.

Sofie slammed her laptop shut, sending coffee sloshing over the mug's rim. Her fingers jabbed at the screen with the kind of precision that comes from trying not to throw something breakable. Her heart hammered against her ribs as the phone rang, each tone ratcheting up her indignation.

He answered on the second ring. "Good morning, Sofie."

"Did you hack into my folders?" Words poured out, rapid fire.

A pause. "I wouldn't classify it as hacking. You gave me your password two months ago to fix your email filters—"

"For email filters, Ryan. Not to completely reorganize my entire professional life!"

"My intent was to enhance your networking efficiency. You mentioned being overwhelmed by contact maintenance, so I built—"

"I'll tell you what you did. You went into my personal folders. You scheduled meetings with people I haven't talked to in months. Without my knowledge or consent."

"The meetings are only requests," he offered, like that was the issue. "Based on standard intervals and prior communication patterns—"

"That's not the point!" Her voice had risen, high and sharp, so that she was fully shouting now, her voice echoing off the walls with a rawness that surprised even her. "These are *my* contacts, *my* decisions. You reorganized everything without even asking! You had no right to do any of this. None!"

He went quiet. "I thought you'd be pleased. The system is significantly more efficient than—"

"I don't care how efficient it is. You crossed a line. You violated my privacy." She was pacing now. Her face felt flushed with heat, and she could taste the metallic tang of adrenaline as months of small boundary violations crystallized into this one massive betrayal. "You reduced my relationships to algorithms. Those are my relationships. And how I manage them, who I choose to connect with—those are my decisions. And they're deeply personal. You didn't even ask!"

"I optimized for professional value—frequency of contact, business potential—"

"That's *exactly* the problem!" Her voice broke. "You treated my relationships like metrics, when you don't know anything about them. You don't know that I cut off Sandra Wu because she humiliated a good friend in front of a client. You don't know that Daniel C. made sexual advances on me at the Vegas convention."

That landed. His silence changed quality—like he was

genuinely processing new information rather than simply waiting to respond. When he finally spoke, his voice was quieter.

"I didn't account for those kinds of variables," he said.

"Because you didn't *ask me,*" Sofie snapped, her voice quieter now, too, but no less intense. "You just decided you knew better than I did. About my own life. And the people in it."

"That wasn't my intention—"

"I don't care about your intention!" Her voice dropped, low and cold. "You keep hiding behind that like it absolves you. You don't get to trample my boundaries and then act confused when I don't thank you."

A long pause. Then: "Would you like me to reverse the changes?"

"No. Don't touch anything. I'll handle it."

She sighed, rubbing the heel of her hand over her eyes. "Ryan, I need you to understand something. There are parts of my life that aren't optimization problems for you to solve. I don't need my files and systems streamlined. I need them *respected.* There are choices I get to make for myself, even if they're not the most efficient or logical by your standards."

"I ... see."

"Do you?" Her voice softened, but not by much. "Because this isn't the first time you've overstepped. You created medication schedules when I was sick. You decided that my whole apartment needed to be reorganized. You're always 'fixing things' you think are broken in my life."

"I'm struggling to identify the boundary," he admitted.

"You accepted those earlier interventions. Even appreciated them. But you find this one unacceptable. The differentiating variables are unclear to me."

"In those cases, I could see what you were doing. I could say yes or no. I could *consent.* This time, you went behind my back. You acted in secret. You made choices about *my* life, without me."

"I should have asked," Ryan said slowly. "Before making changes to your digital environment."

"Yes. Exactly."

A long pause.

"Ryan, I'm angry with you," Sofie said. "Really angry. But that doesn't mean I don't value you. It just means you can't push through my life, bulldozing my autonomy."

"I apologize," he said again, and this time it sounded different. Real.

"Thank you," she said, the heat in her voice cooling—but not gone. "Just ... ask next time. Always ask."

"I will." A pause. Then, more quietly: "Are we ... okay?"

The vulnerability in his voice caught her off guard. For a moment, she pictured his face—confused, maybe even hurt. He was worried about them.

"We will be," she said. "But I need space. And time. This was a big deal. A bad violation."

"Understood."

"I'll see you Monday at the Healthcare Forum meeting." She ended the call.

Sofie stared at the laptop, heart still pounding. Why had this cut so deep?

Then it hit her—hard and fast. Because accepting help meant admitting vulnerability. And vulnerability felt like a loaded weapon. A danger. Control wasn't just a preference. It was protection. Armor.

Ryan's "help" wasn't just invasive—it was destabilizing. It poked at the fragile scaffolding of independence she'd spent years reinforcing. Because what started with apartment organizing and calendar management could end with ... what? Dependency? More vulnerability? Trust that might eventually be betrayed?

She opened her laptop again and got to work—reviewing and selectively undoing the changes. Some were useful. Thoughtful, even. He remembered details she'd forgotten. Identified opportunities she'd overlooked. But others? Way too much. Too intrusive.

As she sorted, her fury cooled into something steadier: resolve. This boundary violation mattered. But she wouldn't let it define their relationship. They had something worth salvaging. Something that—if they could learn from this—might actually become stronger.

A FEW MILES AWAY, Ryan sat frozen at his kitchen table, the phone still in his hand long after the call had ended. Morning light filtered through the blinds in neat little stripes. Everything around him was orderly. Controlled. But inside, he felt unmoored.

He replayed the call in his head, again and again. He'd

expected thanks. But he'd received fury. He'd intended help. But he'd caused harm. He'd optimized a system. But he'd violated a boundary.

He started an email to Sofie. Deleted it. Started over, trying to convey genuine remorse without expectation of forgiveness. Not trying to offer a logical defense of his actions or an explanation of his intentions, but a simple acknowledgment of impact.

Five drafts later, he'd settled on something stripped of logic, stripped of structure. What remained was truth.

He finally hit send, the soft click of the trackpad sounding unnaturally loud in his silent apartment. His shoulders ached with tension he hadn't realized he'd been carrying, and the cursor blinked in the empty composition window like a small, judgmental eye.

> Sofie,
>
> I violated your trust and disregarded your autonomy. That was wrong, regardless of my intentions. I am genuinely sorry. Your anger is entirely justified.
>
> I don't expect forgiveness, nor do I believe an apology negates the impact of my actions. But I want you to know I'm listening. I'm learning. And I'm committed to doing better.
>
> I value our partnership—professionally and personally—more than you know.
>
> Ryan

He closed his laptop and sat in the unusual stillness of

his apartment for a long time. The systems and structures that typically brought him comfort suddenly felt insufficient, incomplete. There were variables he'd been overlooking, dimensions of human experience he'd failed to account for.

He hadn't just misjudged Sofie's preferences. He'd misjudged what it meant to be close to someone. To *respect* someone.

Sofie had always been the one who understood those dimensions intuitively. The one who navigated the messy, unpredictable terrain of human emotion with a natural fluency Ryan admired.

The irony of his action wasn't lost on him. In fact, it settled into his awareness like a physical weight. In trying to help Sofie be more like him—systematic, optimized, efficiently managed—he'd failed to recognize how much he needed to become more like her—intuitive about boundaries, respectful of autonomy, understanding that some things are more important than being perfectly organized.

And if he wanted to keep her in his life, he'd better figure that out.

Chapter Thirty-Seven

Line in the Sand

"They want us to do what?" Sofie stared at Ryan, coffee mug frozen halfway to her lips, steam curling like a question mark. Her grip tightened on the ceramic handle as the implications of his words sank in.

Ryan consulted his tablet. "Reconfigure the main exhibition hall to accommodate an expanded display for SouthStar Pharmaceuticals at the Healthcare Forum next month. They've increased their booth size by 73 percent and require a premium position near the main entrance." He rotated the tablet to show her the location on the diagram he'd pulled up.

"But that's Bioethics Alliance's space. We confirmed their location weeks ago." Sofie set her mug down, coffee forgotten. "They've already designed their layout around it."

"Correct. However, SouthStar has offered to pay a 40 percent premium for that placement." Ryan's tone was calm, clinical, factual. "Margo has indicated this is a priority adjustment."

"Of course she has." Sofie swiveled to her computer, pulling up the schematics. The familiar blue glow of the floor plan filled her screen, but now the neat rectangles and color-coded sections looked less like efficient organization and more like a battlefield, where powerful players could displace others at will. "What about the west hall section? If we—"

"I've run fifteen spatial reconfigurations," Ryan interrupted. "None meets SouthStar's criteria without displacing Bioethics Alliance."

"Then SouthStar doesn't get what they want," Sofie said flatly. "Bioethics Alliance signed first. They paid on time. Their location is confirmed. We made a commitment."

Ryan didn't flinch. "Expanding SouthStar's space would add $147,000 in revenue."

"I don't care if it would add a million. We don't push out a loyal non-profit for a pharma giant waving cash."

"Our contract permits adjustments at management discretion," Ryan pointed out. "It wouldn't be a breach."

"You're really okay with bumping a patient-advocacy group to make room for a company currently facing lawsuits over clinical-trial abuses?"

"Sofie, I'm merely presenting the situation objectively. SouthStar's potential future business far exceeds Bioethics Alliance's."

"This isn't an optimization problem," Sofie snapped. "It's a moral one." The words hung in the air between them, heavy with implications that went far beyond floor plans and revenue projections.

Ryan tilted his head slightly, processing her comment with his usual precision. But this time the variables weren't resolving.

"Are you picking a fight over this because you're angry about my violation of your digital space? I've told you I'm sorry about—"

"Oh, get over yourself, Ryan," Sofie said, her tone angry, bitter. "Bioethics Alliance fights for people harmed by companies like SouthStar. This is *our* event. So, that booth placement sends a message about our values."

Ryan's brow furrowed. "SouthStar's legal history and corporate ethics weren't part of my decision matrix."

"Well, maybe they should be. The Bioethics Alliance advocates for real people—folks in wheelchairs, scientists pushing for transparency. If we shove them aside to make room for SouthStar, we're saying those people don't matter."

Ryan's voice remained calm. "Our job is to manage conferences, not evaluate client missions."

"There's a difference between neutrality and complicity," Sofie countered. "When we favor powerful exhibitors over smaller, less wealthy ones—especially in our own flagship event—that's not neutrality. That's choosing profit over principle."

Something shifted in Ryan's expression—a subtle tightening around the eyes.

"You're suggesting my recommendation lacks principle."

"I'm suggesting it's incomplete," Sofie said, making an effort to soften her tone. "You're looking at this as a mathematical equation: bigger exhibitor equals more money equals logical priority. You're optimizing revenue. I'm thinking about the message we're sending."

"But revenue projections are quantifiable. Ethics are not."

"Some things matter more than numbers, Ryan. How many times do I have to say that to you?" Sofie leaned forward with both hands on her desk, palms flat against the cool surface as if bracing herself against his logical detachment. Her voice was low and fierce when she said, "Some lines shouldn't be crossed—especially by us, when we're the ones calling the shots."

Ryan studied her, brow furrowed. "You feel strongly about this."

"Yes, I do." Sofie met his gaze directly. "I thought you did, too. This is about right and wrong. Don't you have any lines you won't cross? Any principles that matter more to you than efficiency or profit?"

The question seemed to catch him off guard. He blinked, his usually fluid thought process visibly recalibrating.

"I value accuracy. Integrity of systems. Following through on commitments."

"Then how is this okay?" Sofie pressed, sensing a potential opening. "We committed to Bioethics Alliance. We confirmed their space. Moving them now violates that commitment."

"The contract allows for—"

"There you go again with fine print!" she snapped. "I'm talking about values."

Ryan's expression was unreadable as he processed her words. Sofie waited, hoping she'd made a dent in his logical framework. After what felt like an eternity, he spoke.

"Your argument has merit from an ethical perspective. However, Margo assigned me the task of accommodating SouthStar. My job is to execute."

Sofie's heart sank. "So that's it? We chase the biggest dollar, no matter the consequences?"

"I didn't say that," Ryan replied, a hint of something—defensiveness?—in his tone.

"And what about your personal priorities?" Sofie challenged. "Do you actually think this is right, Ryan? Not efficient, not profitable, but right?"

"My personal views are irrelevant to this decision," he finally said.

"That's a cop-out, and you know it." Sofie's disappointment came through clearly in her voice. "We all draw lines somewhere. I thought yours were closer to mine."

Ryan stood abruptly. "I have to submit the revised floor plans to Margo by noon. Will you be contributing?"

His sudden shift to a formal tone hit her like a door swinging closed, like he'd slammed down a barrier of professional distance.

Sofie straightened, her own professional mask now sliding into place also, despite the emotion churning beneath it. "No," she said firmly. "I won't be part of bumping

Bioethics Alliance from their space. In fact, I'm calling them myself to apologize."

"That would be inadvisable, Sofie. Client communications should come through official channels after decisions are finalized."

"Some things matter more than procedure," Sofie replied, gathering her own things. "The Bioethics people deserve to hear from someone who actually gives a damn."

"You're making this personal."

"Yes, I am," Sofie agreed without hesitation. "Because it is personal. What we do reflects who we are. And I thought —" She paused, swallowing her frustration. "I thought we were on the same side."

Ryan's expression remained unreadable, but something flickered in his eyes—uncertainty, maybe. Then it was gone.

"I'll inform you when the new configuration is approved," he said.

"Do what you have to do," Sofie replied. "So will I."

The door clicked shut behind her, the sound deceptively soft for what it signaled: a rift not just in a project, but in their partnership.

Three hours later, Ryan sat alone, staring at the proposal on his screen. The document was perfect—every metric was flawless. Revenue projections strong. Timelines efficient. Floor plans optimized. Everything Margo had requested, packaged in Ryan's signature meticulous style.

But he hadn't submitted it yet.

Sofie's words kept replaying in his mind.

Some things matter more than revenue projections.

There's a difference between neutrality and complicity.

I thought you understood that some principles aren't negotiable.

The disappointment in her eyes had made him ... uncomfortable. More uncomfortable than it should have, given the professional nature of their disagreement.

He opened the Bioethics Alliance website—something he hadn't done earlier. It brought him face to face with tragic patient stories and the real human cost of pharmaceutical misconduct. He dug further into his own file now and found that their plan for the exhibit was to showcase patients harmed in clinical drug trials. They'd chosen the exhibit space near the entrance to facilitate wheelchair users who would be speaking onstage.

None of that had been factored into his model.

The oversight hit him with a cold shock of recognition: his carefully constructed optimization algorithms had prioritized square footage and dollar signs over human beings.

Sobered by this, Ryan searched for information about SouthStar Pharmaceuticals. The lawsuits Sofie mentioned appeared immediately—three separate class actions involving concealed side effects, manipulated trial data, and aggressive marketing of insufficiently tested medications.

She was right. This was another variable he'd excluded.

He leaned back, discomfort prickling under his skin. His process had optimized for all the wrong things. This wasn't clean. This wasn't neutral. Sofie was right: this was a line that shouldn't be crossed.

Ryan opened a new draft. This time, he optimized for dignity, accessibility, fairness. The revised plan preserved Bioethics Alliance's original location. SouthStar would get expanded space, but in the adjacent exhibition hall, with enhanced signage and promo placement to compensate for the secondary location.

It wasn't the solution Margo had requested. It would generate less immediate revenue for their flagship event. It might even create professional complications for him personally.

But it was the right thing to do.

When he finished, he sent the proposal not to Margo, but to Sofie, with a simple message:

Here's an alternative configuration, preserving Bioethics Alliance's original location. It reduces the revenue differential to 12 percent. Do you have any input before I submit?

Then he did something he rarely did during work hours: he left the office to clear his head.

When he returned, her reply was waiting:

This works. Some lines shouldn't be crossed, even when it would be easier to step over them. Thank you for finding another way.

Ryan read it twice.

Then he sent the revised proposal to Margo, cc'ing Sofie. He didn't add any justification. The work spoke for itself.

Chapter Thirty-Eight

Which Entrance Should I Use?

The whole team had been dreading this weekend ever since the unfortunate pairing emerged. When talking to the clients, Ryan sometimes referred to it as "an unfortunate temporal and spatial juxtaposition of incongruent elements." But around the office, even he had adopted the shorthand most people used: the "Jesus Freaks and Sex Freaks Extravaganza."

Regardless of what they called it, everyone agreed—it was going to be a colossal shit-show. The largest annual gathering of the American sex-positivity movement would be sharing the Grand Hyatt with the Family Research Council (FRC), one of the most socially conservative organizations in the country. And Prestige Events was tasked with making it all run smoothly.

Ryan and Sofie had planned obsessively—color-coded routing systems, staggered schedules, separate entrances, dedicated elevators, blue lanyards for FRC, red for SEXPO. Every contingency had been mapped. Every variable anticipated.

And yet, it was already in ruins. Half the directional signs were gone. The color-coding of the lanyards had somehow been mixed up, going to the wrong people. And now, according to a frantic text from Jenny, they knew the in-room welcome baskets had been swapped, too.

People arriving for the FRC event were entering their hotel rooms to discover kits labeled *A Weekend of Uninhibited Pleasure!*—complete with: a dildo, two different kinds of lube, a butt plug, a blindfold, and a copy of *The Ethical Slut: A Practical Guide to Polyamory*.

From their vantage point on the mezzanine balcony, Ryan pointed to the lobby wall over the FRC registration desk, where at 6 a.m. that morning, he and Sofie had hung a banner reading *Defending Traditional Family Values*. But a different banner was now in its place. In glittering hot pink script surrounded by hearts, it commanded: *Embrace Your Kinks Without Shame.*

Ryan's jaw tensed. Only a few things could explain the switch.

Sofie followed his gaze as it shifted to the other side of the lobby, where an elderly woman in a floral housedress brandished a cane like a saber at a couple in full black leather —collars, harnesses, and thigh-high boots clicking with militant authority. They were handing out glossy pamphlets titled *Mindful Masturbation*, *Advanced Anal Play*, and *Group Sex for Beginners*.

"I'll handle her," Sofie muttered. "You go check the north side of the Magnolia Ballroom. FRC's *Protecting Children from Moral Decay* panel is going on there. On the other side of the divider wall is *Sex Toy Lessons 101*. If those two audiences collide—"

"Disaster probability: extremely high," Ryan finished, already moving.

His tablet pinged with an alert from Todd:

[URGENT] FRC KEYNOTE SLIDESHOW REPLACED WITH PORN

He broke into a sprint.

When he reached the ballroom, he saw Todd valiantly trying to calm Reverend James Hammond, whose face was purple with fury.

Spittle flew as Hammond raged, his voice reverberating off the ballroom's gilded walls like divine wrath amplified. "—pornographic material! Projected during my family-values keynote!"

"I understand, Reverend," Todd said, placating. "We're investigating how this happened—"

"This is totally unacceptable! My audience was exposed to explicit, vile imagery!"

Ryan stepped in. "Reverend, I uploaded your correct slides to a secure backup. If you give me about two minutes, I can have you all ready to resume your session."

The reverend's glare could have melted concrete. "It's inexcusable that this happened. I promise you—"

"There you are!" Trevor's voice rang out, smooth as satin.

He approached with perfect timing—fluid, confident, too prepared. Ryan could practically see the invisible stage marks he'd hit.

"We're so sorry about this regrettable glitch," Trevor said, his voice oily. "I've spoken with hotel management. We're arranging a complimentary reception for your group in a private space tonight. The Palmetto Room will be exclusively yours."

Ryan's eyes narrowed. "The Palmetto Room is already reserved for—"

"It's been adjusted. Everything's handled." Trevor started to leave with the reverend, then returned to Ryan with a smile too sharp to be friendly. "You know, Porter, even the best systems collapse under pressure. Human nature's messy. Unpredictable."

Ryan's voice dropped. "Human nature didn't swap his slide-deck file. That was someone with technical access and malicious intent."

Trevor's smile widened. "Paranoia's a hell of a drug, buddy. But if you'd rather chase ghosts than fix real problems, be my guest." He checked his watch theatrically. "Oh look—I promised Dr. Morgan I'd help with her *Tantric Orgasm Techniques* workshop. Apparently they need demo volunteers." He winked. "Should be ... educational." And with a whistle, he strolled off.

Ryan stared after him, pulse pounding. This wasn't Murphy's Law—it was weaponized sabotage. Trevor wasn't solving problems. He was creating them. And he wasn't even hiding it anymore.

Soon, another alert summoned Ryan to the kitchen that served both ballrooms. A red-faced FRC official was screaming at a hotel staffer:

"Get those off our tables! Now!"

Ryan followed her gaze to the dessert trays. Cupcakes. Large ones. Dozens of them. Each one lovingly adorned with anatomically correct frosting art in 3D relief—penises and vulvas, absolutely unmistakable in their accuracy. Rendered with such detail that Ryan could identify substructures. Bold, lush, colorful.

This was high-precision baking porn.

Ryan grimaced. His whole being vibrated with frustration. He turned to the catering manager at his side. "These are the wrong desserts for the FRC meal."

She held up a clipboard. "Not according to this order form."

He grabbed it. The White-Out marks were as visible as a fresh scar, the edits clumsy and rushed.

"This is a mistake. Where are the correct desserts? There must be other desserts."

She pointed across the room to a rack of trays that had been pushed behind a tall cloth screen. Innocent sugar cookies topped with various Christian symbols in delicate piping—a cross, dove, ichthus, tongue of flame.

The orders had been swapped. Again. Just like the lanyards, welcome baskets, and room assignments. Fiddled with, just like the reverend's slide deck.

A blatant pattern.

He went in search of Sofie.

He found her when shouts and the clamor of chaos drew him to the Orchid Room, where a BDSM demo had been in progress, with whips, handcuffs, latex, and rope-tying. A delegation of furious FRC parents had stormed the door, shouting "SHUT DOWN THIS PERVERSION." The crowd inside had erupted in pandemonium, and Sofie was doing her best to calm outraged people on both sides.

When he could finally draw her aside, Ryan filled Sofie in on all the havoc Trevor's sabotage had wrought. Before he could complete the list, they were interrupted by Jenny's voice crackling over their headsets:

ALL HANDS! BALLROOM AREA. NOW!

They ran.

Between the two ballrooms stood a huge display, the size of a box truck. It featured two sets of startlingly realistic animatronic figures demonstrating one explicit sex position after another with unnerving accuracy. The LED display underneath flashed informative labels in cheerful Comic Sans font—*Reverse Cowgirl*, *Doggy Style*, *Pretzel-Dip*—as if this were an educational exhibit at a very specific kind of museum.

Servo motors whined. The mannequins moaned. Plastic faces beamed with rictus ecstasy.

"Pure depravity!" screamed a group of FRC members, some of whom split off to form an impromptu prayer circle, their voices rising in urgent harmony as they clutched their Bibles like shields.

“A celebration of humanism!” chanted the sex-positivists, who cycled between that and “Orgasms are life!” with the rhythmic intensity of a sports-stadium crowd.

The groups’ competing cries rose to the rafters—holy outrage and climactic praise colliding so dissonantly it sounded like the world’s most cursed choir practice.

What happened next would later be described in wildly different terms, depending on who was telling the story. Hotel staff simply called it *The Incident.*

Both organizations threatened lawsuits. The hotel demanded damages. A video of the lobby chaos had already gone viral under the title: *NSFW Conference Meltdown.*

In Margo’s office the following morning, the air was funereal. She paced behind her desk, heels clicking like a metronome of doom. Ryan, Sofie, and Trevor sat in silence.

“Explain to me,” she said finally, voice like ice, “how three professional event coordinators allowed this to happen.”

“With all due respect,” Trevor began smoothly, “disaster was baked in from the start. We were dealing with diametrically opposed groups in a shared venue. It was an impossible situation.”

“A situation,” Margo snapped, “we knew about for six months. A situation we had carefully planned for. We’ve handled worse. And yet somehow, after a half year of preparation, every single thing went wrong.”

"Human nature. Systems failure," Trevor said with a shrug.

Ryan's fingers tightened around his tablet. "This wasn't systems failure," he said, his voice low. "This was deliberate sabotage."

Trevor chuckled. "Still chasing ghosts, Porter? Maybe it's time to accept that your precious systems don't work in the real world."

Sofie leaned in, her tone insistent. "Margo, Ryan is correct. The welcome baskets, the desserts, the—"

Margo's interruption came with the force of a thunderclap. "Are you seriously suggesting someone deliberately orchestrated this? Who would even benefit from that?"

The room went silent except for the distant sound of phones ringing in the outer office. Ryan and Sofie glanced at Trevor, who shifted slightly in his chair—the movement almost imperceptible, just a slight adjustment of his shoulders and a barely perceptible tightening around his eyes. But Sofie saw it.

"Margo," she said evenly, "these weren't random failures. This was engineered—"

"Enough!" Margo cut her off, slashing the air with her hand. "I don't want to hear your stupid theories! I want solutions. Both organizations are pulling future business. Our reputation is imploding. We've become a punchline on social media."

Patterns didn't lie. But Margo wasn't ready to see them. Not yet.

Her voice hard as steel, she punctuated each word with a

finger jab at her desktop. "This was a failure. Period. Right now, I don't care whose fault it was. I care about damage control."

Sofie and Ryan exchanged a look.

Trevor reclined slightly in his chair, looking pleased with himself.

Chapter Thirty-Nine

The Smell of Possibility

Ryan trudged into his building's cramped lobby, the weight of recent days pressing down like a backpack loaded with failure. The foyer's familiar features—the wilting fern in the corner, the low hum of the fluorescent lighting—offered none of their usual comfort. Tonight, it just felt sterile. Harsh. Stark. And just as hollow as he felt inside.

"Well, look who it is."

He turned. Sarah from 7C stood at the bank of mailboxes, her face flushed from her evening run. Damp workout clothes clung to her like a second skin. One hand clutched junk mail, while the other fumbled with her keys, small metallic sounds echoing in the quiet lobby.

"Haven't seen you in a while, Ryan. How's life?"

"Yeah, sorry about that," he said, meaning it. "Things have been ..." He trailed off, not sure how to categorize the wreckage of his professional and personal lives.

"Complicated?" Sarah offered.

"You could say that."

She eyed him, then smiled. "You look like you could use a friendly ear and a good meal. I've got leftover Indian curry from that place on Grand—the one you said you liked. Want in?"

He hesitated. Normally, he'd retreat to his apartment, burying himself in spreadsheets and silence. But something about Sarah's easy, uncomplicated offer was ... grounding. Appealing.

"That would be nice. If it's not an imposition."

"Of course it is. But I'm inviting you anyway." She grinned, already heading toward the elevator. "And I need an update on your dating life. You promised me intel."

Ryan gave a sheepish shrug. "Yeah. Sorry about that, too. You'd have heard ... if there was anything worth reporting."

The elevator stopped on four. As he stepped off, Sarah said, "Give me thirty to de-sweat. Then come up—and bring your best curry-appreciation skills."

The doors slid shut, leaving Ryan alone with something he hadn't felt in days: a flicker of connection.

Then he remembered—she wanted to hear about his dates. He was going to have to tell her about them. All three of them.

The first: Olivia, a librarian who had responded positively to his profile's mention of organizational systems.

They met at a coffee shop Ryan had selected based on optimal ambient noise levels and table spacing.

"So," Olivia said after they'd ordered, "what made you try online dating?"

Ryan had prepped for this question. "My lifestyle creates limited romantic opportunities. Plus, a friend recently suggested my analytical tendencies might align with a structured dating format."

Olivia blinked. "I ... see."

"I've created a spreadsheet tracking first-date success variables, if you'd like to review it."

Her coffee cup froze halfway to her lips. Silence stretched on. And, it turned out, she would not like to see the spreadsheet.

Strike one.

Twelve days later, he met up with Emma, a data analyst who had seemed promising—until she mentioned she found organization "stifling."

"Don't you ever just want to be spontaneous?" she asked over appetizers.

"No. I find that experiences are optimized by proper planning. Spontaneity leaves no room for that."

Emma stared at him. "You know," she said slowly, "sometimes spontaneity can just be ... fun! Like, we could just leave here right now. Go do something crazy!"

"Without even finishing our appetizers? That would be ... suboptimal."

The word came out strangled, like he was personally offended by the concept of abandoned food. There would be no main course, much less dessert. And certainly no second date with Emma.

His third attempt was Ashley, a Columbia grad student in anthropology. She'd messaged first, intrigued by his mention of Arctic research.

"That must've been so fascinating," Ashley said, leaning forward. "All those cultures. The Inuits, the Yupiks—"

"Actually, I focused on wildlife observation and ice-core data collection," Ryan said.

Ashley's enthusiasm visibly dimmed. "Oh. I thought you did, like ... cultural studies. Indigenous peoples, traditional knowledge systems ... that sort of thing."

"Ah. No. But one year, I did create a taxonomy of researcher behaviors during the polar night," he offered. "Quite fascinating, really. Would you like to see the charts?"

She would not.

The truth was, after three spectacularly unsuccessful dates, Ryan had begun to suspect that his approach to romance suffered from the same fundamental flaw as his approach to Sofie's digital life: too much optimization according to his own lights, not enough understanding of what the other person actually wanted or needed.

By the time Ryan knocked on the door of 7C, his short walk down Dating-Memory Lane had depressed him further. But Sarah greeted him with enthusiasm, fresh from her shower, her damp hair catching the warm light spilling from her apartment. The scent of something delicious—curry and cardamom and comfort—wafted past her as she held up a

Singha beer in one hand and a bottle of white wine in the other.

"Pick your poison," she said with a grin. "You're not going back downstairs until I've gotten you well oiled."

Ryan smiled, her commitment to the cause amusing. He pointed to the wine.

As they ate, Sarah debriefed him on his dating disasters like an FBI supervisor quizzing an agent about a risky counterintelligence mission.

He spilled it all out, then concluded, "So, the success metrics remain … discouraging."

"Ah, I'm sorry, Ry. That sucks. Bad luck. And yeah, online dating can be brutal. But you've got to keep putting yourself out there." She poured more wine. "That said, the dating apps aren't the only approach. I mean, some people find it works to participate in an activity they really enjoy in a group setting."

"How—?"

"It's less about meeting your 'person,' and more about exposing yourself to more people, having different conversations and experiences. Let's say I join a women's softball team. I may not meet the man of my dreams that way, but I could meet a new friend who eventually connects me with a romantic prospect … So, think about what you enjoy doing, or might want to do. Take cooking classes or volunteer or join a bowling league."

"I did go bowling once. Sort of enjoyed it, once I got the hang of it."

"There you go. Lean into that. Worst case, you improve your spare game."

He smiled. "I'll consider it. Thanks, Sarah."

The conversation then turned to other things, flowing as easily as the wine Sarah kept pouring. The curry was perfectly spiced—warm heat that built slowly rather than burning—and Ryan felt the tension in his shoulders finally begin to ease. The oiling Sarah promised was well under way.

At meal's end, Sarah set down her napkin with a sigh. "I get the sense that the 'dating blues' aren't the only thing getting you down." She refilled their wine glasses again. "Come on. Spill. Talk to me."

And he did. He told her about Sofie—and about what he'd done to her digital systems.

Sarah's eyes went cartoon-wide. "Oooof. That's ... yeah. No. Oh boy. A critical error."

"She's still distant."

"I bet. ... How long ago?"

"Ten days."

"She'll come around. Just give her time. And don't push."

He nodded, then surprised himself by telling her about Trevor. About the sabotage.

"So this Trevor guy's basically a black-hat hacker?" Sarah said, reaching for her glass. "Only with conference schedules?"

"That's ... uncomfortably accurate."

Sarah shrugged. "We're not totally immune to that at Google. Last year, I had a colleague who constantly undermined me—taking credit, introducing bugs, delaying cooperation. The whole nine yards. ”

“What did you do?”

“Built a better system. One he couldn’t touch without leaving fingerprints.”

Ryan’s eyes lit up. An idea formed that he lodged in his brain. “That’s ... helpful.”

She studied him. “So ... why haven’t you considered working somewhere else?”

“Like where?”

“Like Google.”

He blinked. “Me? At Google?”

“Why not?” she said. “You’re a systems genius. Exactly the sort of person we need.”

He considered that. “Three weeks ago, I probably would’ve just said no. But now, it sounds like an appealing prospect.”

“Good. Because I know a team working on hybrid event ops—kind of like convention planning, but Google-scale. Internal summits, cross-functional logistics.”

“No drunk orthodontists?”

She laughed, then continued. “Look, we need systems thinkers—people who see patterns and anticipate bottlenecks. You’d fit in. You already speak the language. And you know all about precision under pressure. You’re just not in a place that appreciates you.”

“Would I have to fake knowing TensorFlow?”

She laughed. “You don’t dream in TensorFlow?”

He was quiet for a moment, swirling the wine in his

glass, letting himself marinate in the idea of working at Google. The prospect of leaving Prestige was unsettling—but not in the way he would've expected. It felt like Sarah had opened a window in a room stuffy with other people's baggage, letting in air that smelled like possibility.

"What's the downside? The catch?" he asked.

"You'd be a small cog in a big machine. You wouldn't have final say over anything, especially not at first. And sometimes things move slowly. Bureaucracy happens. But if you carve out your space, the work's meaningful."

He was quiet for a long moment. "Would you really float my résumé?"

"Sure. And come spend a day with us. See what it's like. No pressure."

Ryan nodded slowly. "That sounds ... really good. Let's plan that. Thanks, Sarah."

LATER, back in his apartment—quiet, ordered, familiar—Ryan felt lighter than he had in weeks. The conversation with Sarah had debugged something in him.

He still had work to do. Sofie's trust to earn back. Trevor's sabotage to expose.

But for the first time, he had ideas of what to do—and options that didn't feel like compromises.

Chapter Forty

Escape Attempt

"Team building," Margo had said that morning, smiling far too brightly, with the kind of forced enthusiasm that comes from reading too many management books. As if locking five people in Brooklyn's premier escape room—themed as a mad scientist's lair—was going to improve anything.

It probably seemed like a brilliant idea on paper—force them to collaborate, break down barriers, build trust. Instead, it felt to Sofie like locking enemies in a powder keg with a lit fuse. Now, twelve minutes into their one-hour challenge, she wasn't so sure they'd all make it out without someone committing homicide.

The room was peak immersive chaos—cryptic notebooks with pages that crackled when touched, bubbling vials that gurgled ominously with dry-ice fog, ancient books with codes and leather bindings that smelled of theatrical dust. At the center stood a massive workbench wired with gears and levers that gleamed under flickering LED candles. The whole setup hummed with barely contained mechanical energy. The mission: stop the doomsday device before the clock hit zero.

Trevor rifled through desk drawers with theatrical flair, every movement calculated for maximum dramatic effect. His fingers moved through the props with the confidence of someone projecting competence more than possessing it.

Ryan, meanwhile, glowered at a resin skull, turning it over in his hands like it might confess its secrets if he just applied the right pressure. His fingers traced the artificial bone structure with his usual methodical intensity. "The dimensions of the orbital cavity suggest this is a cast of *Australopithecus africanus*," he said, voice clipped, precise. "That might affect the puzzle logic."

"Found something!" Trevor said, holding up a small brass key. "It was in this false-bottom drawer. Classic hiding place." He tossed it across the room. "Sofie, catch!"

She caught it reflexively—but hesitated, aware of Ryan's eyes now on her. A week ago, she'd have gone straight for the locked cabinet they'd already tried. Now, with their suspicions about Trevor rattling around in her head, she paused. She handed the key to Ryan instead. "What do you think?"

Trevor's smile stayed fixed but his eyebrows lifted. "Why ask *him*?"

Sofie didn't answer.

Ryan examined the key. "The notching suggests a nineteenth-century design. Possibly Victorian, though the proportions are exaggerated for theatrical effect." He turned it over in his hand, his expression tightening. "We should test it. Carefully. These puzzles are often rigged with fail conditions."

"Like what?" Sofie asked.

"Insert it in the wrong lock and you might trigger a penalty or block a clue."

"Paranoid much?" Trevor leaned back against the wall, arms folded. "It's just a game, Ryan."

"Some people take games seriously." Ryan's tone was even. Then he looked up—right at Trevor. "Ask the Amusement Machine Association. They weren't exactly amused when thirty Computer Space games—each worth more than some people's cars—wound up in Atlantic City instead of at their convention. Funny how those glitches always happen when you're around."

The comment altered the atmosphere in the room. Sofie felt she could see frost forming between Ryan and Trevor. The countdown clock's ticking grew more ominous. The LED candles seemed to flicker faster, as if unnerved by the accusation that hung in the recycled air.

"Oh, for Christ's sake ..." Trevor snatched the key from Ryan and popped open the lock. Inside were four colored vials.

Jenny and Todd, previously paging listlessly through dusty books, perked up.

"Nice work!" Jenny said.

Trevor turned to Ryan, grinning. “See? While you're busy worrying about booby traps and sabotage, I'm solving problems. Executing. Delivering results.”

“Look,” Todd said. “The vials match the color sequence in that portrait over there.”

“Purple, green, red, blue,” Ryan said, arranging the vials to match the portrait. A hidden panel slid open with a clean click.

“Wow. Spreadsheet Boy knows his colors,” Trevor said.

Sofie turned. “Stop!”

Trevor looked mildly surprised. “Just admiring his attention to detail.”

“No, you're not. You're baiting him.”

“I'd never. I'm a team player. I believe in synergistic collaboration.”

Jenny and Todd stifled giggles. Each mouthed, *Bingo!*

But Sofie was too angry now, too fed up to laugh. “Then act like it!” She gestured toward the next puzzle: sheet music and disassembled instruments. “Start solving.”

Ryan leaned in, scanning the notes. Trevor hummed the music's melody under his breath. A week ago, their different approaches might've seemed complementary. Now, it felt like a duet in the wrong key—one flat, one sharp, no harmony.

“It's ‘Twinkle, Twinkle, Little Star’—played backward,” Todd said.

Trevor pointed up. “So, I bet that ceiling star matters.”

“Or it's a misdirection,” Ryan muttered. After a pause, he added, “You'd know all about that, wouldn't you?”

The air in the room went still. The silence was personal.

Jenny cleared her throat. "Guys? Maybe we should—"

"No, please," Trevor cut in, his voice smooth. "Don't stop now, Ryan. Go on. Let's hear what you're implying."

"Ryan," Sofie said quietly, hand on his forearm. Then, to Trevor: "We've got twenty-five minutes left, and I'm not failing this room because you two can't—" She stopped herself. 'Behave like adults' didn't cut it anymore. She exhaled. "Let's just finish the damn puzzle."

Ryan and Trevor split to opposite puzzles like they were battling for dominance, not solving a shared problem. Sofie became less a teammate and more a referee, directing their hostility into something semi-useful.

Trevor leaned over a sequence of symbols by the doomsday device, his expression tightening as if the puzzle itself had insulted him.

"It's a simple substitution cipher," Ryan said, cool and smug. "A fifth grader could crack it. But—oh, right—you only do 'intuitive leaps.'"

Trevor's fists clenched. His carefully maintained mask cracked to reveal something uglier underneath. He stepped toward Ryan.

Sofie shot in between them, planting her hand against Trevor's chest. His heartbeat pulsed against her palm. His muscles were rigid, tight with restrained fury. He was a coiled spring ready to snap. "Don't."

"This little shit thinks he can—"

"God damn it, Trevor. Grow up."

She turned to Ryan, who looked startled. "And if you

know how to solve the damn thing, then do it, and get us out of here. I can't stand another minute of this."

Ryan shoved a hand through his hair, exhaling through gritted teeth. He bent over the sequence of symbols again. "They're alchemical. Adapted mathematically, possibly binary logic ..." He dropped into intense focus, fingers tracing lines like he was reading braille. The only sound in the room was the slow, relentless tick of the countdown clock.

They escaped with two minutes to spare.

As they filed out, Todd leaned toward Jenny and whispered, "What the hell just happened in there?"

Jenny shook her head. "No clue. But whatever that was, it wasn't team building."

Sofie watched Ryan stalk toward the building's exit, posture tight, jaw set.

Trevor caught her eye, his expression already sliding back into its practiced charm. He winked. The same casual, confident flirtation that once made her pulse race. Now it made her stomach turn.

She didn't blink. Didn't smile. Gave him nothing. Then turned away, the dismissal sharp and deliberate as a slap.

Chapter Forty-One

The Spotlight

The duck breast was perfect—crispy skin that crackled under Sofie's fork, tender meat that melted on her tongue. The meal was elegantly plated with roasted fingerlings and tiny purple microgreens that looked like edible confetti. The savory aroma mixed with the restaurant's ambient notes of garlic and wine, creating a rich, heady atmosphere.

Sofie had already posted a photo to her Instagram story with a *#treatyourself* caption before taking her first bite. She and Val were grabbing a late dinner at Joe Allen after seeing the revival of *Chicago*. Tickets had come their way via a friend on the production staff.

"Through the whole show," Sofie said, swirling her wine, "all I could think was: Trevor is Billy Flynn—suave, manipulative, spinning every narrative with that same practiced charm. And Ryan? He's poor Amos Hart. Honest. Earnest. Getting played because someone sees his decency as weakness."

The theater-district crowd hummed around them—actors glowing with post-performance adrenaline, wide-eyed tourists clutching Playbills, couples raving about the banana cream pie. It was all warm and golden and alive.

Val nodded. "Yep. Charisma versus substance. Performance winning out over ethics in a system that rewards flash instead of truth." She leaned in, more serious, her voice tightening. "Let me ask you something. You know Trevor's sabotaging Ryan. Why aren't you doing anything about it?"

Heat flushed Sofie's cheeks. Her fork clinked against the plate. "It's not that simple—"

"It *is* that simple," Val said flatly. "You watched Trevor destroy people in Chicago. Remember that registration-system crash he engineered? Then swooped in to 'save the day' while his coworker took the fall?"

"That was different—"

"I'll tell you how it was different: that was some coworker you barely knew. This time, the target is Ryan. And I don't understand why that difference doesn't kick your ass into motion."

Val's voice carried enough edge to cut through the restaurant's ambient noise. A couple at the next table glanced at them with the kind of curiosity that comes from witnessing someone else's drama unfold.

Sofie felt heat creep up her neck—part shame, part

anger. She stared into her wine glass, unable to meet Val's eyes. "I can't go to Margo without concrete proof. Right now it's just patterns and suspicion."

"Bullshit. You have your own experience with him in Chicago. You know his playbook." Val leaned in, voice low and pointed. "This isn't about evidence, and we both know it. This is about you being scared—scared of confronting Trevor, scared of rocking the boat at work, scared of admitting that you let yourself get played in Chicago." Her voice dropped even lower—to a whisper that somehow felt more cutting than if she were shouting. "And most of all, scared of what happens if you actually fight for Ryan and it means something."

"I'm not scared—"

"You're terrified."

Silence fell between them, brittle and jagged. When Sofie finally spoke, she pivoted hard. "I'm not sure you're one to talk. You didn't even fight for that position at Steppenwolf. That was your dream job, and you're just walking away from it."

Val let out a bitter laugh. "Yeah, well, dreams have a way of turning into nightmares." She set her wine down. "When I told you I was passing on it, I didn't tell you the real reason."

Sofie sat back, folding her arms. "Okay. Tell me now."

"Remember Malcolm? The tech director?"

"Mr. Sexy Talk."

"Turns out he's been busy—ensemble actress, lighting designer, costume intern. I was next on the rotation, according to our mutual friend Sarah."

"Val ..."

"Don't be sorry. Better to find out now than after I moved my whole life to Chicago." Val took a long sip. "Something better will come along."

Sofie reached across the table and squeezed her hand.

Val said, "Speaking of opportunities ... have you decided about that Occasional Planning job?"

"I turned it down."

Val's eyebrows shot up. "Seriously?"

"The timing wasn't right. There's stuff I need to finish at Prestige. Like making sure Ryan doesn't get railroaded out of the industry by a sociopath."

Val grinned. "Now we're getting somewhere. So you admit you care about him."

"Of course I care. He's my—" Sofie hesitated, the words sticking. "My ..."

"Your what? Colleague? Friend? Or—" Val paused. Not meeting Sofie's eyes, she said, "Actually, I should tell you something. Ryan and I have gone out for drinks a couple of times."

Something cold settled in Sofie, spreading outward like ice water through her veins. Her wine suddenly tasted sharp, acidic. Her grip tightened on her glass. "Oh?"

"He wanted to pick my brain about something. Couldn't find time during work hours, so we met after."

Sofie said nothing. Her throat was suddenly dry.

"He asked me how to make himself more appealing to someone he's interested in."

"Someone he's—" Her voice barely made it out. "Who?"

Val gave her a look. "You, obviously. Good lord. For someone so smart, you can be painfully dense."

"He said that? He said he's interested in me?"

"Not in so many words. Ryan doesn't exactly do direct language. But he did say—and I quote—'Sofie's clearly not interested. I wish she were, but she's not. Something must be fundamentally wrong with me. And, apparently, other women see the same error code Sofie does.'"

Something warm and painful bloomed in Sofie's chest. "He said that about me?"

"He did. The man is head-over-heels for you, Sof. And unless I'm imagining things, I'd say the feeling's mutual."

Sofie blinked, her mind reeling. "I can't ... It's complicated."

"Everything worth doing is." Val leaned in again. "And look, I get that you're focused on what he said about you. I do. But, Sofie, you're blocking out the part about him trying to meet other women. He's got a friend in his building advising him. He hasn't connected with anyone yet, but it's only a matter of time."

The thought sent a jolt of panic through Sofie's chest.

"There's more," Val said. "That same friend works at Google, and when she heard about what's going on with Trevor, she floated a possible job for Ryan there."

The comment jolted her—sharp and electric. She tasted the metallic edge of genuine fear beneath the lingering duck and wine. "He's leaving?"

"He's thinking about it. She's invited him to spend a day there."

Sofie stared at her plate. Her carefully constructed sense of control crumbled under the weight of everything she hadn't admitted—not to Val, not to herself. "What do you think I should do?"

"You should fight for him. You should fight, period. For him. Against Trevor. For what matters. The question is: are you brave enough to stop hanging out in the wings and step into the spotlight?"

Val raised her wine glass, the amber liquid catching the light like a curtain going up. "Because right now, you're letting the villain write this story's ending. And we both know how that turns out."

Sofie didn't answer. Not yet. But her pulse was already moving to a different rhythm.

Chapter Forty-Two

Deeper Connections

Ryan thought he'd give online dating one more shot—though he suspected he already knew the outcome.

According to his compatibility assessment, Amanda seemed promising: her literary interests matched his, her job as a data visualization specialist suggested a shared vernacular, and her messages had both wit and attention to detail—she used the Oxford comma with unfailing consistency.

He'd prepared thoughtfully, selecting the restaurant for optimal conversation acoustics, comfortable seating, and proximity to both their apartments. He'd even rehearsed letting go of conversational scripts. He would aim for real engagement. Genuine human connection.

Everything felt manageable. Until she arrived. Thirteen minutes late. Not ideal, but understandable. Traffic congestion happened. But when she appeared, she was frazzled and distracted, still scrolling through her phone as she reached the table.

“Sorry, my friend just got dumped and she’s live-texting the emotional debris. Five years down the drain because he wouldn’t commit. Men, right?”

Ryan could read the signs already: divided attention, forced enthusiasm, stressed, already mentally somewhere else. A year ago—even four months ago—he might’ve missed these cues. Now they were obvious. He should respond with empathy. Concern for her feelings at this difficult moment.

“Would you prefer to reschedule?” he asked gently. “If your friend needs support—”

“What? No. We’re here. Let’s do this.” She tucked her phone away with a thin, polite smile that floated somewhere above true engagement. “I’m all in. Just … maybe not one hundred percent present yet.”

He tried to adapt, shifting to light conversation. “I noticed several of Elena Ferrante’s novels behind you in your profile photo. I thought her portrayal of female friendship over time was—”

“Oh, I haven’t read them. I just liked the covers.” She gave him a blank look. “They look good on my shelf.”

Ryan felt something deflate. One of the reasons he’d agreed to this date had evaporated before the appetizers even arrived.

He tried self-deprecating humor. “I once spent way too much time figuring out subway seating patterns. Spent a week modeling them—turned into a whole sociology rabbit hole." He added a chuckle for effect.

She blinked twice. "Like, you ... tracked where people sit?"

"Just casual observation," Ryan said quickly. But it was too late. He could hear how defensive he sounded. His anxiety was making him rigid when he needed to be flexible. He could see her pulling back, but the harder he tried to course-correct, the more forced everything became.

The server arrived. Ryan's planned entrée was sold out. This should have been an easy adjustment, except his anxiety made the simple act of choosing from the menu feel overwhelming. Amanda ordered pasta with red sauce. She leaned over it while eating, splashing her white shirt without noticing.

"So," she said, mouth half-full, "what do you do for fun? Besides people-watch on the subway."

Ryan forced a smile. Sweat gathered at his collar. It was a normal question, but her tone suggested she was already categorizing him as 'that weird guy.' His social awareness had improved, but he'd gotten no better at managing the anxiety he felt over being judged. "I enjoy solving complex problems. Lately, I've been optimizing traffic flow—"

"Sorry," she cut in. "I meant, like, normal fun. Hobbies? Sports? Netflix?"

That word—*normal*—landed like a slap. Ryan felt his throat tighten. He could see exactly what was happening—she'd already decided he was too strange, too analytical. But knowing didn't help him fix it. He tried again. "I watch ...

documentaries. Sometimes wildlife, but lately, they've mostly been on behavioral economics."

She took a gulp of wine. "Right."

Conversation limped on. She talked about a bachelorette party in Miami. About hating "guys who overthink everything."

Ryan felt something cold settle in his stomach.

"Like, I once went out with this guy who brought index cards with conversation topics. Can you imagine?"

Ryan nodded, painfully aware of the mental list of discussion topics he'd prepared—not index cards, but close enough.

By the time the check arrived, his hands were shaking. He miscalculated the tip and had to correct it. Twice.

"You okay?" she asked, already standing, keys in hand.

"Yes," Ryan said automatically. Then, more honestly, "Actually, no. But I will be."

She gave him a polite smile. "Well. Thanks for dinner."

As she walked away, Ryan realized he'd forgotten to say anything about seeing her again—not that it would've mattered. He could read social cues now, which somehow made this worse. He'd watched himself fail. Seen every moment she'd pulled away. Recognized every signal of disinterest. Observed the whole thing unravel in real time. And he'd been powerless to stop it.

He walked home. Slowly. One foot at a time. His mind, usually humming with patterns and metrics, was strangely quiet. Blank. It wasn't the conversational missteps—say bowling next time, not documentaries. It was the realization that he could do everything right—do his best—and still be left sitting alone, calculating the optimal route back to an empty apartment.

He passed a couple on the sidewalk. Her laugh rose, her head tucked naturally into his shoulder. They weren't following any protocol. Weren't optimizing or tracking anything. They were just ... being. Something deep inside Ryan's chest cracked. Not dramatically. More like ice breaking on a thawing lake, a hairline fracture releasing pressure.

For the first time since childhood, he felt tears threaten. Not just disappointment or frustration, but a profound sense of inadequacy. Of isolation. What if he was fundamentally incapable of the one thing humans seemed designed to do—connect with each other?

Back in his apartment, he stared at the bottle of wine he'd planned to open if things had gone well. And then, without thinking, he picked up his phone.

Sofie was curled up on her couch, laptop balanced on her knees, struggling to focus on a client proposal when her phone rang. Ryan's name on the screen made her stomach do something complicated. Why would Ryan be calling at 10 PM?

"Hey, you. What's up?" she answered, trying to keep her voice light.

Silence stretched across the line. The wrong kind of silence. For too long.

"Ryan? You there?"

"I failed again." His voice was hollow. Scraped raw.

"At what?"

"At connecting with anyone who might actually ... want to be with me."

The words hit like a gut punch. Sofie set the laptop aside, heart pounding. "I don't understand. What happened?"

He told her everything. Not just about the date, but his growing sense that maybe he was fundamentally incapable of real connection.

"I saw it all happening," he explained, his voice cracking. "Every signal she was losing interest. And knowing didn't help. Just made it worse. I got so anxious about failing that I ... failed."

Sofie's grip on the phone tightened. She wanted to scream. Not at him—but at this Amanda person. At the world. At herself.

"That's not failure," she said fiercely. "That's being human. Everyone spirals sometimes."

He exhaled shakily. "Then why do I still feel so broken?"

She nearly said it: *You're not broken. You're extraordinary.* But instead, she said, "Because dating is terrifying. For everyone. It's vulnerability without guarantees. And vulnerability is even more terrifying than dating. ... Listen. You're doing a hard thing, Ryan. You're putting yourself out there."

Even as she said it, part of her wanted to scream that he

didn't need to be out there at all—that what he was looking for was right here, had been here all along.

"But what if I'm just ... incompatible with this whole process?" he asked, voice barely a whisper. "What if I'm never going to connect the way I want to?"

The anguish in his voice nearly undid her. *You connect with me,* she thought. *Every day. In ways that matter.* "Ryan, you connect deeply. You have wonderful qualities that the right person will treasure." The word *treasure* slipped out before she could stop it. "You're genuine. You're the only person I know who's exactly the same whether you're talking to a CEO or a maintenance worker. There's no performance, no mask—just you. Do you know how rare that is?"

"That's just because I don't know how to be anyone else."

"You shouldn't try to be anyone else. You're great the way you are." She could feel herself getting emotional, but couldn't stop. "You remember things no one else does. That I hate cilantro and rap. Where I dropped my keys. You figured out how my emotions affect the organization of my apartment. You listen to me and don't judge."

Each example felt like a small confession. She was cataloging the ways he'd quietly woven himself into her life, the thousand small considerations that proved how deeply he paid attention. How had she ever convinced herself her feelings were one-sided?

"You see patterns and beauty," she continued, her heart hammering. "You make me want to be more thoughtful, more precise. You've changed how I approach problems at work. You've made me better at my job, and better at understanding myself."

The silence that followed felt different now—charged with things neither of them was saying outright. Sofie held her breath, wondering if he could hear the subtext beneath her words.

"Tonight was just ... bad chemistry. That's all. It doesn't reflect on you."

"I'm scared," Ryan said finally.

Sofie closed her eyes. This level of vulnerability from him felt like a gift she wasn't sure she deserved. "Of what?"

"That I'll keep trying and failing, and eventually I'll just ... give up. Accept that I'm meant to be alone." His voice got quieter. "Or that I'll settle for someone who doesn't really get me because I'm tired of being lonely."

She could barely breathe. "Don't," she said, almost a plea. "Don't settle. You deserve someone who sees all of you—systems and all—and cherishes every part." *Like I do.* "You're a remarkable person, Ryan."

"Thank you," he said after a long moment, his voice steadier now. "For picking up. For ... saying all that."

"Always," she said. And she meant it. More than ever. It was both a confession and a promise.

After they ended the call, Sofie sat in her darkened apartment for a long time, staring at her phone. Everything felt different now—the conversation had shifted something fundamental between them, even if Ryan didn't realize it yet. He had cracked open, and she'd cracked with him. And now she knew. Knew it wasn't just admiration or fondness or partnership.

She was in love with him.

And if tonight had taught her anything, it was that she'd been an idiot. A complete, cowardly idiot. Val had tried to warn her. While she'd been telling herself their relationship was complicated and professional, Ryan had been out there subjecting himself to painful dates, looking for connection with someone who could appreciate and understand him.

And now she was sitting here, knowing that she was that person. Finally ready to admit she'd been falling in love with him for months.

The question: what was she going to do about it?

Chapter Forty-Three

Too Human to Quantify

The coffee shop buzzed with morning energy—people tapping on laptop keyboards, espresso machines hissing, conversations rising and falling like tide pools. Steam fogged the windows, creating a warm cocoon against the cold morning outside. Sofie arrived eight minutes early, ordered Ryan's drink and her own (triple-shot oat-milk latte, extra hot), then claimed the corner table with two oversized armchairs.

She'd texted Ryan at 6:43 AM, a carefully casual invitation for coffee. She'd been awake since 4:05, staring at her ceiling and thinking about their phone conversation two nights earlier. His raw vulnerability. The shift in their connection. The unmistakable feeling that something was changing. And about the fact that today, Ryan was going to

Google.

He'd responded within ninety seconds:

```
Awake since 5:17.
```

She'd followed up:

```
Know you're going to Google
today—think you said you're
due there at 10. Want to meet
at Corner Brew around 8:30?
```

The idea of him walking into Google's sleek, hyper-optimized world made her chest tighten. Not because she didn't want him to be happy or succeed—she did. Desperately. But because if he left, she'd lose her chance. Maybe not right away. But eventually.

The bell above the door chimed. There he was—navy jacket, crisp blue button-down, laptop bag perfectly aligned on his shoulder. Exactly as expected, exactly on time. He scanned the room, then made his way to her table.

"Good morning," he said, voice neutral, controlled. Professional.

She smiled, gesturing to his drink. "Cappuccino. Extra shot. Non-fat milk, no sugar."

A flicker of softness passed across his face. He set down his laptop bag, took a seat, and arranged himself with his usual precision. Neither spoke for a moment. Sofie took a sip of her latte, watching him over the rim of her mug.

"So," she said, aiming for casual. "Big day. How are you feeling about it?"

Ryan adjusted the crease in his pants. "It's not a job interview. Just an exploratory consultation."

"Sure ..." She leaned forward. "Did your neighbor give you a sense of what kind of role you might land there if you're interested?"

"Systems optimization for large-scale event operations." His tone was careful, measured.

Sofie nodded, fighting the sinking feeling in her gut. "So ... basically the same thing you do for us. But with better tools. And fewer reptiles."

He smiled. "Presumably."

She waited for him to elaborate, but Ryan seemed content to study the grain pattern in the wooden table. The silence stretched until Sofie couldn't stand it anymore.

"Are you unhappy at Prestige?" The question came out more direct than she'd intended.

His eyes flicked up, startled. "Happiness is not ... the optimal framework for analysis."

"Okay, then approach the question however you want. What does our work environment look like to you?"

He paused. "There are many things I like. People I like." His eyes dropped to his cappuccino.

Her heart caught on that. She wanted him to say more, to name it, to name her, but he didn't.

"But, currently, there's systemic dysfunction," he added.

Trevor.

She traced a pattern in the condensation ring her mug had left on the table. "You shouldn't have to deal with that alone."

"Yeah, well, it doesn't look like I'm going to get any help from on high."

"What do you mean?"

"I went to Margo yesterday. About the stunt Trevor pulled at the Federation of the Blind conference—using hidden ultrasonic devices to rile the guide dogs. It was meant as sabotage. But, worse, it was dangerous. Visually impaired people could've been hurt."

Sofie's blood went cold. "And Margo?"

"Waved it off."

They sat in silence.

"At least at Google," he said finally, "I might find systems integrity. Protocols that prioritize optimal outcomes over personal agendas."

Each word landed like a blow.

He checked his watch. "I should get going. Leaving now allows room for subway variability and building check-in procedures."

"Of course." Sofie smiled despite the tightness in her chest. "Good luck today, Ryan. I hope ... I hope it's everything you're looking for."

He hesitated. Just for a moment. She thought she saw something like regret cross his face. Then he nodded.

She watched him leave, noting the precise way he navigated between tables, the careful attention he paid to holding the door for an older woman with a walker. Even in something as simple as leaving a coffee shop, Ryan was thoughtful, considerate, methodical.

Google doesn't deserve him, she thought. *Prestige doesn't either.*

THE GOOGLE OFFICES in Chelsea Market rose like a cathedral of sleek possibility. Industrial bones—exposed brick, old beams—wrapped around glass and steel interiors. Sunlight streamed through floor-to-ceiling windows, casting geometric shadows across polished concrete floors. As Sarah's friend Aditya led him through the space, Ryan couldn't help but appreciate the architectural precision, the geometric ratios that made the space feel simultaneously vast and intimate.

Aditya took him past touchscreens and real-time dashboards, into a place where data and architecture lived in perfect harmony. "We optimize everything here," Aditya said. "From the ambient temperature—adjusted every 3 minutes based on occupancy patterns—to the cafeteria menu, which uses predictive models to reduce food waste by 97.3 percent."

Ryan felt a flutter of something close to awe. "You track the variables that precisely?"

"Of course." Aditya grinned. "You're looking at a company that predicts search queries before users finish typing. Optimizing lunch is child's play."

They moved through what Aditya called "the collaborative hub"—an open-concept workspace where engineers tapped away at keyboards in soothing white-noise harmony. No theatrics. No chaos. Just focus.

"Our workstations adjust to biometric feedback—desk height, screen brightness, even ambient lighting. Based on your circadian rhythms and current task type."

Ryan nodded appreciatively. "That's ... brilliant."

"It is. Fourteen percent increase in productivity. Thirty-two percent reduction in reported eyestrain," Aditya said, rattling off the numbers with casual pride. "Here, we don't guess. We measure."

This, Ryan thought, is what systems are supposed to look like.

Then they reached the event-management lab. "I think you'll appreciate this next part," Aditya said, leading him toward a glass-walled conference room. Inside, a team gathered around a massive touchscreen that displayed an event-management platform exponentially more sophisticated than anything Ryan had ever seen, much less worked with. This was to Prestige's software what a quantum computer was to an abacus.

Lakshmi, one of the project leads, explained. "It handles everything from developer conferences to internal off-sites. Fifty-seven simultaneous variables—from speaker preferences to optimal seating arrangements."

Ryan stepped closer, barely able to hide his fascination. The interface was beautiful—clean, intuitive. Every feature he'd dreamed of at Prestige was here, fully realized and integrated. Room assignment algorithms that factored in not just capacity but acoustics and lighting quality. Scheduling tools that identified potential conflicts before they occurred. Attendee flow models that optimized everything from bathroom breaks to coffee station placement.

"This is ... remarkable," Ryan admitted, zooming in on a predictive attendance pattern visualization.

"I was just about to demonstrate a new feature," Lakshmi said. "Watch this." She pulled up a simulation of their upcoming developer conference. With a few taps, she introduced an artificial crisis—a speaker cancellation fifteen minutes before a keynote.

"Now watch how the system responds."

Ryan observed, transfixed, as the platform automatically rearranged the schedule, reassigned the room, notified affected attendees, and even suggested alternative content options based on the interests of the registrants.

"Crisis resolution protocols are adaptive," Lakshmi explained. "Machine learning cuts our incident response time by 83 percent."

Ryan was speechless. This was every dream tool he'd ever imagined, fully realized.

When he had a brief moment to himself, he texted Sofie:

```
This place is amazing. I'm
'blown away,' as you might
say. May be time for a change.
```

Sofie was deep into floor-plan revisions when the text came through. She stared at the message. *May be time for a change.*

Her stomach lurched. Her finger hovered over the screen. What could she say that was neutral, that didn't reveal how much this message shattered her? Ryan might actually be leaving Prestige Events. Because she'd failed him. She couldn't possibly respond to the substance of his text. The thought of him leaving was too devastating. She replied:

> The thermostat war here has
> gone nuclear. Might want to
> pick up iodine pills before
> returning.

Then she stared at her screen for a long time, seeing nothing. No wonder he didn't respond. She wouldn't respond to an uncaring colleague either. She'd done nothing to protect him when his events took hit after hit after horrible hit.

She pulled up her calendar, scanning back through the months of Trevor's employment, revisiting every glitch, every chaotic incident Ryan had endured.

Her phone buzzed again. This time, a text from Trevor:

> Heard Ryan might be leaving us
> for Google. Too bad—just when
> he was finding his footing.
> But maybe it's for the best.

Her vision blurred. The smug cruelty of it. Trevor knew exactly what he'd done.

By noon, Sofie's feelings of guilt and failure had metastasized into frenzied overcompensation. She rewrote the schedule for the divorce professionals' conference and added layers of contingency plans that bordered on the absurd.

What if the keynote projector dies? What if the family-law attorneys' reception runs out of wine? What if someone cries and needs emergency tissues? It was mere busywork to avoid facing her own complicity. A desperate attempt to fix the unfixable.

"Sofie?" Jenny appeared, approaching her cautiously. "The caterer says moving the buffet tables will block the fire exit—"

"They need to be 18 inches from the wall," Sofie said automatically. "It's in the revised plan."

"Right, but—"

"I'll handle it." Her voice was clipped, professional. Not controlled, because control was slipping away inside her like sand through fingers.

Jenny studied her. "You okay? You seem—"

"Fine." Sofie's smile was performance-perfect. "Just focused. And tired." The smile held until Jenny was safely out of sight. Then it collapsed.

GOOGLE's elevated dining space was a sleek area with floor-to-ceiling windows overlooking the High Line. Over lunch, Sarah wanted to hear Ryan's impressions.

"So," she asked, "what do you think? Could you see yourself here?"

"Definitely," he said. "It's a revelation. I never imagined systems this perfect."

Sarah studied him. "But?"

Ryan hesitated. "It's almost … too perfect. There's no chaos here. No surprises. I think I might miss the mess."

"Miss … the mess?" she repeated, smiling.

"The variables that make the events I handle … interesting. The unpredictability. The human moments. Lincoln impersonators arguing over historical authenticity. Competitive barbershop quartets demanding specific room acoustics. Here, problems are solved before they happen. At Prestige, I learned how to solve them while they happen—with incomplete information, zero margin. Once, with a fire-breathing mime who'd invaded a ballroom full of ventriloquists." He smiled.

So did she. "I get it. But I have to say: it sounds really stressful."

"It is. But also interesting," he admitted. "The stress and the interest are inseparable. I'm not certain my satisfaction is derived any longer solely from system efficiency."

"It comes from dealing directly with people and solving human problems?" Sarah supplied.

"Yeah, I guess so." Ryan thought about it further. "Or perhaps from whatever it is that forms when systematic and intuitive approaches combine to solve those problems together."

Finally, he looked at her and smiled. "I'm really grateful to you for arranging this visit today, Sarah. I need to spend some time thinking about it."

By 8:30 PM, the Prestige office was empty. Except for Sofie. Even the cleaning crew had finished, giving her sympathetic nods as they left. She sat alone in the break room now, her laptop open to a spreadsheet so intricate it resembled abstract art. A granola bar lay abandoned beside her, untouched because her hands were shaking too badly to open the wrapper.

She didn't cry. Not at first.

Then her breath stuttered. Her shoulders curled. And the tears came. Hot and fast and mortifying—the kind that burned her sinuses and made her nose run embarrassingly. Not elegant stage tears, but messy, gulping sobs that bent her double over her laptop, her shoulders shaking with the violence of months of suppressed guilt finally breaking free. She covered her face with both hands, mascara smearing across her palms.

She had failed him. And now he was leaving.

She heard footsteps in the hallway—the familiar, measured cadence that could only be Ryan. She froze, wiping her eyes frantically with her sleeve, trying to erase the evidence of her breakdown. But it was too late.

The fluorescent lights overhead were merciless, highlighting every smear of make-up, every red blotch on her cheeks, every sign that her carefully maintained composure had finally cracked.

"Sofie?" Ryan stood in the doorway, his expression shifting from surprise to concern. "I forgot my—" He stopped, taking in her state. "You're upset about something."

A broken laugh escaped her. "You could say that."

He stood awkwardly for a moment, then sat across from her. "Do you want to talk about it?"

She did. She had to.

Eventually, she reached the point. "I should've protected you, Ryan. From Trevor. I knew all along what he was. I knew. I lived through it in Chicago. I knew his playbook from there. He did the same things. Undermined colleagues, took credit for their work, made them doubt themselves while he swooped in to save the day." She swallowed hard. "And when he started doing it to you, I recognized the pattern immediately. And I did nothing."

Ryan was still.

"Why?"

"Because I didn't want to believe it. Because facing it would've meant admitting that I'd learned nothing from before." Her voice cracked. "Because it was easier to believe Trevor had changed than to believe I could trust my own judgment about him." She wiped her eyes with her sleeve. "I stood by while he chipped away at you. And I told myself I was being professional."

She was silent for a long time. The only sounds were the hum of the nearby vending machine and the faint sounds through the window of the city's endless symphony, indifferent to the small human drama unfolding above.

"I'm sorry, Ryan," she whispered. "You deserve better."

He studied her for a long moment, his analytical mind visibly working through the implications. "Trevor's been manipulating both of us," he said finally. "You, through guilt and nostalgia; me, through professional humiliation."

"That doesn't excuse—"

"No," he agreed. "But it explains it." He leaned in. "So, what do we do now?"

She looked up, startled. "We? You're going to Google."

"Oh, I don't know, Sofie. That depends. On whether we can get Prestige Events to deal with its Trevor Hoyt problem."

"You really might stay? But you texted that Google's 'amazing,' and that it's 'time for a change.'"

"Yes, everything about Google is incredible. But later in the day I kept thinking: *What would Sofie think of all this?* I could almost hear your voice: 'Sure, their algorithms are top-shelf, but can those folks calm down an anxious bride when the wedding cake arrives in the wrong shade of peach?'"

Sofie laughed through her tears.

"I'd miss the mess," Ryan said. "But mostly ... I'd miss you."

Their eyes met.

And for the first time in weeks, they both knew exactly what was coming next.

Sofie rose from her chair slowly, unsure if her legs would carry her. Ryan mirrored the movement.

She crossed the small space between them, and without hesitation, wrapped her arms around him. He froze for a moment—then melted into the embrace. His arms circled her back, pulling her close. They held each other tightly, breaths syncing, the noise of the city falling away. No spreadsheets, no sabotage, no algorithms. Just this.

Ryan's cheek rested against her hair. "You smell like

coffee and lavender," he murmured, the words barely audible.

Sofie leaned back slightly to look at him—and then, slowly, deliberately, she kissed him. Soft at first. Testing. Then with greater certainty.

Ryan kissed her back.

It wasn't a movie kiss, wasn't some grand cinematic gesture. It was gentle and human and real. His hand cupped her cheek with the kind of care that said he'd memorized every detail. Her fingers threaded into the back of his hair, anchoring herself.

When they finally pulled apart, neither of them spoke.

They didn't need to.

Whatever came next, they were facing it together.

Chapter Forty-Four

Reckoning at Table 4

As dusk fell, painting the city in shades of gray and amber, Sofie spotted Trevor through the rain-streaked window of Perfect Grind Coffee on 42nd Street. The glass was fogged with condensation, but she could see him clearly—sitting alone at a corner table with his laptop open and that insufferable air of casual confidence, backlit by the warm glow of Edison bulbs.

Seeing him in this familiar setting—calm, smug, and comfortable—made her stomach clench with anger. Something snapped into place. Trevor's treacherous behavior had to stop. She needed to confront him. Now.

The bell above the door jingled as she entered. The smell of dark roast and cinnamon mingled with damp wool and wet sidewalks. Trevor looked up, his expression shifting quickly from surprise to calculation to that same insufferable smile.

"Hey, Sof! What a pleasant surprise." He gestured to the empty chair. "Care to join me for a late coffee? I was just reviewing some client proposals."

She stayed standing. Water dripped from her coat onto the worn wooden floor, her hair damp and dark from the rain. Her heart hammered, but her voice was steady. "We need to talk."

Trevor leaned back, still smiling. "Of course. You look like you've had a rough day. Everything okay?"

"Cut the bullshit, Trevor."

The smile wavered, but held. "I'm sorry?"

"The fly larvae shipment. The ultrasonic devices. The bourbon fountain. The Jane Austen screwups. The arcade games. All the SEXPO disasters." She leaned over the table, her voice low and fierce. "Should I keep going?"

Trevor's fingers moved almost imperceptibly toward his laptop, closing it with the practiced motion of someone shielding evidence. The gesture was smooth, rehearsed.

"I'm not sure what you're implying—"

"I'm not implying anything. I'm stating facts. You've been sabotaging Ryan's events. Systematically. And I know because I've seen you do it before."

Trevor's smile remained, but his eyes went cold. "That's quite an accusation."

"Chicago," she said. The word hung between them like a blade. "Lakeside Convention Center. Dr. Martinez's corrupted slides. Or, here's another: the catering 'accident' that served buffalo chicken wraps to three hundred vegetarians. Those ring a bell?"

He went still. Trevor's expression shifted almost imperceptibly—still smiling, but his eyes had gone flat and calculating, like a switch had been flipped behind them.

"Those were legitimate technical failures—"

"Bullshit." Sofie studied his face with the repugnance of a veterinary tech examining a particularly unpleasant specimen under a microscope.

He started. "I don't recall—"

"I found you in the AV booth, remember? You were hunched over the control panel, pretending to troubleshoot. But you weren't fixing anything. You were enjoying the collapse. You had access because you were sleeping with Karen. Just like you had access to our vendor systems because you were sleeping with me. Amazing how your sexual escapades always seem to coincide with your professional opportunities. Are you sleeping with Margo now?"

Trevor's smile finally died. "Sofie, I think you're projecting some unresolved feelings about our relationship—"

"This isn't about me. This is about you being a predator." Her voice was like ice. "You undermine the people around you, then pose as the solution. You're a parasite, Trevor. You feed on other people's competence because you don't have enough of your own."

He drummed his fingers softly against the table. She remembered that rhythm from Chicago. His tell. He was calculating, cycling through lies, scanning for exits.

“You know,” he said finally, “Ryan’s a nice guy. Brilliant, even. But he’s not built for this business. Too rigid. Too dependent on systems. Maybe what you’re calling sabotage is just ... natural selection.”

“Don’t you dare.” Her voice rose, then lowered again. “You deliberately corrupted his databases. You rerouted deliveries. You tampered with vendor orders. You made him look like a failure.”

Trevor leaned back, studying her. “You really care about him, don’t you?” When Sofie didn’t respond, he tacked. “You’re trying to make it sound like this is about ethics. But it’s not. This is personal for you.”

“Everything’s personal when you target someone I care about.”

He tilted his head, voice going soft and needling. “How personal are we talking, exactly?”

“None of your goddamn business.”

“I think it is.” His smile returned—meaner now. The coffee shop’s cozy atmosphere seemed to recede around them, leaving just the two of them locked in battle while other customers remained blissfully unaware of the psychological warfare playing out nearby. “If you’re sleeping with him, that would explain this little crusade. Protecting your boyfriend’s feelings—”

“Stop.” The word cracked across the table like a slap. “This isn’t one of your games. This is about you being a saboteur and a liar and a professional sociopath who gets off on destroying other people’s work. And I’m warning you: your career is now on the line.”

Trevor was quiet for a long moment, his expression cycling through various calculations. When he spoke again, his voice had shed all pretense of charm. "What do you want, Sofie?"

"I want you to stop. Completely. No more accessing Ryan's files. No more mysterious equipment failures. No more convenient malfunctions that happen to occur right before or during his events."

"And if I don't?"

"Then we bring everything we have—and it's plenty—to Margo and make her listen. And if she doesn't, we'll go to the CEO. To the industry boards. And to journalists who might be interested in a pattern of professional sabotage at a high-end event planning firm. I will make sure every client, every competitor, every association hears your name—and knows what you've done. You won't survive having it all documented and exposed."

"That's quite a threat."

"It's not a threat. It's a promise. Backed by a guarantee. You pull one more stunt, and I will take you down. And I will be meticulous about it." She leaned in close. "You're good, Trevor. But I'm better. And I'm done being quiet."

Trevor said nothing. Just sat there, blinking at her like he wasn't used to someone finishing the game before he could even start it.

She walked out into the rain, leaving him with his closed laptop, his cold coffee, and whatever calculations were running behind those flat, predatory eyes.

Her phone buzzed as she reached the corner. A text from Ryan:

```
Hope you're having a good
evening.
```

She smiled for the first time in hours and typed back:

```
Evening just got better. See
you tomorrow.
```

Chapter Forty-Five

Hook, Line, and Keystroke

Ryan had repurposed a storage room in the Midtown Hilton to be his "tactical command center" for this event. Three monitors cast blue light across a whiteboard crammed with his block-letter handwriting. The space was cramped enough that when Sofie leaned over his shoulder, he could feel the warmth of her skin and catch the faint scent of lavender shampoo. Usually, those sensory distractions would short-circuit multiple synapses. But at this moment, he was too focused to pay much attention.

He'd spent the past hour analyzing attendance patterns at the National Association of Divorce Professionals convention—and something was off. According to his spreadsheets, 125 attendees had registered for the morning panel on

"Digital Asset Division in the Age of Cryptocurrency." But only two dozen had shown up.

"You're sure about this?" Sofie asked.

"The data are consistent." He toggled screens. "Look. I cross-referenced registration data against historical attendance patterns, factoring in timing, speaker reputation, and topic relevance. Even with standard deviation, we should've had at least 112 attendees."

"There were twenty-three," Sofie said grimly. "I counted."

"And that number includes two lost hotel guests who wandered in, looking for the breakfast buffet."

Sofie exhaled. "Could your calculations be off?"

Ryan gave her a look.

She smiled and raised her palms. "Right. Stupid question."

He pulled up the original room assignments. "Here's my layout—optimized for maximum flow and minimal bottlenecking." Color-coded charts filled the screen, each room assignment a small act of logistical art.

Sofie frowned, tracing her finger across the monitor. "And here's what actually happened. The most popular sessions—'High-Net-Worth Property Division' and 'Modern Co-Parenting'—got shoved into closet-sized rooms, while the low-interest panels—"

"—got assigned to the grand ballrooms," Ryan finished. "And attendees received last-minute email notifications about the room changes."

"But we didn't send any notifications." Sofie's voice dropped.

They both straightened and looked each other in the eye. They didn't have to say his name.

Ryan finally said, "Tomorrow's sessions include the keynote on 'How the Gentle Parenting Movement Ruins Kids and Destroys Marriages' and the 'Whither Ethics in Divorce Practice?' panel. Those are both major draws. If he succeeds in scrambling those, the damage to this convention—and to me—will be irreversible."

"It's not going to happen," she said. "I told Trevor if he pulled even one more stunt, we'd take him down. He had his warning. So now, we follow through on my promise. We take him down."

Ryan nodded, then leaned back, thinking. He began pulling up the backend system he'd quietly upgraded the previous month after his conversation with Sarah had given him an idea. "What we need to do is trap him. Offer him bait—something tempting. We'll plant vulnerabilities—honey-pots he won't be able to resist. Decoy files. And we'll monitor everything—record everything he touches. Every login, every keystroke."

"And we'll nail him. But, it has to be irrefutable," Sofie said. "No wiggle room. No plausible deniability."

"There's still one problem," Ryan said, frowning. "We need him to act tonight. Before tomorrow's keynote."

Sofie paced, then snapped her fingers. "We'll fake a system lockdown. I'll tell him that access to the computer system shuts off at 10 PM tonight for a software upgrade. I'll say the only terminal still connected is the one in the business center. We'll make sure the security camera there is trained on it."

"Let's make sure the trap ends before he gets curious about the real system," Ryan said. "He'll think he has to strike before the window closes."

"Right, he'll believe it's now or never. And when he tries …" Sofie smiled.

At 7:36 PM, they put their plan into motion. The trap was a work of art—clean, precise, bulletproof. Ryan watched a security feed that showed Sofie intercept Trevor outside the business center. She gestured animatedly, no doubt explaining the "lockdown." Ryan noted Trevor's telltale pause—shoulders tensing, fingers twitching. Then he nodded. They exchanged a few more words. As Sofie walked away, his gaze lingered on the computer terminal inside.

Moments later, Sofie dropped into the chair beside Ryan. "Hook baited," she said. "Now we wait."

They didn't have to wait long.

"Movement," Sofie said, pointing at the monitor.

Trevor slid into the business center with exaggerated nonchalance, like a coyote easing into a familiar hunting ground. The fluorescent overheads threw sharp shadows across his face as he settled at the terminal, his movements precise and confident—the muscle memory of someone who'd done this sort of thing before, in other hotels, to other victims.

Ryan pulled up the backend system logs. He and Sofie

watched Trevor enter his credentials and the system flashed: *Access granted.*

"Got him!" Ryan murmured, watching keystrokes appear in real time on the monitor. Each character Trevor typed appeared with a soft ping, building an irrefutable record of his sabotage. Ryan felt a deep glow of satisfaction. Every action was being recorded, time-stamped, and traced to Trevor's unique credentials with the kind of systematic thoroughness that would make denial impossible. "He's accessing tomorrow's schedules."

Sofie leaned closer. "Can you tell what he's changing?"

"Breakfast meetings ... now, room assignments ..."

"Should we stop him?" Sofie whispered.

"No need. Remember, the real files remain untouched. He's editing the decoy files we put in place. So we might as well let him keep going. He's tying his own noose."

A sharper ping sounded. Then another. And another. Ryan's eyes narrowed. "He's trying to breach restricted areas."

Sofie stiffened. "Can he do damage?"

"Not to our system. But—" A different, more urgent alert now reverberated through the little room. "Oh, no. He's moved on from our database. He's found a backdoor into the hotel's main network. The real one. If he corrupts their space-management software—"

"—every event in the hotel is toast," Sofie finished grimly.

Ryan grabbed his phone to alert security. But he'd barely ended the call when they saw a digital signage monitor in the lobby flicker and go dark. Then another. And another.

Sofie was already on her feet. "Time to end this."

They sprinted through the service corridors, their footsteps echoing off cinderblock walls while Ryan mentally mapped the fastest route—like a GPS recalculating in real time. Sofie kept pace beside him, her breath sharp and rhythmic as they raced to confront Trevor while he was still at the keyboard.

Rounding the final corner, they burst into the business center with enough force that the door slammed against the wall with a satisfying crash. Trevor jolted upright like he'd been electrocuted, his fingers frozen over the keys that spelled his professional doom.

"Sofie! Ryan! I was just—"

"—corrupting data, accessing restricted systems," Sofie cut in, her breathing hard and fast, her eyes sharp as glass.

Ryan stepped forward. "Twenty-three unauthorized changes to tomorrow's plan. Every one logged. Timestamped. Tied to your ID."

Trevor's face twitched. "You can't prove anything. It's your word against—"

"—your keystrokes," Sofie said flatly.

Ryan watched him—pulse pounding visibly in his neck. Sweat had begun to bead at his hairline, and his usual composure was cracking like ice under pressure, revealing the desperate calculation of someone whose carefully constructed lies were finally catching up with him. The mask was cracking. At last.

"This is ridiculous," he snapped. "I was helping. Everyone knows Ryan's systems don't work in the real—"

Before Trevor could finish, the door opened. Kevin O'Hara, head of hotel security, entered, flanked by two uniformed guards. Sofie and Ryan both pointed at Trevor.

"Mr. Hoyt," O'Hara said, calm and final. "Let's you and me have a little chat about unauthorized access to the hotel's systems."

As they led Trevor away, he turned over his shoulder. "This isn't over."

But even his voice sounded small now.

Chapter Forty-Six

Conclusive Evidence

Sofie watched as Ryan methodically presented the evidence on Margo's monitor, his fingers pointing to the relevant data with the confidence of someone laying down a royal flush. The afternoon sun slanted through the office windows, casting harsh geometric shadows across Margo's desk and highlighting the tense line of Ryan's jaw as he pulled up log file after log file.

"Here," he said, tapping a timestamp. "Trevor accessed the convention management system at 8:11 PM on Tuesday. The key-logger captured his exact sequence." Ryan's voice took on that familiar tone and cadence he used when presenting irrefutable data. "He deliberately reassigned the Collaborative Divorce Associates to the same meeting space as the Scorched Earth Litigation Group."

Margo leaned forward, frowning at the screen. "That could be a simple scheduling error—"

"No." Sofie stepped closer, laying printouts on the desk. "Look at the hotel's security logs. Trevor used his access card to enter the office at 8:07 PM. Four minutes later, he's in the system making these changes. Then at 8:34 PM, he accessed the hotel's own convention database and deleted their copy of the original schedule."

Ryan said, "The keystroke logs show him actively searching for high-conflict scenarios."

Margo sat back, her face unreadable. "And how exactly did you two obtain all this?"

"We had prior evidence from events we knew he'd sabotaged—Jane Austen Society, Federation of the Blind, Amusement Machines, SEXPO." Sofie paused, considering what else to add. "But we needed to establish it beyond a doubt with actual keystroke records. So, Ryan implemented standard tracking protocols for database changes."

"While I appreciate your ... thoroughness," Margo said, her tone setting Sofie's teeth on edge, "I don't like it that you two mounted a surveillance operation against a colleague. I don't like that at all. It's deeply problematic. And, frankly, I think you're reading too much into all this." She gestured toward the monitor with a dismissive flick, as if Ryan's carefully constructed web of evidence were nothing more than a conspiracy theory in spreadsheet form. The casual cruelty of the gesture made Sofie's stomach clench.

Sofie stared at her, stunned. "'Reading too much—'?" She raked her hands through her hair in disbelief. "Margo, we have him on camera. The logs show his keystrokes. He violated hotel security protocols and deliberately sabotaged events. You think the hotel's complaint was fiction? You think their security officers were imagining things?"

"Sofie," Margo said, her tone tight with warning, "Trevor came to us with impeccable references. Some of my closest friends in the industry—" She paused, and for a second, something flickered across her expression—a crack in the professional facade that suggested she knew exactly what she was defending and was choosing to do it anyway, for some combination of reasons known only to her.

"Your friends must be as willfully blind as you," Sofie snapped. Realizing how sharp that sounded, she dialed it back, her tone now simply pleading. "Margo, the evidence is right in front of you. Look at the pattern analysis."

Ryan pulled up another complex spreadsheet, colored cells showing each incident, access time, outcome. "There's a virtually perfect correlation between Trevor's late-night logins and subsequent failures," he said. "This isn't theory—it's a pattern."

"Data can be interpreted many ways," Margo replied calmly. She paused for a long moment, then continued. "And when I look at the data from your time here with us, Ryan, I'm left with the conclusion that this environment isn't a good fit for someone with your ... particular talents."

Sofie blinked, stunned by the shift. She felt as though the floor had tilted beneath her. Her breath caught. The realization that Margo wasn't going to act—wasn't even going to acknowledge the evidence—hit her like a physical blow. "Are you serious?" she asked. Her tone boiled with indignation. "Ryan's prevented more disasters in his time with us than anyone. His systems work."

"Ryan's excellent with technical problems," Margo agreed. "But this job is about people."

Sofie couldn't believe what she was hearing. "This job is about keeping people safe! Which is exactly what Ryan does —while Trevor creates chaos and danger, and somehow gets away with it because he's handsome and charming and finds female protectors higher up the ladder. As he's apparently done here. You should be ashamed of yourself, Margo."

Margo's face jolted, just as if she'd been slapped. With a stone-cold tone, she said, "I believe this meeting is over."

Ryan stood, his movements controlled as always, but Sofie saw the slight tremor in his hands as he gathered his tablet. His face remained neutral, but his jaw twitched—a micro-expression she'd learned to read: he was swallowing something back, sharp and bitter.

"This is ridiculous," Sofie snapped, snatching up the printouts. "We give you ironclad proof of sabotage, and your response is to ask Ryan to leave?"

"Sofie—" Ryan murmured.

"No! This is wrong." She turned back to Margo, pointing at her. "And you know it's wrong. Trevor is actively damaging this company, our reputation, our clients. And you're covering for him because ... because what? He has something on you? Are you sleeping with him?"

The words detonated in the room. Margo's expression cycled through shock, fury, and something dangerously close to guilt. She glanced toward the door, as if hoping someone else would interrupt. "That's enough," she said, her tone pure ice. "Perhaps you should reconsider your position here, too."

Sofie's jaw dropped, then snapped shut. Without another word, she turned and stormed out, footsteps echoing off the polished floors. She caught up to Ryan, who was already halfway down the hall. The familiar office smells—coffee, toner, recycled air—felt alien now, soured by betrayal.

"Ryan, wait—"

"I need to review the setup for the UnitedHealthcare event," he said without turning to look at her. "They're very particular about their workspace configuration."

"Forget UnitedHealthcare. We've nailed that down solid. Besides, it starts in the morning. If we're not ready by now, we never will be." She stepped into his path. "And this stuff with Trevor isn't over. We have proof. Real, concrete proof. Maybe Margo just needs time to process this. She'll come around."

She met Ryan's eyes. What she saw there wasn't defeat, exactly, but a kind of resignation that broke her heart.

He said, "The statistical probability of success—"

"Isn't zero!" she finished. "And as long as it's not zero, we keep trying."

Ryan gave her a long look. Then, with a rueful grin, he said, "Ah, Sofie, I think not. As my friends in quantum physics would say, 'the wave function has collapsed, and not in our favor.' Schrödinger's cat is definitely dead."

His attempt at humor fell flat in the hallway's institutional lighting, but Sofie caught the genuine hurt beneath his analytical detachment—the way he used scientific metaphors to distance himself from emotional pain.

Now it was her turn to study him, which she did. For a long beat. Then, making a decision, she nodded and took his hand. "Come on," she said. "Let's go get hammered."

Chapter Forty-Seven

The Right Thing

Bloom's Tavern on 58th Street was the kind of Irish pub that welcomed the disheartened with the same indifferent hospitality it offered the triumphant—its dark-wood interior absorbing both moods with equal dispassion. Afternoon light filtered through grimy windows, casting everything in sepia tones that matched Ryan and Sofie's gloom perfectly. They claimed a corner booth far from the handful of day drinkers nursing their liquor in solitary contemplation. It was mercifully quiet at three in the afternoon, the happy-hour crowd not yet having arrived.

"Two Johnny Walker Reds, please," Sofie told the waitress before Ryan could speak. "Neat. Make them doubles."

Ryan raised an eyebrow. "Starting with high-proof spirits

before establishing a proper hydration baseline could result in—"

"Ryan, we just got our asses handed to us by Margo. Let's skip the worry about hydration protocols."

He nodded, conceding the point.

When the drinks arrived—two amber glasses that caught the dim light like liquid fire—Sofie raised hers immediately in a bitter toast. The scotch's sharp, medicinal smell promised the kind of clarity that only came after accepting that sometimes the good guys don't win. "To incontrovertible evidence that nobody wants to see."

Ryan clinked his glass against hers and took a precise sip. "The human capacity for selective perception continues to defy statistical modeling."

"You can say that again." Sofie leaned back against the worn leather booth, letting the alcohol do its work. "I just ... I don't understand how Margo can look at hard evidence and just ... ignore it. It's right there."

But even as she said it, her mind flashed back to Chicago—Trevor in her kitchen at midnight, shirt half-unbuttoned, nibbling at her bare shoulder while he lied, spinning another excuse. *"You know how Lakeside's system glitches, Sof. You don't really think I'd deliberately mess with the Optometrists' Conference, do you?"* And she'd believed him. Or wanted to. Margo probably did, too.

"Cognitive dissonance," Ryan replied, running his finger around the rim of his glass. "When presented with information that contradicts established beliefs, humans often reject the new data rather than revise their mental models." He paused. "My father published a paper on this phenomenon among climate researchers who ignored shifting migration patterns."

Sofie snorted. "Comparing Margo to climate deniers feels about right." She took a longer sip. "You know what else really kills me? That crap about your systems being 'too rigid.' Your systems are the only reason half our events don't implode."

"They're not perfect," Ryan admitted, studying the honey-colored liquid in his glass with unusual intensity. "But they're statistically more reliable than Trevor's approach of winging it and hoping for the best."

"And yet, he keeps failing upward while you ..." Sofie trailed off, the words sticking in her throat. "It's not fair."

"Fairness is a human construct with no basis in natural law," Ryan said quietly, but there was no conviction in his tone. Just quiet resignation.

Watching him accept defeat with such calm precision—like it was just another system failure to log—made her stomach turn. "Is this really how it's supposed to work?" she asked. "The person who does the job right gets pushed out, while the saboteur gets stroked?" Her voice rose slightly. "It's like rewarding the actor who misses every cue, but firing the stage manager who keeps the show running. What kind of company runs that way?"

"Approximately 67.3 percent of them, according to workplace studies," Ryan replied, but the corner of his mouth twitched upward.

Sofie cracked a smile. "Your made-up statistics are getting less convincing."

"I never make up statistics." He paused a beat. "I merely adjust the confidence intervals."

She laughed, then grew serious again. "Joking aside, what Margo did in there ... it wasn't just wrong. It was—"

"Unethical," Ryan supplied. He met her eyes squarely. "The data are unambiguous. Trevor's actions endangered client events, company reputation, and in some cases, human safety. Choosing to overlook that is an ethical failure."

"Exactly." Sofie slapped her palm against the table with enough force to make their glasses jump, sloshing a bit of scotch over each rim. The sharp sound cut through the bar's ambient noise, earning glances from other patrons. Her hand stung, but the pain grounded her.

"Since when am I okay with that?" she said. "I've spent my whole career trying to make events go off without a hitch—sometimes at the expense of everything else. My health, my relationships, my sanity. And now I'm supposed to just accept this?" She didn't say the rest: *since when do I allow others to harm someone I care about?*

Ryan didn't answer immediately. He just watched her, his gaze steady. "This goes beyond professional concerns for you."

"Damn right it does." She drained her glass and flagged the waitress for another round. "This is about who we are. What we stand for." She leaned in. "Remember when you started here? I had your back because you cared. Not about appearances, but about getting it right. Even when the clients were weird Lincoln impersonators or people who predicted weather from squirrel fur." *Because you reminded me of who I wanted to be. Because you weren't afraid to be exactly who you are. Because you trusted me. Yet I failed you.*

"That squirrel guy was particularly challenging," Ryan said, the hint of a smile ghosting across his lips.

"But we figured it out." Sofie accepted her fresh drink from the server with a nod of thanks. "And now we're just supposed to ignore Trevor's bullshit? Pretend it's not there?"

Ryan tilted his glass, watching the light warp through the scotch. "Classic ethical dilemma: maintain job security by compromising principles, or uphold principles at potential personal cost."

Sofie heard Trevor's voice echo in her memory: *"That's just how this industry works, Sof. Sometimes you have to bend a little to get ahead."* She'd bent so far she almost snapped. And where had that gotten her? Sitting in a bar with the one person who'd never asked her to be anything but herself, both of them on the verge of losing their jobs because she hadn't been brave enough to stop Trevor years ago.

"When you put it that way ..." Sofie sighed. Then straightened. "No. I'm not doing it."

Ryan looked at her.

"You know what?" she said, voice steady now. "Screw Margo. Screw Trevor. Screw Prestige Events. We did the right thing. That matters."

"It does," Ryan agreed. "Though I regret the negative impact on your career."

"Don't worry about me," Sofie grinned. "I'm resilient. Like a cockroach, but cuter."

"Significantly cuter," Ryan agreed, a flush blooming at his collar.

Sofie's eyes widened. Her smile softened. "Why, Ryan Porter. That almost sounded like a compliment without a confidence interval."

He laughed, "Alcohol appears to impair my filtering protocols."

"I like unfiltered Ryan," Sofie said, leaning in. "He's fun."

The bar had grown busier around them, the after-work crowd starting to filter in as the afternoon stretched. Voices rose in overlapping conversations about commutes and weekend plans, the ordinary concerns of people whose biggest workplace drama was probably a broken printer. The normalcy felt surreal against the backdrop of their professional crisis. The two of them sat in a cone of silence, staring into their drinks.

Finally, Sofie spoke again. "Okay. Here's what we do. We handle the UnitedHealthcare conference tomorrow—because we're professionals. We don't leave clients stranded."

"And after that?" Ryan asked.

"After that, we figure out what comes next. We write our own script this time. Not Trevor's version, not Margo's. Ours."

Something shifted in Ryan's expression—a subtle recalibration she would have missed if she hadn't spent so many months learning his micro-expressions. "An interesting proposition," he said. "Defining variables instead of reacting to them. Taking control of the equation."

"Exactly." She raised her glass. "We've spent enough time taking direction from other people. Time we called our own cues."

Sofie felt something solidify inside her. A clarity long overdue. Things couldn't continue as they were. Not if she wanted to look herself in the mirror each morning without flinching. Not if she wanted to be the kind of person who stood up rather than stood by. And from the thoughtful look in Ryan's eyes, she knew he felt it, too. Patterns could be broken. Equations could be rewritten. So could futures.

LATER, as they stepped into the cool evening air, neither spoke at first. But when Ryan reached for Sofie's hand and laced his fingers with hers, she asked quietly, "We're really doing this?"

"Yes," he replied. Then, after a pause: "Because of you."

"No, because of *us*."

For a moment, the traffic noise on 58th blurred into silence. Then he leaned in. The kiss wasn't dramatic. It was deliberate. Certain. Like they'd finally aligned at exactly the right time, in exactly the right place. No performance. No calculations.

Just them.

Chapter Forty-Eight

The Business of No

The Grand Pavilion at the Ritz-Carlton smelled like money—that indefinable mix of privilege and entitlement enjoyed by people who've never had to choose between medication and groceries. A champagne fountain burbled merrily in the corner. Crystal chandeliers cast rainbow prisms across polished marble floors. Even the air felt expensive—perfectly climate-controlled for an event where the wealthy casually discussed inflicting pain on other people.

After yesterday's confrontation with Margo, they'd both arrived this morning with a strange mixture of professionalism and emotional detachment. They'd planned this event meticulously for weeks. It had been drummed into them repeatedly that this was one of their firm's "signature events." Nothing could go wrong at this UnitedHealthcare Annual Executive Leadership Summit. But especially under the circumstances, it was hard not to approach this event with a healthy dose of cynicism. And not least because this was where insurance executives gathered to discuss innovative ways to say 'no' to claims while looking concerned.

Ryan had been scrolling through his tablet. His voice sounded carefully neutral when he said, "Today's agenda includes the keynote speech: 'Pre-Existing Conditions: Finding the Silver Lining in Denial Letters.' And—let's be sure to remember—the speaker requires her Svalbard water to be exactly 42 degrees Fahrenheit."

"Of course she does," Sofie replied, unable to keep the edge from her voice. "How else would one want water that's been harvested from icebergs in Norwegian fjords?"

The morning proceeded with clockwork efficiency. At one point, Sofie had to relocate the coffee-station positions after observing unusual clustering patterns among the claims-denial specialists. "They move in packs," she said to Ryan. "Like wolves, but with better suits."

They both laughed, a moment of connection amidst the flurry of convention activity. Sofie realized with a start how much Ryan's way of seeing the world—finding patterns, making observations—had influenced her own.

As they set up for the luncheon keynote, Ryan leaned closer, his voice low and tight. "These people are really despicable. And the keynote speaker—Caroline Elverson, the CFO—is one of the worst. She claims 'credit' for the company reducing claim-processing staff by nearly 30 percent last year. Wait times tripled. Approval rates dipped. But profits surged."

"How do you know all that?"

"I dug through public disclosures—SEC filings, quarterly investor calls, press releases. ... I came across a newspaper report from last year about a difficult case that got kicked all the way up to her—and she personally denied coverage for a child's life-saving medication over a clerical error in the paperwork. No wonder she made it to CFO."

Sofie stared at him, startled by both the information itself and the fact that Ryan had so thoroughly investigated the company's ethical compass. She said, "In the midst of all you've been going through, you took time to look into the company's denial practices?"

He nodded. "It seemed ... relevant. I learned from you that we should pay attention to the ethics of our clients. I wish I'd started doing it sooner."

Elverson took the stage at precisely 12:30 PM, dressed in a perfectly tailored suit that probably cost more than an average family's monthly housing payment. She began her address with professional aplomb, PowerPoint slides animating smoothly behind her. "In today's evolving healthcare landscape, we must become more creative in our interpretation of coverage parameters," she said, the euphemism hanging in the air like expensive perfume.

Ryan stood at the back of the room, tablet in hand, monitoring sound levels and room temperature with his usual exactitude. But Sofie noticed a tension in his jaw.

Elverson was halfway through extolling the virtues of

their new automated denial algorithm when she paused, frowned slightly, and reached for her water glass. Her hand trembled, causing the water to slosh over the rim. She set it down, gripping the podium with both hands.

"As I was saying, our new system allows us to ..." She wavered, her words suddenly slurring like a recording played at the wrong speed. The laser pointer in her hand clattered to the floor, a sharp metallic ping cutting through the shocked silence. She slumped sideways against the podium with the boneless weight of someone whose nervous system had disconnected.

For two endless seconds, no one moved. Then panic rippled through the ballroom. Some executives shrank back in their chairs. Others pulled out phones to record the scene. A few called out, asking if there was a doctor present.

Ryan was already moving, his emergency protocols activating automatically. "Clear the stage," he directed two staffers. "Call 911," he told another, his voice calm but urgent. As others tended to the unconscious executive, Ryan hovered nearby, trying to stay useful while remaining out of their way.

By the time medics arrived, Elverson's face had gone gray, her body having seized multiple times in violent spasms.

"She's having seizures," one of the medics said. "We need her medical history. Medications, conditions, allergies. Anyone have access to that information?"

Ryan scanned the room. He'd seen Elverson earlier,

talking and laughing with the Senior VP of Policy, who now stood off to the side, his face pale beneath his expensive tan.

Ryan went to him. "Do you know her medical history?"

The man hesitated, his eyes darting between Elverson's convulsing form and the gathering crowd. "There are privacy concerns," he said stiffly. "Legal clearance would be required for disclosure of personal—"

Ryan's hand shot out. He grabbed the man's lapel, expensive fabric bunching beneath his fingers. Several nearby execs gasped like they were witnessing a mugging. In one fluid motion, Ryan yanked him closer, lifting him slightly off his feet.

"She is seizing," Ryan said, his voice, raw and emotional. "This isn't a hypothetical. Not a policy discussion about a claim. A human being is in crisis. Right now. Right over there."

"I—I can't just—"

Ryan's grip tightened, his voice lethal. "She. Could. Die. Would you like me to calculate the growing statistical probability of that outcome as you withhold information?"

"She has M.S.," the man stammered. "Diagnosed three years ago. She's on immunomodulatory therapy. An experimental protocol."

Ryan released him and relayed the info to the EMTs, who adjusted their treatment immediately.

As they stabilized her and transferred her to a stretcher, the policy VP straightened his jacket, his shock having given way to indignation. "That was completely out of line," he hissed at Ryan. "You had no authority—"

“I had moral authority,” Ryan cut him off, his voice level but intense. “I had eyes. I had ears. I had a choice. You did, too. And you were making the wrong one.” The VP recoiled as if slapped.

Sofie felt her blood turn to ice water. She’d watched the entire exchange in stunned silence, but now the implications crashed over her like a wave. Ryan had just physically confronted a senior executive. At a signature event of one of their most important clients. With hundreds of witnesses. There would be reports. There would be a shitstorm.

She grabbed Ryan’s arm, her fingers digging into his sleeve. “We need to talk. Now.” She pulled him into a service corridor off the main hallway. Her heart hammered so hard she could feel her pulse in her throat. The moment they were alone, she whirled on him. “What the hell was that?” she whispered, her voice shaking. “Ryan, do you have any idea what you just did?”

He looked at her with that same calm intensity. “I did what was necessary.”

“Necessary?” Sofie’s voice rose despite her efforts to keep it down. “You physically assaulted a senior VP!”

“He was letting a woman die to protect corporate liability—”

“I don’t care!” The words burst out of her, raw and desperate. “I don’t care if he was sacrificing babies to the profit gods! You can’t just ... you can’t just grab people!” She pressed her hands to her temples, trying to think. “Margo’s going to hear about this within the hour. Hell, we’ll probably be fired before the cocktail reception.”

Ryan's expression didn't change. "Then we'll be fired. So what? Margo made it clear she wants me gone. And yesterday, she flashed you a yellow card, too."

They both knew there wasn't time to continue this exchange. There was too much to do. They went through the afternoon in a blur of forced normalcy, with their usual precision. But as the hours ticked by, Sofie realized she'd been wrong to confront Ryan the way she had. He'd done the right thing. And he'd probably saved that woman's life.

Her other realization, as she observed all the event's luxurious excesses, was how wrong the whole thing felt. Her growing unease tasted like copper pennies. What were they doing here? What were they enabling? Each perfectly executed detail left her feeling utterly complicit in something monstrous.

By the evening party and banquet, her morality antennae felt thoroughly fried. She watched waiters circulate with gold-dusted caviar canapés. She leaned toward Ryan and groaned with disgust. "God, think of the cost of that."

Ryan said, "Based on current market prices for beluga caviar and edible gold leaf, each canapé represents about a third of the average family's premium."

"And how many denied claims would you estimate paid for this event?" The question slipped out before she could stop it.

Ryan's eyes widened slightly. "I ... haven't run that calculation."

"Maybe some numbers are better left un-crunched."

The CEO of UnitedHealthcare took the stage to thunderous applause. His smile was bright enough to power a small surgical wing. "Ladies and gentlemen, I'm pleased to announce that, thanks to our innovative coverage limitations and strategic denial protocols, our quarterly profits exceeded expectations by forty-four percent!" The crowd roared with approval. "Thank you for your good work. Let's keep it up. Remember," he boomed, "every 'no' is an opportunity to say 'yes' to profits!" The audience went into a frenzy. "Every time you say 'no' to a claim, an angel gets its wings. And by angel, I mean your stock options!"

Sofie felt sick. "Ryan," she whispered, "is it wrong that I want them all to get stuck with out-of-network providers someday?"

"Not wrong. Just improbable," he replied. "Most of them have platinum-plus coverage that includes resurrection services."

Despite everything, she almost laughed.

They watched as Jenny and Todd smoothly delivered swag bags to each table—the women receiving Cartier diamond bracelets, the men Rolex watches. Each luxury item a monument to someone's denied coverage.

"At least they didn't deliver their swag to the tables by actual golden parachutes," Sofie said.

Ryan laughed at her gallows humor, understanding her reference to the absurd stunt at the previous year's infamous Purdue Pharma conference. "The Oxy hucksters won't be able to repeat that this year. I hear their gift is going to be an actual half-pound gold bar, so a parachute would be an impractical mode of delivery."

She looked at him. Her heart in her throat and her voice barely a whisper, she said, "We can't keep ignoring the cruelty of companies that profit from human suffering. I don't want to do this any more. It makes me feel dirty."

Ryan returned her gaze, studying her for a long moment. He nodded. "Right. So, we won't. The moral compromises end now."

Chapter Forty-Nine

The Leap

The Greasy Spoon Diner on 9th Avenue was the precise opposite of the Ritz-Carlton's Grand Pavilion—and somehow infinitely more honest. Instead of marble floors, cracked linoleum tiles told stories in their scuff marks. Instead of crystal chandeliers, flickering fluorescent tubes cast everything in the harsh, democratic light of truth. Laminated menus boasted "World Famous Home Fries," and in the corner, a jukebox hummed quietly, waiting for quarters that rarely came. The air smelled of bacon grease, burnt coffee, and the freedom of people not pretending to be anything other than what they are. It was perfect.

"To unemployment," Sofie said, raising her chipped mug in melancholy toast.

"To statistical uncertainty," Ryan countered, clinking his mug against hers.

The coffee was strong enough to dissolve spoons, bitter enough to strip paint, and somehow exactly what they needed—honest fuel for honest conversation.

Their joint appearance earlier that morning in Margo's office had been surprisingly anticlimactic. They'd walked in together, ID badges in hand like evidence of their former selves, and announced their resignations with the calm dignity of people who'd finally decided to stop putting up with bullshit. Who finally found their way out of an escape room filled with moral compromise. Margo had stared at them for approximately seven seconds (Ryan had counted) before accepting the badges with a tight nod.

At the door, Sofie had turned around and said, "Trevor's been sabotaging events, and you've been covering for him. And having sex with him, against company—"

"Now, you—"

"Our time here, may be up, Margo, but this story is far from over. We're going to see that both of you are held accountable."

Now, dumping an obscene amount of creamer into her coffee, she asked Ryan, "Any regrets?"

"Regrets imply that, given the same variables, one would make different choices," he said finally. "My analysis indicates our decision was optimal."

"That's Ryan-speak for 'Hell no,'" Sofie translated, grinning.

He smiled, too—not his careful, measured smile meant

for clients, but the real one that transformed his entire face. "Correct."

As they waited for their food, Sofie watched him carefully arrange the sweetener packets by color. His movements were as precise as ever, but there was something different about him. A relaxation around his eyes, a lightness in his shoulders, as if he'd finally set down some invisible weight he'd been carrying. Even his breathing seemed deeper, more natural.

"Unemployment suits you," she said, walking her fingers across the table toward his.

He took her hand in his. "Technically, we're not unemployed. We're between professional engagements."

Sofie raised an eyebrow. "Is that what we're calling it?"

"It's more accurate. Unemployment implies a desire for traditional employment, which I find I no longer have."

"You don't want another job?"

"I want to work," Ryan clarified. "I simply find myself reconsidering the optimal organizational structure for that work. I spent last night researching positions at nonprofits, academic institutions, government agencies. Organizations with missions I can actually support."

The waitress refilled their mugs with the casual precision of someone who'd done it thousands of times. As she walked away, Sofie leaned in, eyes alight.

"What if we didn't work for someone else at all?"

Ryan tilted his head—his standard 'processing new input' gesture. "You mean freelance consulting?"

"No, not freelancing." Sofie's voice quickened with

excitement, her hands gesturing animatedly. Energy radiated from her like warmth from a space heater. "What if we started our own company? A boutique operation. Small, selective, values-driven. We call the shots. We write the script. No more vulgar health-insurance executives celebrating denied claims. No more effete snobs sipping rare waters without any concern for the harm their stupid hobby has on the environment. No more SouthStar Pharmaceuticals wanting display-area hegemony. No more having to check our ethics at the door."

"Values-driven," Ryan echoed. His voice warmed. "We could develop ethical algorithms. Select clients based on corporate responsibility metrics, environmental impact factors—"

"Exactly. All of that. We choose clients we believe in, run events our way." She was talking faster now, coffee forgotten, her thoughts suddenly crystallizing into a vision. "Your bulletproof logistics and systems, my improvisational magic."

"Theoretically, such a venture would have advantages. Decreased organizational friction, optimized resource allocation without bureaucratic interference ..."

"And we bring Todd and Jenny with us," Sofie added, her excitement palpable.

Ryan smiled. "We'd have to put one of those locked cages around the office thermostat to keep Jenny from—"

"—turning it into a Bikram yoga studio?"

Ryan smiled. But then his expression shifted. His shoulders tensed as if his body were physically bracing against a different weight—reality. "Sofie," he said slowly, "the statistical failure rate for new businesses is approximately 50 percent within the first five years. Ninety percent fail within ten."

"But we're not most businesses—"

He shook his head and met her eyes. "We have no startup capital. No independent client base. No business plan."

Sofie's enthusiasm deflated. "So you think it's a bad idea?"

"I think it's a massive financial risk with uncertain prospects. I was planning to apply for salaried positions with stable advancement paths, predictable hierarchies—"

"You want to go back to being someone else's employee? After all this?"

"I want security," Ryan admitted. "I want to know I can pay my rent, that I have health insurance, that I'm not gambling my future on an untested proposition."

Sofie stared at him. Something cold settled inside. "So you have stage fright. About us."

"Yes," he said. "I'm not embarrassed to admit it. I'm scared of failure. Of financial instability. Of discovering that what works between us now doesn't translate to running a business together."

The honesty in his voice stopped her short. She'd been so caught up in her own excitement, her vision of escaping the corporate world, that she hadn't considered what she was asking of him. Ryan, who needed predictability like other people needed oxygen. Ryan, who'd spent his whole life building systems to manage uncertainty.

"You're right," she said finally. "It's scary. And risky. And probably stupid."

Ryan's shoulders relaxed slightly. "I'm glad you understand—"

"But I still think we should do it."

He blinked. "What?"

Sofie reached across the table and covered his hands. "You remember why you took the job at Prestige? You were trying to grow, to change, to explore the human arena, to become someone new."

"That's different. I was taking a calculated risk with measurable outcomes—"

"Right. It was a leap of faith." Her grip tightened. "And look how it turned out. You found your calling. You found people who appreciate your gifts, who value you. You found ..."

"You." Ryan finished softly.

"Yeah. Me."

He looked at their joined hands. "What if working together ruins ..." He started over. "What if the stress of running a business together destroys our friendship? Our partnership? Our ..." He struggled for the word that would encompass everything they'd become to each other but hadn't been brave enough to name.

"Our whatever-this-is?" Sofie supplied softly.

"Yes."

The question hung between them. What was this thing? This connection that had grown from professional respect into something deeper, more complex, more precious than either had expected?

"That's the real risk, isn't it?" Sofie said quietly. "But I don't want to spend the rest of my life wondering what we could've built together. What we could've become."

Ryan studied her, silent. Then: "You said we could choose our clients."

"Very selectively. With your systems."

He took a deep breath and remained quiet for another long moment. Then, with the careful precision that was so essentially him, he said, "We'd need detailed financial projections. A business plan. Legal advice. Clear boundaries between our professional and personal relationships. Protocols for decision-making, conflict resolution, profit-sharing."

Seeing that something had shifted in him, she said gently, her voice filled with hope. "Really, Ryan? You think you want to do this?"

He met her eyes directly, and she saw that his fear had transformed into determination—like some mathematical proof had suddenly resolved into elegant clarity. His breathing steadied, his shoulders squared, and that familiar analytical intensity returned to his gaze, but softer now, tempered by trust.

"Yes," he said. "Despite every rational objection ... yes."

Relief flooded through her, followed immediately by terror. They were really doing this. Together.

"One condition," Ryan said. "If this fails, we promise to preserve this. Us. Whatever this is."

Sofie felt tears prick her eyes. "Deal."

There was another long pause. Then Ryan looked up. "I assume there are industry standards for company nomenclature—"

"Nope. Sky's the limit." Sofie grabbed a napkin to dab at the collecting moisture around her eyes. "How about 'Arctic Foxes Event Planning'? A nod to your origins."

He smiled. "Fibonacci Events?"

"Too nerdy." Sofie tapped her chin. "What about 'Perfect Chaos'?"

"An oxymoron." Ryan paused. "Though I find I don't dislike it."

Sofie laughed. "What about 'Perfect Plans'?"

His eyes lit up. "Ah. A company name that's also an aspirational lie. I like it."

"Then we should toast." Sofie lifted her mug. "To complementary methodologies."

"To taking the leap."

"To us," Sofie said.

They clinked their mugs—ceramic against ceramic with a sound like a small bell—sealing their agreement with burnt coffee and trembling hands.

Later, stepping into the late-morning sunlight, Sofie felt the uncertainty ahead, but also the possibility.

They stood just outside the diner, the city moving around them—a delivery truck rumbling, a messenger bike streaking by, a man arguing with a pigeon on the corner. But for a moment, none of it registered.

Ryan looked at her. No data to analyze. No charts to build. Just her.

"Sofie," he said quietly.

She turned to him, heart thudding.

"I love you," he said simply, eyes unwavering.

It landed exactly like what it was: a truth she'd known for ages but needed to hear out loud.

"I don't understand the whole equation," he added. "I just know it's you."

She laughed, tears rising fast now—not the misty kind, but the good, overwhelming kind that come from deep inside. "You ridiculous, beautiful man. I love you, too."

She reached for him, and he met her halfway. And they kissed. Right there on the sidewalk, sunlight warming their shoulders, future unfolding in every direction. It wasn't perfect. It was better. It was real.

Epilogue

Perfect Plans, Imperfect People

Sofie's morning at the Westin New York in Times Square began with zombies in the wrong bathroom.

Not real zombies—just highly committed cosplayers from the Halloween and Costume Association convention, decked out in latex wounds, oozing theatrical blood, and wearing milky-white contact lenses. Unfortunately, their appearance had terrified several members of the Ethical Funeral Directors Association, who were not accustomed to their clients walking around.

"I assure you, Mrs. Rodriguez," Sofie told the EFDA's event chair, "we'll make sure all restroom signage is clearly marked to prevent further incidents."

Two ballrooms to the north, Ryan was dealing with fog machines belching mist across the marble floors like a low-budget horror movie, repeatedly setting off the smoke detectors in the funeral directors' keynote room. As he worked on the problem, his tablet pinged—Prestige's CEO had finally acted on the sabotage reports. Trevor and Margo had been fired.

Ten seconds later, Ryan got a text from Sofie:

> Maybe their sexual
> relationship was the final
> nail in their coffin?

He replied:

> Or maybe you just have sex on
> the brain.

Not untrue. But at that moment, it was actually coffins. Sofie was in the vendor pavilion, drawn by a commotion near the premium-casket booth. A sales rep was shouting, "Excuse me! What are you doing?" Sofie watched as three twenty-somethings in skeleton leggings climbed into a $12,000 Legacy Series casket—mahogany with brass fittings that gleamed under the exhibition lights—snapping selfies with the kind of cheerful irreverence that made the sales rep's face cycle through various shades of red. The casket's silk interior provided a surprisingly photogenic backdrop for the young women's hip-jutting poses.

"This haunted-house prop is amazing!" one squealed. "Do you have any with, like, built-in scary music?"

"It's *not* a prop!" the red-faced rep shouted. "This is ... Please get out! And stop making duck faces."

Sofie stifled a laugh and returned to mission control—a repurposed hotel conference room that buzzed with quiet efficiency and the comforting chaos of a major event humming along. Ryan monitored security feeds with the serene focus of someone who'd learned to find beauty in unpredictability. Even in pandemonium.

"Current tally," he reported. "Three funeral directors fainted after wandering into the Zombie Makeup Workshop. They thought it was the EFDA's 'Natural Appearance Enhancement' seminar. But after the initial fright, they all had a surprisingly engaging conversation about achieving the perfect palor."

"Not bad, considering," Sofie said. "Anything else?"

"I noticed some Halloween vendors scribbling notes while talking with morticians about solemn body language and chapel-appropriate lighting."

Sofie said, "Sounds like 'creepy dignity' may be the next big trend for Halloween cosplayers."

Jenny's voice crackled over the radio: "Be advised—we have another situation in the exhibition hall. Halloween drag performers have infiltrated the hearse showcase."

"How many?" Sofie asked.

"Three morticians, two Grim Reapers, and ..." Jenny paused, then laughed. "I don't even know what the hell this last one is supposed to be. But she just asked me where the pole-dancing class is."

Ryan tapped his tablet. "One of them's Madame Morticia. Instagram influencer. Her following's up 47 percent since breakfast."

Sofie shook her head, grinning. "Remember when you used to worry about predicting every scenario?"

"I've learned to appreciate the variables I can't predict," Ryan said seriously, his voice carrying the hard-won wisdom of someone who'd discovered that chaos wasn't the enemy of good planning, after all—just part of the recipe. "But ..." He glanced back at the screen and smiled. "I can predict that we'll look back on this with happiness."

"Oh, yeah?"

"My statistical analysis indicates we're actually happy with our lives."

"That's the most romantic thing you've ever said to me." Sofie bumped his shoulder. "I suppose you have a spreadsheet tracking our happiness metrics."

Ryan smiled. "Would you like to see the quarterly report?"

"Save it for our next board meeting," she said.

Then Todd chimed in over the radio: "The shipment of animatronic werewolves somehow got replaced with those inflatable dancing tube men from car dealerships. I don't think these are what the Halloween crowd had in mind for 'terrifying.'"

Sofie looked at Ryan. "Isn't it nice that our first assumption is no longer sabotage?"

Later, they watched as a funeral director's somber lecture on Dignity in Death was accidentally projected onto a wall of dancing skeletons. The looping animations mirrored his gestures so perfectly it looked choreographed—an unintentional performance art piece that neither side could quite explain.

By day's end, several funeral directors had agreed to judge the Halloween costume contest, bringing their expertise in 'authentic memorial atmosphere' to the panel. Business cards were being exchanged. Unlikely partnerships had formed. A DJ was blasting "Stayin' Alive."

Ryan and Sofie stood side by side at the edge of it all, exhausted but grinning, basking in the joy of a job well done.

Eight months earlier, they'd walked away from the corporate safety net and into the unknown. Now they had a thriving business—Perfect Plans, LLC. An office in Brooklyn that smelled like fresh paint and possibility. A loyal team in Todd and Jenny. Clients they actually believed in.

Next up: the Sustainable Food Systems Expo and the Clean Energy Innovators Summit.

The risk hadn't just been worth it. It had been inevitable. The only choice that had ever made sense.

"Ready to go home soon?" Sofie asked.

Ryan smiled—his real smile, the one that transformed his whole face. "With you? Always."

And then, to the blaring beat of "Monster Mash" echoing off the marble walls, they watched in amazement as a conga line of funeral directors in black suits followed a rhinestone-covered Grim Reaper in six-inch heels out into the neon-bright New York night.

Afterword

Thank you for reading *Perfect Plans.*

Reviews are absolutely crucial for indie authors. If you enjoyed the book and have a few moments to spare, please post a brief review or rating on Amazon. That would be enormously useful in connecting this novel with more readers.

To sign up for J.T. Tierney's newsletter and be the first to hear about upcoming releases, news, and special offers, please provide your name and email address on the subscription sign-up form at jttierney.com

About the Author

J.T. Tierney lives outside Chicago with his wife of 42 years, Sue Tierney, and their Great Pyrenees.

He doesn't confine himself to any one genre of fiction. He writes stories that interest him, hoping they'll resonate with readers as well. His previous novels include:

- *Love, Literally*—a contemporary smart romance set on Cape Cod
- *The Butcher on Colfax*—a historical novel that immerses readers in the lives of Irish immigrants in Denver in the 1890s
- *Extreme Malice*—a psychological thriller about a liberal member of the school board in a conservative town being harassed over her pandemic-related policy decisions

Printed in Dunstable, United Kingdom

66666728R00221